LOVE ME LOUDER

CHRISTINA LEE

Copyright © 2018 by Christina Lee. All rights reserved.

Thank you for buying an authorized edition of this book and for complying with copyright laws by not reproducing, scanning, or distributing any part of it in any form without prior written permission by the author(s), except where permitted by law.

LOVE ME LOUDER is a work of fiction. Names, characters, places, and incidents either are the product of the author's imagination or are used fictitiously, and any resemblance to actual persons, living or dead, business establishments, events, or locales is entirely coincidental.

All products and/or brand names mentioned are registered trademarks of their respective holders/companies.

Published by Christina Lee in the United States of America

Cover design by X-Potion

Cover photography by Eric David Battershell

Edited by Keren Reed

Proofreading services provided by Lyrical Lines and Judy's Proofreading

To Kelley Nyrae,
for helping me brainstorm and shape the finer details of this story. Your friendship is a bright, glowing, and comforting presence in my life.

1
NOAH

Noah Dixon opened the online invitation sent by his oldest friend, Tony Malone. He had posted in a private group on Facebook, so Noah had been tagged with an alert. His mouse hovered over the *yes, no,* or *maybe* response box.

Hey, all.

Throwing a massive party for Matt's thirtieth at the beach house. No gifts required. He'd rather you donated to one of his favorite charities, links below.

There will also be a surprise you don't want to miss. But don't tell Matt. I'd hate for anyone to spoil it. Please RSVP and let me know if you're bringing a guest, so we can get a good count for food and beverages.

Hope to see you soon.

Tony planned to propose to Matt at his birthday party; after all, Noah had had enough conversations with Tony about rings, nerves, and proposal ideas over the past few months. Tony and Matt had been dating for three years. They were both financial analysts and had crossed paths in the same circles until they finally spoke to each other at a charity event, fell in love, and the rest was history. Noah knew how much Tony loved Matt and wanted to spend his life with him.

Noah stared at the RSVP on the invitation again. Tony always threw extravagant affairs at his house in Fire Island Pines, and this would be no different. Noah sighed, that familiar nauseating feeling taking root in his stomach. No way could he get out of this one, even though it would only be more of the same: Beautiful men everywhere. Beautiful half-naked men frolicking by the pool or at the beach. No one giving him a second glance, especially if he was brave enough to take off his shirt. And most days, he absolutely wasn't.

He didn't blame anyone; he wasn't anything special to look at, even without the ugly scars lining his torso. He'd had his share of hookups over the years, even one stab at a relationship in college, but too many ended awkwardly, and he certainly didn't relish being the only single one in the bunch. Again.

Maybe one of his friends from the city would tag along with him. Except going all the way to the Pines required a level of commitment—after riding the train to Long Island and then taking the ferry to the island, once you arrived, all you wanted to do was take a load off for a day or two. Besides, Tony would never forgive him if he didn't plan to stay all weekend. They didn't get much time together nowadays with their busy schedules, and ever since Tony had gotten completely immersed in this engagement idea, there'd been little else to talk about.

Noah closed the invite window; he would decide later how to respond to Tony.

He and Tony had been friends since childhood, and their

families spent many summers together on the island. Tony's parents would be there to help make the party a lavish event, but if his memory served him well, his own parents would still be traveling in Europe, which was a relief. Noah's relationship with his parents had become strained in recent years. After the accident, they became the ultimate helicopter parents, always hovering, interfering, not allowing him to make decisions or mistakes on his own.

And though he understood it, he felt suffocated by them. Add in his coming out at eighteen, as well as choosing a less savory career path of his own as a sales associate at a Home and Hearth store, and his parents didn't know how to relate to him anymore.

Not that they didn't accept his sexuality. It was more that they were so desperate to keep him safe that somehow their logic felt mislaid. Not only that, but Noah could never shake the idea that his dad was disappointed in him. For pretty much everything.

Noah absently ran his fingers against the scar tissue below his right ear, then finished buttoning up his shirt. The collar covered his neck for the most part, and his hairstyle did the rest, so he normally didn't have to entertain stares from customers every day.

Noah waved to a neighbor as he left his apartment on the Upper East Side and headed to Midtown by train. He whistled a tune as he skirted around the saxophone-playing panhandler at the top of the stairs, and threw the change from his pocket into his empty case.

He definitely considered himself a happily single gay man. Most of the time. Weekend invites to Fire Island or similar-type events only served as a brutal reminder that he was alone.

His parents still kept property on Fire Island, a more modest dwelling in Cherry Grove than the one from his childhood summers, but they traveled so much now, it seemed a shame to leave it empty. So they rented it out practically every weekend in warmer months, which meant Noah couldn't even use it as an escape from Tony's parties. Regardless, the island rarely held good memories for him anymore, not since the accident.

It wasn't that he couldn't get dates or hookups; they just never amounted to much. His longest relationship had been about four months, and it had taken him about as long to feel comfortable enough in their intimate moments. But the scars were too much for plenty of men, and his parents pushed too hard, making most situations uncomfortable. If he failed at finding himself a respectable guy, he'd rather fail on his own.

It'd been at least ten years since his last skin graft, which was his eighth surgery, and after that he decided he couldn't take much more. His hand scratched across his chest as he balanced himself against the train door during the bumpy ride, that phantom stinging sensation still remaining so many years later. The scar tissue extended from his rib cage over his shoulder and up the side of his neck to his ear. He'd been told countless times by his doctors that it could've been so much worse. His face might've been equally impaired, his hearing too, damage to his organs even, and the biggest kicker of all? He could be dead.

He tried remembering that fact, no matter how discouraging life could be at times. Sure, these parties on the island made him want to run back to the city and disappear into his life, where he didn't have to try to be more than he was. But he wouldn't let it put a damper on his spirits. Besides, he needed to be there for his best friend.

He exited the train and climbed up the stairs to street level near Saks Fifth Avenue, where he paused briefly to admire their whimsical flower display before crossing at the busy light.

Truth was, he loved his job in retail at Home and Hearth, an upscale lifestyle store featuring furniture, lighting, art, and modern hardware. He always had an eye for design, so he enjoyed creating displays on the floor, and he wasn't opposed to the hard work of lifting and stocking shelves. It wasn't the best pay—certainly not to his parents' standards—but it helped him afford his modest apartment, which he'd furnished quite nicely over the years.

His job was the only thing he looked forward to during the week. That and the lemonade served by the hot Asian guy at the bagel shop next door. Coffee only made him jittery, and he could stand for less of that. He sipped his sweet drink as he stepped inside the store and took in the warm and inviting bedroom display he'd helped design back in June. The manager had decided on a dorm-room college theme, even though summer had barely begun. But that was how it went in retail. You always anticipated the next season.

The store was large enough for several staff to be on shift at once, and he noticed that Samantha and Michelle were on the floor with him today. Michelle was a bit of a gossiper, but Samantha was chatty and easygoing, and that would help for any lulls in the schedule, though those happened pretty rarely during peak tourist season. William Crossen had just punched in as well. *Call me Will*, he'd said his first day on the job a few months back, and Noah thought that was a sign of how friendly he'd be. Not exactly the case.

Will was definitely easy on the eyes. Noah could stare at his perfectly sculpted cheeks, dimpled chin, and luscious lips all day. But of course, it was all one-sided, not only because Will was more than likely straight, but because outside of work niceties, he had probably not spoken much else to Noah unless he was pushed for details. But he was a hard worker and good with the customers. He just never shared anything of himself with anyone and rarely went for a drink with the group. Maybe he had stuff to keep private—and didn't Noah know all about that?

Soon enough, they all got busy on the floor as the customers poured in. They were a mix of tourists, apartment dwellers, and families who seemed to be getting their kids set up at NYU or Columbia, parents looking for smaller bedroom sets for their young adults or help with decorating rooms vacated by grown children.

There was a line at the cash register all evening, and by the end of the shift, Noah's feet ached. He was relieved to lock the door behind the last customer so they could clean the floor and cash out.

Noah grabbed his bag from his locker in the staff room, and in his side view noticed Will checking messages on his phone. He'd seemed more reserved than usual that day, not that Noah knew him well enough to understand his moods, but now something he was listening to on his voice mail made his eyes light up. Probably a hot date. Will checked the clock on the wall and then quickly grabbed for his bag. He fished a small white card out of his pocket, scribbled on it, and then scrambled toward the door.

He muttered a rushed goodbye over his shoulder, and it wasn't until Noah looked down to retie his shoelace that he noticed Will had dropped the card he'd just written on.

Noah reached for it and couldn't help reading what was written on it.

Gotham City Escorts
Louise, 10 pm, 22 Park Avenue
All sorts of bells began clanging in Noah's ears.

He stood up suddenly, blood rushing to his cheeks. No way he'd catch Will now, but as he distractedly made his way to the stairs of the train station, he looked around the street just to be certain. He pocketed the card, hopped onto the train, and thought about Will the whole way home. Will was an escort?

He imagined him heading to Park Avenue to meet his client tonight.

Holy shit.

He speed-walked to his apartment, barely looked at his mail as he retrieved it in the lobby, and was lost in his own thoughts all the way up in the elevator to the fifth floor.

While he was reheating sesame noodles from last night's leftover Chinese takeout, he reached for the imported beer he got on his last grocery-store trip, and fired up his laptop.

After a few forkfuls to fill his stomach and some hearty swallows of his beer, he looked up the escort site. Just out of curiosity.

The logo at the top of the page was a play on the Gotham City Batman theme with an outline of the skyline. The site was easily readable and packed with information.

Need a date for an event? Lonely for some company?

Consider hiring a professional escort.

You can expect your companion to be polite, attentive, and courteous.

They'll always put their clients' needs first.

There were tabs up top that took you to the escort page. There were no photos, only simple stats about each of the employees: first name, hair color, height, weight. He didn't see Will's name listed anywhere, which made him wonder if he had been mistaken about him being an employee. Maybe Will was the one doing the hiring. But that didn't make sense. He pulled out the card again. It specifically said *Louise*, so probably a client.

When he glanced back at the site, he noticed an LGBTQ tab on the far-right side and clicked on it.

Discretion is our number-one priority.

Noah stared at the screen for a long time before admitting to himself that the idea of hiring an escort for his weekend at Fire Island sounded mighty appealing. But no, he couldn't possibly do such a thing, right? How much would it even cost? He clicked around a few more pages and saw that the prices varied depending on the escort and event, some raking up a three-hundred-dollar hourly rate.

He loaded his dishwasher, his mind a whirlwind of possibilities, his stomach fluttering with nerves. Did a night with an escort require other things, like sex? That couldn't possibly play into it. After all, they weren't prostitutes hired for sexual exchanges. According to the site, escorts provided companionship, and wasn't that what Noah wanted? Just somebody to hang with him, pretend to be his date so he could get through the weekend and not feel so unattached?

He sat down heavily on his couch, the breath practically knocked from his lungs.

Was he really that hard up? And what if something went terribly wrong?

Maybe if he approached Will discreetly, he could ask how safe it was. Scratch that. If it wasn't safe, would Will really be doing it? He barely knew the guy, but he doubted these companies would stay in business if they didn't provide their employees and customers a measure of security along with discretion. Besides, did he really want Will to know how lonely he felt sometimes?

Now it made a hell of a lot of sense why Will didn't want anyone to know his business.

Noah tried to read through a home-decorating magazine, but he could barely concentrate. Instead, after another swallow of beer, and definitely in a moment of courage, he clicked open the party invite from Tony, checked *yes*, and wrote 2 for the number of attendees.

2

WILL

Damn, he'd dropped the business card somewhere between the store and the train station. Oh well, at least he got the details memorized; besides, all he had to do was listen to the message again or pull up the latest email where he received a receipt of the transaction. Whenever he saw those dollar signs, he knew he was doing the right thing. It gave him a renewed sense of purpose.

Tonight he had a regular client by the name of Louise. She was the CEO of a large financial corporation and always had tons of events to attend, but she admitted she sometimes felt too single and wanted someone to accompany her, someone who wasn't with her for her status or wealth.

It was good money, and mostly easy money. Keeping someone company, showing them some courtesy and respect. It hadn't all been roses, and he'd been placed in some uncomfortable situations over the past year, but he had the backing of the company, which seemed to be on their employees' side for the most part.

He walked to his apartment building on the Lower East Side, retrieved the mail, and walked up three flights of stairs to the place he shared with his mom. Most men he dated didn't understand that he lived with his mom to keep his eye on her as well as to get a handle on their finances. It was his motivation for taking the escort job last year. It took time and expense to stabilize her meds after she was hospitalized again. She suffered from schizophrenia, and his greatest fear in life was not only that he might lose her in some tragic way, but that he might have inherited the disorder. Statistics showed that kids who had the propensity showed early signs, sometimes in their teens. But it was a fear that continued to plague him, along with them getting in over their heads again financially.

His mom did well on her meds, but it was when she randomly decided to go off them that all hell broke loose. Add in paranoia and delusions, and they were right back where they started so many years prior. It was the reason his father walked out on them when Will was only a kid. Will used to rent his own shitty place after college but moved in with his mom three years ago so he could keep his eye on her as well as save money on rent. Besides, it was only the two of them, and he needed to keep her safe.

"Everything okay, Mom?" he asked as he keyed into the door and took a quick glance around the place. Nothing seemed out of order. His mom sat on the couch in the clothes she had changed into that morning and was watching something on the history channel. She loved documentaries, but it sometimes contributed to her paranoia, if not about government conspiracies, then about aliens invading the earth.

"Yes, honey," she replied in a distracted voice. "There's some leftover pizza on the counter." She attended an adult day-treatment program a couple of days a week, and volunteered at a food bank one bus stop away, which she enjoyed. He hoped she could support herself again someday, but he wasn't sure if it would ever be entirely possible. The social-security checks helped, but they definitely didn't cover everything.

"Just stopping home to change. I'm, uh, going out tonight." He wasn't ashamed of his escort job but preferred to keep the information to himself. His mother would no doubt worry relentlessly, whereas others would disapprove, especially his old theater friends. Most wouldn't get it, but honestly, it was nobody's business.

When he broke up with his ex, who was one of the stars of an Off-Broadway show, Will decided to also walk away from his backstage-assistant job. Truth was, he needed a break. He had his Fine Arts degree, but after shelling out money over the years for voice lessons, acting classes, headshots, and then obtaining the right work history to actually get into the actors' union, let alone in an actual small role onstage, the pay was dismal at best. According to some friends who'd been in bigger productions, the salary doubled, but it wasn't much better. Most actors he knew had side jobs. He finally found some steady work backstage on a production, but it was a tough business and he wasn't sure if he always loved it. He wished he would've chosen a different career that wasn't so cutthroat, especially in a big metropolis. He'd heard it was easier in smaller cities and theaters.

He sat down beside his mom with a slice of pizza on a paper towel so he could gulp it down and be on his way. "What's this one about?"

"The JFK conspiracy," she replied absently, and he couldn't help his antennae from standing at attention. Except as he looked her over, she didn't seem overly agitated as she got sometimes when she was feeling suspicious or off-kilter. As far as he knew, she was taking her meds like clockwork every day. Admittedly, sometimes he counted the pills just to make sure. Now who was the suspicious one?

Maybe he should've chosen the field of psychology, given how much he'd learned about his mom's condition as well as the social services provided in the city. Still, every now and again the past year since he'd quit theater, he'd head to Midtown just to be around the big lights, and if he had extra money, he'd stand in line at TKTS to see if he could score some discounted tickets to a newer production.

It fed his need for a little while, and besides, it wasn't so bad working at Home and Hearth. Everyone was decent, and sales were a little bit like performing—as was being an escort, for the most part. He knew how to play his cards right and not to lay it on too thick, though he had nothing on his coworker Noah Dixon, who was probably the top sales earner in the store. Pretty damn annoying, if he was being honest.

Customers seemed to gravitate toward Noah, and if he had to guess, it was because of his over-the-top sunny confidence. The guy was like some character in that *Pleasantville* show, if they'd allowed gays. Perfectly dressed in his khakis and button-downs. The only thing that seemed out of place was the hairstyle he kept chin-length and a bit unruly. Will would kill for that head of copper-brown hair because of how it caught the light, but honestly, it was the only interesting thing on him.

Pretty average-looking Noah exuded this charisma as soon as the customers stepped through the door. Could probably charm a snake into buying venom. Fucking unbelievable. Most days Will barely kept from rolling his eyes if he had to work with him. He wondered if he ever turned it off and just relaxed, for fuck's sake.

He imagined Noah's home was like a Pottery Barn catalog, and couldn't help wondering what Noah would make of the apartment Will shared with his mother—clean but shabby, comprised of secondhand furniture and worn carpeting.

He shook himself out of his thoughts as he remembered he had a paying client he needed to get to.

After he got dressed in the only decent slacks and jacket he owned, he slipped out the door, hoping his mom didn't pay him any attention or ask too many questions. Luck was on his side, as she barely gave him a side glance when he said goodbye.

"Nice to see you again, Max," Louise said in greeting as he leaned in and kissed both her cheeks. "Sorry about the last-minute notice. Glad you were available."

Max was the name he used for the escort business—sort of like a stage name—and it helped keep just enough distance between him and his clients.

"You look lovely, Louise," he replied, and she blushed at the compliment. It made him wonder just how much authentic interaction she got from the opposite sex as a high-powered business woman.

They walked out the front door to the waiting car service that would drive them across town to the fundraiser. He could schmooze with the best of them, but he had to admit how much of a bore it all was. So he focused on the end result. The money and his mother's well-being.

They stayed for a couple of hours as Louise worked the room and introduced him as her date. He held her hand at certain points or placed his palm on the small of her back because she liked that; she was responsive to his attentiveness and chivalry, especially when he held out her chair or left her side to order them drinks from the open bar.

Once back at her place, he wondered if she would invite him up. A couple of times in the past she had, and she'd urged him to kiss or hold her. She'd never requested sex, and he was glad for that. Sexual relations were left up for negotiation between the parties entered in the contract. The escorts were within their rights to refuse and had the backing of the company. It was one of the reasons he decided to sign with them. He was warned, though, that he might not be asked back by a repeat customer if he refused intimacy, and he was fine with that, although the tip he was left after one of those closed-door encounters was usually a really nice bonus.

But this time, Louise chastely kissed his cheek after a long yawn, which told him she was too tired for a nightcap.

After he got home and checked that his mother was sleeping soundly, he was too keyed up to go to bed. He headed back out to the corner coffee shop to get some tea concoction his friend Oren had turned him onto for sleepless nights.

As he pushed through the glass entrance he waved to Oren, the barista who was also a theater major consistently auditioning for gigs. He was the only one who got why Will had quit; Oren had a baby to support, so he also needed steadier income.

"I need some of that..." Will waved his hand as he looked up at the board for the tea.

"Tranquility Tea?" Oren asked with a raised eyebrow. He looked him up and down, noticing his dressier getup. "Rough night?"

"Not anything out of the ordinary," Will replied, and as Oren began making the concoction, he threw Will a knowing glance. Oren was the one who'd suggested the escort gig in the first place. He'd been working at Gotham City himself until he got more serious with his girlfriend.

"What's in it anyway?" he asked as Oren handed him the cup.

"Chamomile and sarsaparilla," he replied.

"Sarsa—what?" Will quipped.

Oren laughed. "Something to put your ass to sleep."

"Sounds perfect." He waved as he went out the door.

He sipped the tea as he played around on his laptop, finally pulling up some gay porn and muting the sound. It had been weeks since he had a hookup or even a male client from the escort service. Cock in hand, he jacked himself to climax to a scene between two average-looking guys. Those were his favorite setups because they seemed more authentic. Not everyone could be muscled and gorgeous. He'd trade someone who sought the spotlight for a real guy any day of the week.

3

NOAH

Between work, the gym, and the online merchandising class he'd recently signed up for to keep himself fresh, Noah had nearly forgotten about the escort service until three days later. Will was on the same schedule at Home and Hearth, but it took until the end of their shift to work up the nerve. As they were leaving the store that night, he stopped Will on the street. Fishing the business card from his pocket, he handed it over to him. "So, hey. You dropped this the other day, and I, uh, wanted to return it to you."

Noah noticed how Will's cheeks pinked immediately before he squared his shoulders and looked him directly in the eye. Almost in defiance, or maybe it was pride.

"Yeah, okay. Thanks," he replied, taking the card and pocketing it.

He turned to walk away, but Noah followed him down the pavement, swearing under his breath because he'd been hoping for more of a conversation. But he should've known better, based on how private Will seemed in general.

"Hold on a minute," Noah said, and Will stopped abruptly, causing Noah to have to veer around him. "You work for them?"

Will's eyebrows knit together. "Yeah, so? If this is about..." He aimed his thumb toward the darkened Home and Hearth store. "It's none of their business what I do on my own—"

"No, that's not what I mean," Noah sputtered. He was absolutely giving Will the wrong impression. He needed to start over again, or Will might refuse to speak to him after this encounter, and he so rarely spoke freely now. But damn, getting the right words out was difficult at best. "I was only trying to..."

Will looked down at his feet and then kicked at a random stone on the ground. "What do you want, Noah?"

"I just wanted to know if...if they're a good company...because I..."

"Looking for a new job?" Will asked with an arched eyebrow.

Was Will poking fun at him? Noah's face instantly heated.

"No," he replied and then motioned to himself. "I mean, are you kidding me?"

He was going for self-deprecating, but Will didn't seem to get it, which Noah sort of appreciated in that brief moment as Will looked him up and down. It reminded him how most people didn't immediately notice his scars, and he definitely liked blending in when it came to his body issues.

Not that he could ever pass as any sort of escort even *without* his scars. He was average at best. No impressive height or muscle mass to speak of, and never was that more evident than standing in front of Will, who was tall, fit, gorgeous, and could've easily passed for a runway model. And given they lived in the city, that idea wasn't so far-fetched.

Will folded his arms, apparently waiting for him to get his mouth unstuck.

"I'm asking because I have this *friend*...who has an event coming up, and he was looking into hiring an escort..."

"A friend, huh?" Will replied, attempting to hide his smirk. Noah stared down at the ground, unable to meet his gaze. "It's a decent company. I've never had any problems, if that helps."

Noah wanted to ask so many other questions, about intimacy or expectations, but he held himself back. He'd blow his front, plus it didn't really feel like Will was eager to talk about more than the basics. It made him realize just how much about his coworker he didn't know. Was this the reason why Will never seemed to hang out on nights when some of them kicked back with a drink at Chauncey's around the corner? Was he too embarrassed, too proud, too...*busy*?

The idea of Will being an escort made Noah shiver. The notion that even tonight Will might be off to meet a client. Did he charm them with his looks or words or body? He was more than curious now, but it was really none of his business.

"Okay, cool." Noah breathed out, glad the conversation was finally moving along. He didn't know how much more squirming he could stand. "I actually looked up the site the other night and saw it has a gay section, so I thought he would be cool with that... my *friend*..."

Christ. Noah was out and proud, so that most likely wasn't news to Will. But his attempt to hide his own interest in the escort service was ridiculous at best.

"Yeah, they definitely offer same-sex services too." Will absently scratched his head, as if considering his query. "Your friend might be actually better off with an all-gay escort service, like the one called Queer in the City...I think that's the name."

"Oh, um, okay...thanks for that tip. I'll let him know," Noah said, still unable to look at Will properly. "Hey, could you not..." His voice trailed off as he glanced over at Home and Hearth, which was still as dark and locked tight as last time he checked.

Will rolled his eyes. "I know how to be discreet, in case you haven't caught on to that."

"Yeah...yeah, sure. Sorry." Feeling all kinds of awkward, he mumbled a quick thanks and took off down the street.

When he got home, he pulled a quart of ice cream out of the freezer, along with some lunch meat for a sandwich. After downing his dinner, he sat on his couch with a spoon and the container of cookies 'n cream, instead of dishing it into one of the new bowls he'd excitedly purchased from Pottery Barn last week. He silently cursed Will for his perfect hair and lips and body. Bet he'd never have to use an escort service for a date. Some people needed to work harder for it, he guessed. Some people also weren't scarred on over thirty percent of their body.

He suddenly felt completely self-conscious, even alone in his apartment. He imagined himself on the arm of a beautiful, unattainable guy doubling as his escort and felt sick to his stomach.

He wasn't going to compare ab muscles or his workout routine, which was bare minimum. Though since switching up his routine, he was beginning to see some depth in his arms and shoulders, maybe even his back. Still, he'd rather walk ten blocks than lift weights in the gym around the corner from his apartment, where men gawked at all the eye candy. Story of his life.

But he wanted to be able to relate to the man in some way, for Christ's sake. He hoped they could have intelligent conversations, laugh about similar things, and find some common ground if they were going to be spending a whole weekend together. Hell, more and more this was sounding like a bad idea.

A half hour later, he decided to pick up the phone and call Gotham City Escorts instead of using their online form. And while he was speaking to the kind and patient lady who answered the call, he felt better. He had given her his middle name, James, out of sheer panic, but he figured he could explain that to the escort once they talked.

By the end of the phone call, he had scheduled an entire weekend with a gay escort named Max. The woman asked if she could give Max his email address—which was generic as well, he realized—so they could communicate about the details prior to the time they would be spending together. The price was steep for someone who was frugal with his funds, except when it came to home furnishings, of course. Only the top brands would do for products that might last you a lifetime.

Jesus, he sounded like a cheesy infomercial.

But Noah had been saving for years, ever since he told his parents he wanted to make it on his own in the city, so he could afford to splurge just this once for peace of mind. All the guy had to do was pretend to be his date, for fuck's sake, and they'd be all set.

Hopefully he was a good actor.

A COUPLE OF NIGHTS LATER HE RECEIVED AN EMAIL FROM MAX—HIS pretend boyfriend for Matt's birthday party on Fire Island. Holy hell, was this seriously his reality? Had he really followed through with hiring someone? Soon enough his bank account would reflect that fact, if he decided to go through with it.

He was so relieved he hadn't been on schedule with Will the past two days after that uncomfortable conversation outside the store. Hopefully Will didn't ask for a follow-up about his *friend*. But knowing the little he did about the man, he figured that was unlikely. Apparently, discretion was the way Will preferred things, and at this stage, Noah could definitely appreciate that.

His pulse thumped in his ears as he read the professional-sounding message.

HEY, JAMES!

Thanks for signing up with Gotham City Escorts. Meeting in person is generally the best idea before hiring someone for a long weekend. It would be important for me to understand what you require as well as getting to know you a bit better before spending so many hours together.

It's also a good idea for you to make sure you're comfortable with me, and vice versa, and whether I'm someone you'd want to take for a weekend to meet your friends. Believe me, the opposite is not ideal, and it would be a shame for you to have regrets or be miserable all weekend long. Of course, meeting prior to our arrangement is completely up to you. A phone call could work just as well.

Best regards,
Max

MEETING HIS ESCORT BEFOREHAND WAS CERTAINLY NOT SOMETHING Noah had even considered, but it sure made a hell of a lot of sense. What if they were like oil and water? He supposed that could work for a couple of hours, but an entire weekend? A shiver rolled through him. He'd certainly been in awkward situations with hookups or blind dates over the years, and he definitely wanted to avoid something similar at all costs. Except this guy would only be pretending, which in so many ways felt worse.

He hit the Reply button and poised his fingers on the keyboard.

MAX,
Nice to hear from you. Thanks for this suggestion because I think it's a great idea! I'd want to make sure you're just as comfortable with me as well as with our arrangement. Going alone to these types of events has been awkward for me, and it would really be great not to feel like such an outsider. Of course, I can explain more when we meet. How about Saturday morning for coffee somewhere in Midtown? The Starbucks on 40th works for me, or feel free to throw out another suggestion. I'm flexible.
James

HE IMMEDIATELY DELETED HIS NAME AT THE END OF THE EMAIL AND

considered deleting the feeling-like-an-outsider business but ended up keeping it. As soon as he met Max, he would tell him his real name if he felt comfortable enough. Besides, he'd have to. His friends only knew him as Noah, and his escort was about to learn a whole lot more about him too.

4

WILL

Will had a new client to see the following Friday, an older woman who got a little handsy after one too many drinks in her hotel room. As soon as he got home, he took a long, scalding shower, thoroughly scrubbing his skin. He didn't feel that way too often; normally customers were pretty respectful, but sloppy-drunk clients were the worst. At least he was able to fend her off long enough until she passed out completely. Then he shut the door behind him and hightailed it out of there.

Will wasn't going to mince words—most of his clients were just lonely. They merely needed simple human contact in a hotel room they rented for the night. A couple of times they'd become too attached, and when that happened, the service stepped in to sever the relationship and protect his identity.

When Will received nightly arrangements from gay guys, it was usually from men well past their prime, whose clubbing days were long over, Grindr days too, and they just wanted some company in a safe and nonjudgmental environment. Several asked to ogle his body while they jerked off or for permission to touch him. It was insane the number of requests Will received for blowjobs. Some probably reveled in the fantasy of it, or just wanted to experience the good old days, or maybe to see if they still had it—to make another human being feel good with their hands or mouths. It was the part of the business the escorts he'd come across usually never spoke about—except maybe over a few shots of whiskey—even though it happened more regularly than one would assume.

So Will had no idea what to expect as he stepped off the train on Saturday morning, headed up the stairs to street level, and walked inside the Starbucks to meet his newest client. He glanced around the space but couldn't place the guy, and he cursed himself for forgetting to at least inquire about his hair color. And since photos were forbidden on the escort site to protect employee privacy, his client wouldn't know what he looked like either.

As he walked down one aisle to glance at the row of booths, he was suddenly taken aback to see Noah Dixon sitting there, his head bent and his gaze buried in his phone. Will considered saying *fuck it* and leaving the coffee shop, except Noah glanced up at that same moment and tensed when they made eye contact.

Noah glanced all around the coffee shop in a seeming state of panic, his gaze darting side to side as if either hoping for an out or putting some pieces together in his head.

"What are you doing here?" Will blurted out, but he already knew the answer.

Fucking hell.

"Christ. Are you M-Max?" Noah asked unsteadily as he eyed him over his straw. His fingers shook the cardboard cup in his hand. He must've preferred iced coffee, Will noted absently while having a mini freak-out inside his head.

"Are you *James*?" Will replied through gritted teeth. Holy shit, this was not happening. "I thought you said you were *asking for a friend*."

"You knew it was probably a lie," Noah retorted before his gaze dropped to the cardboard lining on his cup as he nervously picked at it. "Fuck...you can just go. We can pretend this never happened, believe me."

Will nodded and twisted toward the entrance to leave. But he was struck by a moment of sympathy for Noah. How hard had it been for him to reach out to Will in the first place? To ask questions and then decide to make the leap and hire an escort?

"*Going alone to these types of events had been awkward for me, and it would really be great not to feel like such an outsider.*"

Will was being unfair, all because he had developed some preconceived notions about his annoyingly perky coworker who was way too good at his job and probably had things easier than him in life. At least that was what he thought before he stepped foot inside this place. He'd admit the other night when Noah flagged him down and asked him questions about his agency, he thought he was probably being...nosy. Afterward, he was half afraid Noah was going to tell all his coworkers about his job as an escort, and he'd either have to quit or just suck it up. He hadn't even considered the possibility that Noah would be just as mortified to be discovered as the one asking the questions. Why else would he use a fake name?

Will sighed and then slid into the booth across from Noah.

Noah's eyes widened. "What are you doing?"

"Helping you out," Will said with a shrug. "Maybe I can suggest someone else from the agency, someone who comes highly recommended. Another guy I would trust."

For some reason that seemed of upmost importance to him now. No way he'd want Noah to have a bad experience out of this. After all, it was him who initially vouched for the company, and he knew of a couple of other escorts who were well respected.

"Okay, sure," Noah replied with what looked like genuine gratitude in his gaze. "Thanks."

After another awkward beat, Noah leaned forward. "So...you're gay?"

"Bi," Will replied. "Mostly into guys, but it certainly helps book jobs. The company likes that I'm...flexible."

Noah blushed a scarlet shade, and Will realized he had just given him one hell of a visual.

After Will ordered his own drink and stirred in some sugar and cream, he noticed how Noah nervously played with the sugar packets in front of him. "So tell me about this event you're hiring an escort for."

Noah took a deep breath. "My friend Tony, who has a place on Fire Island, is throwing a huge birthday party for his boyfriend, Matt. What Matt doesn't know is that he's also going to propose that weekend."

"Cool," Will said with a smile. The entire concept felt completely foreign to him. Not only a party at a beach house on Fire Island, but the notion of some extravagant proposal. It only confirmed to Will his suspicions about Noah's lifestyle. Like out of some Ethan Allen catalog. "So, if the party is at your friend's place...why do you need an escort?"

Will felt like it was a fair question even though it was none of his business. But he still thought it would help him decide which of the other escorts would work best for him. Plus, he couldn't help that his curiosity was piqued. It was one of the only times he'd seen Noah out of sorts, and he wasn't sure exactly what was causing such distress.

"Have you ever been to the Pines or Cherry Grove?" Noah asked with a faraway look in his eyes, as if he were remembering his time spent on Fire Island. The two areas he mentioned were known as gay magnets for many years now in the state of New York.

Will squinted, trying to recall the last time he'd been there. It had only been a couple of times because trekking to the island was practically a luxury for someone like him with limited funds and time. It was a picturesque escape from the city and right now sounded pretty damn good to him. August could be sweltering and miserable in Manhattan, especially using public transportation. Plus, he hadn't gone on any sort of getaway in years. "Sure I have. It's a gay man's paradise."

"Maybe for someone like you," Noah replied, frustration obvious in his voice.

Will's eyebrows knit together as he studied Noah. He wasn't certain if he was referring to looks or lifestyle, but if he had to guess, he meant Will's appearance because his lifestyle was nothing to write home about. Except, it wasn't as if Noah was bad-looking, so Will was unsure where his annoyance was coming from. "Not sure I follow. You'd be able to get plenty of—"

"I can hook up for a night, definitely. But it's never..." Noah remarked, cutting him off, then mumbled, "Maybe for a pity fuck."

"That's a bit of a stretch, isn't it?" Will replied with some disbelief, but as Noah shifted his eyes away from him and flexed his jaw, Will noticed for the first time that Noah was wearing a regular T-shirt and jeans today. Crisp and neat, of course, like straight out of J.Crew, but normally it was a button-down, collared shirt with khakis for work.

And as Noah scratched his shoulder, Will zeroed in on his neck right above the collar area. His skin was thicker and appeared almost layered right below his ear. Will had never noticed it before, and he barely could now with Noah's thick hair nearly obscuring it.

A pity fuck? Bells and whistles clanged in his ears as he glanced in that general direction again, but he didn't want to be caught staring at the leathery skin on Noah's neck, leading down to his shoulder. Did Noah have a birth defect, or maybe he'd been in some sort of accident?

"I mean, don't get me wrong..." Noah was saying, but Will was barely able to keep up between his swirling thoughts. "My family owned property in the Pines pre-Stonewall era, before it became more popular than Cherry Grove as a gay resort. That was how I first met Tony, and we share mutual friends from our summers spent there. But that was a long time ago, and since then…I'd just rather be doing my thing in the city. But a birthday party and a proposal? I can't miss something like that. It's too important, you know?"

Noah had paused and was waiting for him to respond, but too many things were swirling through Will's brain, so he just mumbled in agreement and tried to process what he had figured out thus far. Noah spent summers at Fire Island with his family, so they probably had some money. Except Noah worked in a regular retail job for barely above minimum wage. Something must've happened. He wasn't sure what. But Noah no longer enjoyed spending time there.

And he made it sound like guys only slept with him out of pity. So that factored into his reasoning for hiring an escort. Will would've never guessed this was the same cheery, obnoxious guy he'd worked with at Home and Hearth all these months. He was the picture of a Midtown city type but obviously had some things to hide. And didn't they all?

"So what do you think?" Noah asked suddenly, breaking him out of his heavy thoughts. He was tapping his fingers on the table, and Will realized that his own coffee had practically gone untouched. "Is there someone else you have in mind? All he'd need to do is pretend to be my date, and I'd only expect… Well, I don't know yet; we'd have to figure out the details. It would just be nice not to have to go alone."

As Noah stared at him across the table, his deep blue eyes open and earnest, Will considered what a simple assignment that weekend might actually be. At least he knew Noah. It seemed like easy money.

"How about… I mean, if you're not too opposed to it…" Will gulped. Was he really going to suggest this? "How about I go with you to Fire Island after all?"

Noah shook his head. "Don't do it out of mercy. *Please.*"

Will's heart rose to his throat as he glanced at Noah's pleading eyes.

Damn, he felt like shit in that moment. And he imagined Noah saying something similar to other people in his life. But it wasn't pity. It was empathy. Understanding. He had some shitty stuff going on in his life too.

"Of course not," he said in a throaty voice, trying to dislodge the boulder planted there. "The more I think about it... It'll just be easier. Because we're acquaintances, and now I sort of know what you'd need from an escort."

Noah stared at him for the longest minute, as if trying to read something behind his eyes. Then slowly...slowly, he reached out his hand toward Will. "Okay, then. Deal."

5

NOAH

Noah felt calmer than he had thirty minutes ago when he first spotted Will in the same Starbucks as him. What the hell were the odds? But then he all but spilled his guts to the guy because as it turned out Will was easier to talk to than he'd imagined. Once he got past his detached exterior, which he guessed was sort of a front to hide behind, he kind of had this soothing vibe that Noah latched on to with both hands.

Once they finished their drinks, he headed toward the busy sidewalk, following behind Will. The guy who'd just agreed to accompany him to a weekend getaway on Fire Island as his escort. Holy shit.

"What are your plans today?" he asked, just to have something to say. But also because he was pretty curious about Will's life. More curious than ever before.

Will turned to face him and then glanced at the time stamp on his phone. "I was actually headed over to this Off-Broadway show called *Revive* to see some old friends in the production."

He didn't know why this surprised him. "Cool. I've heard good things about that show."

Will's eyes suddenly seemed to light up. "You, uh, interested? I have two tickets waiting in case I wanted to bring a friend."

Noah waved him off. He certainly didn't want Will to feel obligated to be friendlier now that they had an arrangement. "No, it's okay. You wouldn't normally want to hang with me, so it's all cool."

Will bit his lip as if thinking how to word something. "But... maybe we should? It might help us look more...natural."

Noah stared into his eyes to see if he was only humoring him. He did have a point. If they could show up for the weekend looking like they at least enjoyed each other's company instead of just tolerating each other, it might make the whole thing easier. "Yeah, okay. Good idea."

"Let's go." They walked two blocks to the train that would get them to Union Square. It was awkward at first, like two people stuck together for a common goal, and Noah considered backing out. Except, how would he ever get used to Will if he didn't at least get to know him better? Once they got to ground level again, they casually strolled through a farmer's market in the square. The sun felt warm on his skin, and Noah thought it was turning into a pretty nice day. He was doing something different, something out of his comfort zone, but it wasn't so bad. He was actually sort of enjoying himself.

"Ever come down here on weekends?" Will asked, glancing over his shoulder at a vegetable stand.

"Nah, usually I can catch a good street fair closer to my apartment...if I feel like weaving through a shitload of people."

"Tell me about it," Will replied. "Not many places without crowds in the city, though."

"True. You couldn't pay me to walk through Times Square on a weekend night."

"Not unless you're there for a show," Will said, and there was a spark in his gaze. Theater meant something to him, and now they were headed to a production to see *old friends*, who had apparently reserved tickets for him. Was he a theater major, or did he just enjoy live productions? Noah's interest was definitely piqued.

There was a short line waiting to get into the show, but it went fast, and as soon as they stepped inside, Noah noticed how small the space was, which was typical for these types of productions.

Off-Broadway shows weren't as well attended, unless it was a runaway hit, and Noah wondered if marketing was one of the reasons. But he'd definitely heard of this one; it had been getting good buzz the last few months, even though given the size of the theater, which looked like it would probably seat less than a hundred people, it was more than likely considered an Off-*Off-*Broadway show.

As Noah sat in the dead-center middle seats of the theater with Will of all damn people—or should he call him Max?—he was still shell-shocked that his own coworker had been the one to meet him at the coffee shop out of so many possible outcomes. How naive had he been to think Will would use his real name? He'd anticipated this day going totally differently but was still pleasantly surprised nonetheless.

In its own way, it was somewhat of a comfort that Will was someone Noah knew and not some creeper or potential serial killer. Not that escort services hired serial killers. And suddenly that got him thinking about the job from Will's point of view. Was it just as intimidating from his end too?

Noah wanted to ask Will all sorts of questions. But before he could ask anything more, the curtain rose and the show began. And it was riveting. Completely entertaining. And Noah realized why this low-budget production had gotten so much buzz. He just wished they had better attendance as well as backing. He knew actors were hardworking, but most also needed second jobs to make ends meet. He understood a little better why.

When the lights came on ninety minutes later, Will turned with a smile toward Noah. "Did you like it?" he asked with dreamy eyes, leaving Noah with the impression that theater lit him up in a special way.

"It was amazing," Noah replied. "Thanks for inviting me."

"Yeah, sure," he remarked, standing up and straightening his shirt. "They definitely put on a good show."

Suddenly Will raised his hand in a wave. The main actor of the performance was peeking out of the curtain and motioning to Will. "That's my friend. Do you mind going backstage for a few minutes?"

"Not at all." Noah had never been behind-the-scenes of a production, and he found it all pretty fascinating as they walked through the tiny hall, past backdrops and lighting, to the dressing rooms. A couple of behind-the-scenes people greeted Will or clapped him on the back like they were well-acquainted.

Will knocked timidly on the main dressing-room door, and when they heard the okay, they stepped inside. The star of the show, a handsome guy with brown hair and a nice smile, pulled Will into a hug that somehow seemed more intimate than a friendly gesture. Did these two have a history?

"It's good to see you," the star said, and suddenly Noah felt like he was intruding, so he stayed back. "We miss you around here."

"I miss it too sometimes," Will responded, drawing back from the tight grasp. "The show is still as good as ever."

When the man looked over Will's shoulder, Will turned as if suddenly remembering he had brought Noah with him. "Len, this is my...coworker, Noah."

Noah stepped forward to reach for his hand. "Nice to meet you. Great show."

"Thanks for coming," he replied, but then his eyes turned back to Will, and they apparently had a lot of catching up to do, so Noah stood nearby and listened to them discuss lighting and props and actors they both knew as he took in the tiny dressing room that was a bit messy and cramped. He couldn't help wondering...so many things. As it turned out, Will was a mystery, and Noah was suddenly glad he'd had the opportunity to spend an afternoon with him.

Afterward they strolled back through the farmer's market, where Will claimed he was famished, so he bought some apples and grapes while Noah purchased some crusty bread and cheese, and they sat on a nearby bench, having an impromptu picnic of sorts.

"Go ahead and ask," Will said after taking a bite of his Granny Smith, the juice dripping down his chin. "I know you want to."

Noah used a plastic knife to cut off a piece of cheese for Will. "What do you mean?"

Will motioned toward the theater. "Why did I quit? How am I an escort? Am I right?"

"Well, now that you mention it..." Noah shrugged, feeling a flush line his cheeks. "Seems you and Len have some sort of history. Like maybe he's your ex?"

Will stopped chewing and swiped at his chin. "That obvious, huh?"

"It wasn't that hard to put together," Noah said as he reached for a grape.

"We broke up last year. It just wasn't working between us, and I had a bunch of family shit going on anyway. That's when I decided to walk away from theater too. Clean break, fresh start," Will said, and when Noah only raised his eyebrows, he continued. "The pay is way better, and as for the store, it offers more regular hours."

Noah nodded and chewed on a piece of bread as he considered what Will had shared.

"Did you give up your dream?" Noah asked, and Will sucked in a shaky breath.

"Not sure yet. For now, it's a break...while I get some other things in order."

They remained silent for another beat, each lost in their own thoughts. Noah stared straight ahead, watching a juggler who had set up his act near the street corner and laid down a hat for tips from passersby.

"Do you like it at least? Being an escort?" Noah winced as he asked, not sure if he had overstepped bounds. But they had already been so frank with each other at the coffee shop, so why stop now? It was refreshing, really. No expectations, just the plain truth.

Will shrugged. "Sometimes. It's sort of like acting—performing a role. Helps me shut off other parts of my brain."

Shit, he hadn't considered the whole acting part, but it made sense. His stomach tightened, wondering if Will would be performing with him as well.

"Do you ever fear for your safety?" The question rolled off his tongue before he could stop it.

Will turned in his seat and scrunched his nose. "You plan on pulling a knife on me? Threatening to stab me if I don't suck your cock?"

Holy fuck. Noah turned beet red and nearly choked on a grape at the mere mention of anything physical happening between them.

"Just messing with you." Will chuckled and then stood up and stretched. "I gotta get home. But I'll walk with you to the train."

They threw away their scraps on their way to the subway. Once down the stairs, they'd be heading in opposite directions.

"Well, this is me," Will said, motioning to the side heading downtown. "I'll see you at work."

"Sounds good," Noah said. "And...thanks again."

But strangely, he wasn't ready to part ways yet. What if Will had questions? What if there was something they needed to talk about?

Noah turned to leave, but then stopped and called to Will over his shoulder. "Hey, wait!" It had to be normal to exchange numbers, right?

He pulled out his cell and stepped closer to Will so passengers could get around them. "If anything changes or you have questions before that weekend, let me know. Otherwise I can meet you at Penn Station, and we can ride to Long Island together."

"Good idea. It'd be too suspicious to do that at work."

After quickly exchanging numbers, they went their separate ways. Noah was grateful for the turn of events as well as for the nice afternoon—it was totally unexpected, and he couldn't help whistling all the way home, thinking about his weekend at Fire Island. He maybe even looked forward to it.

6

WILL

Will thought the next couple of weeks leading up to the Fire Island party were sort of surreal. Although he worked some shifts with Noah, they didn't speak much out on the floor and didn't make any significant eye contact either. He did catch Noah staring at him a couple of times before he quickly looked away. But Will was guilty of the same thing.

He wasn't able to notice any more scarring on Noah, especially since his collar and hair covered it all too well, but he couldn't help studying him more closely regardless. Noah was the same happy, confident sales associate he always was. His style was different than Will's, that was for certain, and as a result, Will had always considered him a bit obnoxious. Noah sought people out with a cheery greeting the moment they stepped into Home and Hearth, whereas Will always hung back and let the customer get the lay of the land first before approaching them.

No doubt Noah sold the most on their team and was probably on the fast track to management. Will was fine with average sales —it wasn't his passion, after all; as long as he enjoyed the job for the most part and received a steady paycheck, that was all that mattered.

Will wasn't sure how their weekend together would go and if it would make him avoid Noah even more afterward. Why had Will made this decision in the first place? They were coworkers, for Christ's sake, and in another few days there would be a paid transaction tethering them together.

But Noah had looked so vulnerable that day at the coffee shop, and Will felt this visceral need to help the guy out. Maybe even protect him. If he was being honest, the idea of suggesting a different escort made his stomach sour. Besides, he'd be getting paid for an entire weekend on Fire Island with perfect beach weather, if they were lucky.

They both asked for the same couple of days off the schedule, but they interacted so infrequently that nobody batted an eye. Regardless, it was the first time he made a request to rearrange his schedule since he started working there, so the manager was cool about it.

Will and Noah may not have communicated much inside the store, but outside of work seemed different. They actually texted occasionally, asking random questions leading up to their weekend. He had enjoyed his afternoon with Noah in Union Square, so it almost felt natural to bounce things off him.

Maybe they both felt braver when they weren't face-to-face.

So what do I wear? Will asked one night while lying in bed. **Is this a formal gig?**

Nah, parties are usually pretty chill. Shorts, beachwear mostly.

Cool. And how about sleeping arrangements?

There was a long pause that made Will wonder if he had thrown Noah off.

Um, I'm not sure? I've always stayed in the same upstairs bedroom at the beach house. I assume it's a similar arrangement. But hey, if you want to get a hotel or plan for a separate room, that is totally cool.

He could almost picture Noah getting all flustered like he did at the coffee shop. Completely different from how he was on the sales floor.

No worries! I'm supposed to be pretending to be your date, remember?

God, this is so stupid. I'm sorry if you feel put on the spot.

Deep breaths. Unless you're an obnoxious snorer, I've slept in plenty of beds with "friends" before. It'll all work out.

It was the first time Will really wondered what Noah wanted out of this arrangement besides the companionship part. He was going to strongly guess it would be hands-off, which worked just fine for him. No need to make this more awkward than it was, especially at work.

Besides, Noah had looked completely mortified when Will had joked with him at the farmer's market.

All right. Just make sure you let me know if something feels...off or uncomfortable.

How about just letting this happen naturally? Let's not overanalyze. And remember, I've been doing this a while, and I'm pretty decent at this job.

Will could see the dots as Noah typed, but the short message didn't match the time it took him to compose it.

Okay...and thanks again.

Will chalked it up to nerves, which probably meant it was a good idea that they get more used to one another.

The following Sunday, when the store closed early for the day, he and Noah both walked out at the same time behind Kara, their manager, and after they said their goodbyes, Will turned to Noah, who also seemed to be dragging his feet; maybe he had the same notion.

"Are you headed straight home?" Will asked.

"Yeah, was gonna grab something to eat and then clean my apartment," Noah said, scrunching up his nose like it was an unpleasant chore, which totally went against the picture Will had formed of Noah. He figured his place was spotless and organized.

But there he went with his assumptions again. Besides, you could still have a nice place and not like cleaning. Who the hell loved scrubbing toilets anyway?

"Hey, guys," their coworker Samantha said, startling them. She must've gone into the bagel shop for the steaming cup of coffee she was now sipping from. She glanced guiltily between them as if she'd interrupted their conversation, and then abruptly said good night.

Noah must've picked up on it as well, since he called after her. "Where are you off to tonight?"

She turned and smiled. "To meet the boyfriend in SoHo for dinner."

"Have fun," Noah replied as she took off toward the subway. Noah blew out a breath as he turned back to Will. "So, you were saying?"

Maybe this was a bad idea after all. Except why couldn't they have a conversation? They were coworkers, for Christ's sake. "I'm in the mood for dumplings from Veng's. Feel like coming with so I can ask more questions? We can hop on the A and get off at 34th."

Noah's eyes widened as he swallowed roughly. For a split second Will thought for sure Noah would turn him down, and he wanted to kick himself for even suggesting it.

Noah glanced toward the nearest cross street. "Sure. Feel like walking?"

Relief soared through him. "Perfect."

Will didn't have any plans that night, and his mom was out to dinner with a friend who visited her every few weeks. He had a couple of extra hours to kill, even though he could've gone home and scrubbed the toilet too. But what fun was that? He had enough responsibilities between the two jobs, and he hated being away from his mom too many nights in a row in case she got stir-crazy in the apartment. It just felt better when he could physically check on her—which led to his anxieties about the weekend at Fire Island. Plus, the more he knew, the better.

They made small talk as they navigated the crowded street away from Rockefeller Center.

"So hit me with your questions," Noah said once they got more room between them on the pavement.

"Want to tell me about the friends I'm going to meet next weekend?"

"Good idea." They narrowly missed a taxi that'd careened through the busy cross street, and Will marveled that there weren't more accidents. "Like I already mentioned, I've known Tony my entire life. Total player until he met Matt."

"The man he's going to propose to?" Will asked.

"Right." Noah nodded. "He fell hard for him, and I'll admit they're perfect together."

"Cool," Will said, and it vaguely made him wonder how many relationships Noah had been in over the years, especially given the way he talked about his dating life now. "So...your friends are bound to ask us questions, like how we met."

"Crap. I didn't even consider that." He took several measured breaths as if to calm himself down. "You're good at this."

Will was now glad he asked Noah to join him. He was more nervous than Will had first suspected.

Will chuckled. "It definitely helps to be on the same page, especially if you're going to an event where you have to meet people," he explained. "If it's only going to be me and the customer, it obviously doesn't matter."

Noah faltered on the pavement. "Wait, so sometimes it's just you and them alone together?"

"Well, yeah," he replied warily, as if he had to be careful what he said next or it might scare Noah off. "Sometimes my customers just want...company."

"Yeah, okay. Makes sense," Noah said, and then they walked on in silence for a couple of blocks, which left Will wondering what in the hell Noah was thinking. Was he comparing himself to those clients or reconsidering the entire weekend?

"Does that bother you?" Will finally asked, figuring it was better to get it out in the open.

"I don't think so?" Noah responded, as if he was unsure. "Just stuff I haven't thought about before. And besides, I'm pretty much doing the same thing."

"Right," Will replied cautiously. "Companionship to get you through an uncomfortable time."

There was a heaviness to the air between them as they turned the corner onto Park Avenue.

"Would it be stupid to just say we met through work?" Noah asked, apparently thinking hard about it. "It's the truth at least."

Will looked off in the distance as if considering it. "It's not stupid, but it's…boring. If we're going to pretend, might as well go big or go home."

Noah cringed. "Big how?"

"Let me think on it," he said with a devilish smile. "Maybe a fated thing like you see in romantic comedies. Our eyes met across the room, something like that. Because, why not?"

Noah shook his head as if balking at his idea, even though Will was really only trying to lighten the mood between them.

"No way they'd buy something like that," he scoffed. "*I* certainly wouldn't."

"What, you're not a romantic at heart?" Will jested.

"Fuck no," Noah replied, rolling his eyes. "I'm a realist, obviously."

"Oh, I hear you," Will agreed and fist-bumped him.

"So just the met-at-work idea, then?" Noah asked.

"Totally cool. I was mostly just messing around."

"Oh. Duh." Noah's cheeks turned red, and for some reason, Will found it endearing. "Okay."

After they placed their dumplings order at Veng's, they took their bag of food across the street to a tiny park, where they shared a bench and ate them.

"These are the best dumplings I've had in the city."

"Told you so," Will said, wiping his mouth with a napkin. "Thanks for coming with me."

"You're welcome," Noah replied, smiling shyly as he used more sesame sauce.

Once they were sated, Noah stood up to throw away their empty containers. Will's phone buzzed with a text from his mom. **I'm home, honey.**

That was his cue to leave. He texted back. **Be there soon.**

"Well, I better get going," Will said, standing and stretching. He was surprisingly bummed. Hanging with Noah was a nice reprieve from his normal routine.

"Yeah, me too," Noah replied as they walked to the nearest subway station. "Text if you think of anything else before the weekend."

A FEW NIGHTS LATER, WILL GOT HOME REASONABLY EARLY FROM Home and Hearth and stopped for takeout from his mom's favorite Thai place in the East Village.

"Hey, Ma," he said as he came through the door, holding up the bag. She was on the couch, watching one of her favorite reality shows that featured housewives from different cities. She looked calm and content even though she was still in her nightgown from that morning.

After she helped him pull the containers from the bag and he retrieved a couple of forks and plates from the kitchen, she patted the cushion beside her. "Come sit by me. A catfight is about to break out between these two."

Will stared at the screen as the two women began yelling over each other. "I don't know how you can stand the arguing."

His mom chuckled. "Sometimes it helps me remember that my life can be pretty calm in comparison."

"I see what you mean," Will replied as he leaned over to kiss her cheek. His heart quickened as he realized that they indeed had a calmer couple of months even with the recent change in dosage the psychiatrist had prescribed. There were a couple of shaky nights where she didn't seem to be herself, but then she appeared to snap out of it.

"So remember, I'll be gone this weekend."

She glanced over at him. "Remind me again where you're going?"

"To a party on Fire Island," he replied. "With my friend Noah. I work with him."

"Noah? Why have I never heard of him before?"

Will stiffened at the question. "He's a newer friend."

"Well, that's good, honey. You work too much anyway. Time away will be good," she said and then laughed at something on the screen.

"Anyway, I leave in the morning," he reminded her again and then stood up to clear their plates.

"Sounds like fun. And maybe fancy too. You have something nice to wear?"

"Yeah, I think I'm all set," he replied as he absently washed the dishes and then sat back down to watch more of her show with her.

He couldn't even remember anything leading up to bedtime, he was so preoccupied with his weekend plans.

By the time the morning rolled around, Will felt like he had tossed and turned all night, and anxiety had taken hold again. Especially about leaving his mom. He should've visited Oren for some of his tea concoction, but he feared he'd spill his guts and maybe even talk himself out of it.

"Remember," he said while she stood at the counter in her robe, pouring herself a cup of coffee. "You can always text or call."

"You worry too much," she said around a yawn and then patted his cheek. "You're a good son, William. I wish you'd find someone nice to make you happy."

His heart banged in his chest. He got irritable with her sometimes, especially when she was careless about her meds. But damn, she'd been dealt a tough hand. She'd always been a good mom, and even when she was delusional, she wasn't harmful to anyone but herself. When she would wander out into the street or hide in make-believe bunkers because the government was out to get her, she was putting herself in danger. He was always terrified she'd get mowed over by a car or someone would get pissed off enough to beat her up and leave her for dead.

"*You* make me happy; that's all I need for now."

Will left their apartment and went down to the first floor, where he knocked on the superintendent's door. The building was owned by an older couple who'd been decent to his mom—and as long as he slipped them some extra cash with their rent, all was good. "I just wanted to remind you that I'll be gone the entire weekend."

Mr. Wilkens smiled. "Go enjoy yourself. She'll be fine. The wife will be sure to check on her a couple of times."

Will nodded. "You still have my number—"

"Yes, of course; programmed in my phone," he said in a sterner voice. "Now go on. You deserve to have fun."

Will passed him an additional twenty just to be sure.

Mr. Wilkens quickly shoved it in his pocket before looking both ways and creaking the door shut. "Get going, kid."

Kid. Christ, he was shy of twenty-nine.

Will raced down the steps to the train, feeling like maybe all would be okay. He'd only left town with a client once, and he'd been so nervous, he balked at any out-of-town assignments ever since. But this was close enough—well, a couple of hours out of town instead of a plane ride away—that it felt doable.

He met Noah at Penn Station so they could ride to Sayville

together and then catch a ferry to Fire Island. Noah's smile was sort of wooden, and he kept wiping his palms on his thighs, so Will knew Noah was nervous too. But today he was dressed more casual, with some cut-off shorts that were frayed at the hem and a soft-washed T-shirt that brought out the color of his eyes. He was actually glad to see that Noah let loose a bit when he was with his friends.

Instead of talking Will's ear off, like he might've done with customers at work, Noah was unusually subdued on the train. But *Max* was on the clock now, and he had a role to perform. He had plenty of experience making his clients feel at ease, and hopefully he could work his magic with Noah as well.

7
NOAH

The only word that came to Noah's mind on the ferry ride over to Fire Island was *awkward*. What in the hell had he gotten himself into? Had he lost his common sense to not only hire an escort, but to also actually think he could pull this arrangement off in front of his closest friends?

He suddenly felt sick, like he needed to vomit, so he hopped off the bench and headed toward the railing of the ferry, which would be pulling up to Fire Island in another twenty minutes. It would be just his luck to puke his guts out in front of Will.

No, *Max*. Max was his escort name. They'd decided during a text conversation two nights ago to use his escort name this weekend because it might be better that way, easier. He could be his Max persona while he pretended to be Noah's date, and when they got back to the city and to Home and Hearth, he would be Will again. The separation, Will had reasoned, might help them compartmentalize this event in their brains. Noah agreed because he certainly didn't want them to be uncomfortable around each other at work after this.

He stared out at the water and swallowed back the warm bile in his throat.

"Hey," Will said from behind him, and Noah's shoulders bunched up. Christ, what had he done?

Will's fingers danced lightly against his forearm, and he resisted the urge to cower away. "Just say the word, and I'll catch the next ferry back. No sweat. People change their minds all the time. I know this feels strange, especially since we work together."

And yet the idea of showing up solo, *again*, didn't sit well with Noah either. He was a head case of conflicting thoughts.

He turned and faced Will. "Really?"

"Well, yeah," Will said, scratching his neck. "Wait, which part?"

A grin tugged at Noah's mouth, but he tamped it down. "About people changing their minds."

"Definitely," Will responded, leaning his forearms on the railing and staring out at the water. "It might seem like a good idea at the onset, but people get nervous, chicken out…freak."

"I'm not a chicken or a *freak*," Noah bit out. The phrases had been a source of contention for him since he was a kid, so he couldn't help himself. "I just—"

"Sorry, wrong choice of words." Will shook his head. "It's just that you hired me for a whole weekend, so I can understand if it suddenly feels a bit too much for you."

Noah licked his lips, measuring his words. "I was actually thinking it might be too much for *you*."

Will's eyebrows knit together. "What do you mean?"

"Too much for you to, you know, *pretend*…that you're attracted to me." Noah winced and found he couldn't look him in the eye.

He was startled when Will snickered, and his gaze snapped to him. He narrowed his eyes. Fuck him for finding this funny.

"You obviously think you're some sort of troll," Will said in disbelief. "Christ, who ruined that for you? I'd like to give him a serious ass-whooping."

Noah glanced away. No way did he want to get into how one

of his first crushes practically destroyed him by acting completely disgusted by his scars.

"I'm just being realistic. You'll see what I mean soon enough," Noah muttered as he studied Will's appearance, much like he did the first time he noticed him at Penn Station that morning. His T-shirt pulled nicely across his physique, and Noah imagined how his friends would respond to seeing him with such an attractive guy. "You'll fit in perfectly."

Will's fingers suddenly grazed his shoulder directly below his scars. "Is this the reason? You're worried what people think when they see you?"

Noah shrugged away from Will's touch and immediately saw the regret in Will's gaze. "It's not a worry; it's a fact. Men either ignore me or give me a wide berth. Always been that way."

Will sighed. "Well, then it's their loss."

Noah swallowed and turned away, eyes focused on how the ferry cut perpendicularly through the waves.

He could feel Will's warm brown gaze on him but didn't want to face him right then. The kicker was that Will was hired to act the part of an attentive date, and wasn't that exactly what was wrong with this whole arrangement? He took a deep breath. Too late now. He needed to accept what he'd done. Maybe it wouldn't be too bad. Will wasn't an asshole, after all. In fact, it hadn't been a hardship spending time with him thus far.

"Since we have a few more minutes before we dock, tell me what Tony's place is like."

"Okay, sure." They sat back down on the hard bench near an older couple holding hands. "It's a large beach house that's been refurbished in recent years."

"Expensive taste?" Will asked.

"Definitely." Noah nodded. "Not gonna lie, my family has money too, but I... I've been doing things on my own terms the past few years."

"Is there a reason for that?" Will asked in a hesitant tone. "Not that it's any of my business."

Noah winced. "Too long of a story. But in a nutshell, my parents can be...overbearing at times."

"Got it." Will looked off in the distance as if considering it. "Will they be at this party?"

"Last time we talked they were traveling in the UK for my father's company and meeting up with my half sister, Amanda, who lives in London." He last saw Amanda during the holidays a couple of years ago. She was thirty-three—five years older than Noah—and married to a museum curator. His dad loved to brag about his daughter from his short-lived first marriage; despite his father's divorce from her mother, their families had always remained close. "Plus, my parents rent their place in the Grove practically every weekend all summer long." People paid a premium to stay out there for the summer.

"Maybe I should be thankful I don't have to meet the 'rents?" Will asked with a cocked brow.

"Ha! For sure."

Will winked, and it made Noah feel fleetingly buoyant, like maybe this weekend would work out as he envisioned after all. At least they'd be in it together, and wasn't that exactly what he wanted? Someone to share his time with, even temporarily?

"You look nice, by the way," Will stated in a serious tone. "And I'd definitely kill for your hair."

Noah absently pushed behind his ear a stray lock that continued getting tangled in the wind coming off the water. His hair had a natural wave to it, and wearing it a bit longer always felt like a shield from the outside world. "Thanks. Um, are you already in escort mode?"

"Because I said I liked your hair?" Will scoffed. "Guess you need to learn how to take a compliment. I mean, you dress better than anyone I hang with, and somehow your eyes are a color I've never seen. And today they really stand out against the water."

At this point Noah would've normally felt like the guy was laying it on pretty thick, but Will sounded so sincere that he allowed himself to relax and let down some of his defenses. He'd heard compliments about his clothes before. Once or twice about his eyes as well, which he knew were an unusual shade of blue gray. But he mostly dressed to hide his scars, so hearing otherwise actually felt nice.

"Well, thanks," Noah muttered, his cheeks growing warm.

"You're very welcome," Will said with a smile, and it was catching. Noah found himself grinning back.

"So who else will be there this weekend?" Will asked after another minute, and as he leaned in, Noah decided he liked the way the man smelled—soapy clean and a bit like saltwater as well, which had everything to do with being on a ferry driving them across the Atlantic.

Noah considered the question a moment. "Usual crowd. Some guys who like to party and others who are sort of shallow. Hooking up for the whole weekend."

"And you've never done that?" Will asked in a lower register that made him shiver.

"I just…" Noah shook his head once, conjuring up that miserable feeling from the pit of his stomach from so many of these damn parties. "It's like getting picked last in gym, you know, and after a while you don't want to be somebody's sloppy seconds. Can we just…leave it at that?"

Will nudged him with his shoulder. "Thanks for entertaining my questions. It helps me do my job better."

Noah grew motionless and almost wished he didn't have the reminder as a constant backdrop. That Will was only here because he hired him to be.

Will sensed his change in mood immediately. "I promise I'm here for you too, as a friend. I mean, now that I've gotten to know you a bit better. I hope you believe me."

Noah nodded and then pasted on a bright smile. "I just want to feel comfortable and have a good time. Think we can do that?"

Their eyes met for a long, drawn-out moment. "Definitely."

8

WILL

After grabbing their bags and departing the ferry, they strolled down the main boardwalk to the section of Fire Island known as the Pines. From what he'd heard, gay men and women began inhabiting the Pines in the sixties to keep their sexuality more private than they could in Cherry Grove, which by that time had become known as the gay mecca. It didn't take long for the Pines to become the destination for gay men and women of a certain status, which was evidenced by stories of legendary parties in equally legendary houses built for just such occasions.

But the island still drew all types of beach lovers, with traditional families inhabiting some of the more suburban parts of the island spanning about thirty-two miles along the coast. And according to Noah, his family had been vacationing on the island for years, and that was where he met his friend Tony.

Will was again taken in by the vibe and charm of the island, as well as the modern, clean lines of the homes and businesses in the Pines, which—if he remembered this right from his previous visits—contrasted Cherry Grove's more understated style. And he definitely understood what Noah was getting at with all the beautiful men. They had already passed several on the street, some holding hands, others in skimpy Speedos, and by the time Will considered that maybe the two of them should show up with their fingers clasped so there was no question about them, the picturesque beach house had already come into view.

"Damn, that's gorgeous," Will remarked, staring at the two-story mini mansion. The home boasted an outdoor patio and pool area and wall-to-ceiling windows facing the ocean—basically something for everyone to envy.

"Noah, you made it," a tan, fit man wearing blue swim trunks called out as he stood near another handsome guy just inside the sliding glass doors.

"Wouldn't miss it," Noah responded in a tight voice that alerted Will to his renewed anxiety. Will placed his hand on the small of Noah's back and murmured words of reassurance as they walked up the small stone stairway from beach level. Several pairs of eyes turned toward them as they passed by the beach chairs lining the pool.

After Noah's friends drew him into friendly hugs and claps on the back, he turned to Will. "Um, this is my friend Tony and his boyfriend, Matt."

Will waited for an introduction that didn't quite come in time to avoid an awkward silence from descending. He stepped forward and offered his hand. "I'm Max."

"Fuck, sorry," Noah blurted as if he'd suddenly snapped out of a trance. Will noticed how Matt smirked at Tony as they eyed their friend. They had to have recognized his nerves as well.

"It's nice to meet you, Max," Tony replied. "Glad you could make it."

"Thanks," Will said. "I'm sure you hear it all the time, but this place is amazing."

Tony smiled. "Yeah, it's pretty cool and perfect for parties. It belongs to my family, so we've been coming here for years."

Will nodded. "Noah told me that's how you know each other."

"That's right. We go way back," Tony acknowledged as they

followed them into the large, modern kitchen, done in gray tones with black and white fixtures and fitted with stainless-steel appliances.

"Want to put your stuff in your bedroom?" Tony asked, and he must've picked up on Noah's hesitation because he added, "Unless we read this wrong? Noah hadn't exactly mentioned who he was bringing, but if you're the new guy in his life, we couldn't be happier."

"Or more surprised," Noah mumbled under his breath, and Will could feel the slight tension between the friends. Noah's love life was apparently a thorny subject between them.

"You know Noah," Matt added. "Probably didn't want to jinx anything. But glad to have you."

"Thanks," Will replied, nudging Noah so he'd snap out of it. "Going to the room would be great."

Suddenly he wondered if this was such a great idea after all. Would Noah be this wooden the entire weekend?

Will felt completely out of his element as Tony ushered them through the lavish great room with the stone fireplace, tall ceilings, and exposed wooden beams. *Must be nice to have money at your fingertips.* But he squashed down the envy. It never solved anything. Besides, he was good at being a chameleon. In fact, much of his clientele were well off—otherwise they wouldn't be able to afford to pay an escort regularly.

Still, the realization had painted Noah in a new light. Noah's family was well off; they owned property on this island, and given the expensive house they were staying in, that meant Noah was used to this sort of extravagance. He mentioned that his parents were overbearing, but why make such a clean break by working for base pay as a sales associate?

Thoughts spinning, Will followed Noah up the grand staircase to the bedroom at the end of the hall. As soon as they were alone, all Noah's pretenses seemed to melt away as he relaxed his jaw as well as his posture. It was almost as if he'd arrived in a suit of armor, and Will desperately wanted to understand why. Outside of what he'd already shared and Will pieced together, there had to be more.

Hand planted on the doorknob, Noah bit his lip in a demure sort of way that appeared almost virginal. Gone was the overconfident sales associate from work, as well as the robotic man from downstairs. Now it was the bashful, awkward guy who'd hired an escort after admitting he'd rather not show up here alone. "Are you sure this is okay? There's a nice hotel down the block if you—"

"I'm cool if you are," Will reiterated and then nudged him to open the door by placing his hand on his shoulder. He felt Noah tremble, so he used a soothing tone. "But thanks again for offering."

They stepped inside to a plush king-size bed, a Jacuzzi tub, and a large couch. When his gaze snagged on the French doors leading to a balcony with a view of the ocean, his jaw dropped. "Holy shit, this is unbelievable."

Noah blinked as if taking it all in through new eyes. "Yeah, guess it is. Been coming here for so long, suppose I sort of…got used to it."

"Not sure this is anything I could ever get used to," he muttered through a clenched jaw, that same envy rearing its ugly head.

Will threw open the French balcony doors and stepped out, riveted by the view. He glanced below to the pool area, which was more crowded than when they first arrived.

It was only Friday, and the party wasn't until tomorrow night. "Will it be this packed all weekend?"

Noah sighed. "Yeah. Tony and Matt are cool with it. But sometimes I hate the freeloaders."

"What do you mean?" Will asked as he watched a gorgeous couple spreading lotion on each other.

Noah folded his arms. "Some will come right off the beach,

crash the party, or pretend they're with someone and have a right to be here."

"Well damn," Will replied as he studied Noah's clenched teeth. "Has that happened to you? Someone pretending to be with you in order to—"

"Too many times to count." He turned from the balcony, walked to his bag, and began unloading toiletries. Will's stomach dropped. No wonder he wanted some sort of...what, companion?

But wasn't Will doing the same exact thing? Pretending?

Except it was all on Noah's terms, he supposed, so maybe that made it okay. He could control what he wanted out of this arrangement. But if they were ever going to fool anyone, Noah was going to have to loosen up.

9
NOAH

Well, now Noah had gone and done it—made Will feel sympathy for him. He might've been honest to a fault about the way things were, or at least the way he perceived them to be. But being here always stirred up so many memories for him that felt too close to the surface. He certainly didn't want to go into any details about his scars, though he had caught Will studying his neckline more than once. And not about his parents or the fact that he spent many summers on the island as a kid. After college, he knew he wanted to make it on his own, without their help, and now he had something to show for it. Though some wouldn't think it was much.

Besides, it wasn't exactly like Will was opening up about the details of his own life. That wasn't what this arrangement was supposed to be about anyway. Far from it.

"So what's the lineup for the weekend?" Will asked as he opened his bag and removed some clothes. Noah had shown him which empty drawers to use. He'd always seen this as his room, and outside of random hookups, it felt rather strange to have another man sharing space with him.

"Some people will arrive tonight, and others won't make it

until tomorrow, so Tony wanted to wait until the middle of the party for his surprise proposal," Noah replied as he folded a pair of shorts into a drawer. "So today we'll just help where we're needed and *chill*."

"Got it. So what do people do to chill around here?" Will asked as he gave himself a once-over in front of the vanity.

"Lie on the beach, swim in the pool, *drink*," Noah explained as he glanced in the linen closet, making sure there were enough towels for both of them. "We can also walk around town if that's your thing."

Will's gaze met his own in the mirror. "My thing is your thing."

Noah's cheeks flushed. He couldn't remember anyone being so agreeable, but Will seemed the type of guy who would go with the flow—not that he had any other choice. Noah was fine with lounging around, but honestly, he wasn't much for the beach or pool, not in that sweltering heat. Going shirtless took some courage, even around people who'd known him for years. Besides, the UV rays were not so good for his scars. He was always encouraged to use protection and limit his time in the sun.

"Tonight we'll probably head to a bar in town, but we can play the afternoon by ear," Noah suggested. "And right now, I'm thirsty. How about you?"

"I could definitely use a drink." A dimply smile split Will's face. Damn, he was cute. It would not be a hardship to stare at him all weekend long. Noah only hoped to make it tolerable from his end as well.

"Let's go," Noah said, heading toward the door. "I know how to make a good frozen margarita."

"Sounds perfect." Will clapped his hands together. "Just one more thing."

"What's that?" he asked, turning toward Will.

"I just... I know this has got to feel awkward on some level, but it might not go over too well if you're constantly shrinking back when I get too close."

Noah shook his head, his stomach tightening. "I know. I'm sorry. I'll get used to it."

"It's okay," Will replied, stepping closer. "I just need to know if anything is off-limits for you. I don't want to make you feel uncomfortable."

"No. It's nothing like that. I've just rarely had somebody...so attractive...make the effort—" He briefly shut his eyes and breathed out.

Will reached out and tentatively squeezed his shoulder. Will's cheeks were flushed, but Noah wasn't exactly sure why. "Deep breaths. We'll get through this together."

As they made their way down the stairs, Noah noticed that additional guests had arrived, as evidenced by the chairs taken near the poolside as well as stools around the large kitchen island. Matt had the music turned up; that was always his specialty, since he also dabbled in amateur performance art. He loved dressing in drag or doing open-mic nights at clubs.

Noah said hello and introduced Max to a few men he knew from prior seasons, some old hookups in the bunch as well. Then they went into the kitchen, where Noah reached for a pitcher and made them some margaritas with plenty of crushed ice that was bound to melt quickly in this temperature. He filled a couple of fancy glasses, handed one to Will, and they clinked them for a toast. Will took a sip—Noah didn't know why it mattered what Will thought of his concoction, but when he gave him a thumbs-up in approval, Noah preened like a peacock.

Someday he'd love to throw lavish dinner parties of his own, but they would need to be on his own terms, not at a beach house with beautiful naked men who didn't have a vested interest in him. In fact, before Will became his coworker, Noah had hosted a couple of holiday parties at his apartment and was pleased to admit they were a success.

Noah passed margarita glasses to a couple of random guests around the kitchen island before making another pitcher and storing it in the coolest part of the fridge.

Heading outside, they found two empty chairs in a corner and sat down. After a few minutes of the sun beating down on them, Will took off his shirt just like every other man around the pool, some in nothing more than skimpy Speedos.

One couldn't help admiring Will's smooth skin and nice physique. Noah stopped short of following the trail of dark hair that ran to his belly button and beyond. He reached for the sunscreen on the side table and handed it to him, almost offering to rub it on before he chickened out.

As Will spread the lotion over his arms and neck, he glanced at Noah, who had his knees bent to his chest and his sunglasses on. "Aren't you hot?"

It wasn't a question he hadn't heard before. "Yeah, sure, a little."

"Maybe you should…" He motioned to his shirt.

"Maybe later," Noah replied and then looked away as he took another sip of his drink.

Besides, he didn't want Will to see him like that, his ruined skin on full display. Not yet, maybe not ever. Tony knew how sensitive the topic was for him, and as if on cue, he and Matt pulled up a lounge chair near them and shared the seat, Matt's back to Tony's front. They were always pretty physical with each other, and he'd admit they looked good together.

After making small talk about traffic in the city and their jobs on Wall Street, Matt asked the inevitable question. "So how did you guys meet?"

Before he could fumble his way through their prepared response, Will jumped in with both feet. "It was all me. I work at the Whole Bagel shop near Home and Hearth, and he comes in like clockwork every single day for his cuppa."

Tony raised an eyebrow in Noah's direction, possibly because he knew his friend wasn't a coffee drinker. Shit.

"They have the best lemonade," Noah supplied and threw Will a pointed look. It wasn't like they ever discussed their coffee preferences.

But Will was quick on his feet and caught on to his blunder right away. "Fresh squeezed every day." He delivered the line with a wink. "Anyway, he has the prettiest blue eyes I've ever seen, so one day last month I wrote something on his cup and hoped he'd notice it after he left the shop."

Tony leaned in as if riveted by the story, and Noah's neck burned hot.

"Oooh, what did you write?" Matt asked.

Christ, this was getting ridiculous. Noah wanted to dig a hole in the sand and come up for air later.

"I wrote," Will replied and then paused for effect. "*Meet later? I get off at 6.*"

Noah's cheeks flushed hot. He wondered if his friends would ever let him live it down.

Matt turned toward him in his chair. "So...what did you do?"

Noah's eyes met Will's, and he clenched his fists like he wanted to strangle him. *Go big or go home.* Wasn't that his sentiment the night they walked some twenty blocks for dumplings? He was going to kill him. "I mean, look at him. How could I pass that up?"

Tony thumped Noah's shoulder and chuckled. "You mean, you didn't roll your eyes or try to call his bluff? Shocking."

"Whatever."

Will seemed to watch their exchange with interest. Tony knew Noah well and would always call him on his bullshit. But Noah couldn't help being completely skeptical of any advances or come-ons after so many shitty experiences.

"Eh, he could've easily turned me down," Will said suddenly.

"He didn't really know me or my personality...whether or not we'd click. And that shit is important."

Noah knew what he was trying to do, but goddamn, it pissed him off. No need to get all philosophical about *connecting on a deeper level*.

"True," Tony replied, and Noah nearly rolled his eyes but kept himself in check.

When the pair noticed Tony's parents had arrived, they jumped up to greet them near the sliding glass doors. As soon as they were out of hearing distance, Noah glanced at Will. "Nice story, but such bullshit."

Will furrowed his brows. "Besides the made-up part, what else was BS?"

"You acting like personality is so important when you first meet someone," he replied through a clenched jaw. "You know damn well looks are number one on the list for literally *everyone*."

Will shook his head. "I know plenty of pretty men who are ugly inside."

That was true enough but so not the point. Noah dug his nails into his palm.

"I'd rather be with someone who makes me laugh than someone who only looks nice."

"Okay, fine. I'll concede to that," Noah huffed out. "There are plenty of other things to consider too."

Will tilted his chin. "Such as?"

"Shared values. Sexual compatibility," Noah said, going through the list in his head. "Or how about something as simple as kissing. Because to me, kissing is a big fucking deal."

"Yeah?" Will said with a slight chuckle as if surprised by Noah's response. "What kind of kissing meets your standards?"

Just as Noah was about to answer, Will sat up suddenly and reached for Noah's hand.

"What are you doing?" Noah asked, the urge to snatch his hand away strong.

"Pretending I'm here with you. *Christ.* You're still stiff as a board." Will leaned toward him and lowered his voice. "No one will buy this between us if we aren't even touching."

Noah released a breath. "Okay, true. I just don't want you to feel—"

"I don't." Will squeezed Noah's hand, and it felt...*nice.* "So go on—with the kissing."

Why the hell had he even brought it up in the first place? "I don't know... A lot of tongue ruins it for me. Don't get me wrong, tongue is good when you're in the moment."

"Like during sex?" Will threw out.

Noah nodded, his stomach swooping a bit at the turn of conversation. "It's sexy as hell in the heat of the moment, but not right off the bat. I don't like anyone slobbering on me."

Will casually lifted Noah's hand and brought it toward his mouth. "So...like this?" He kissed the middle of his palm, which sent a shockwave through his system. Before Will pulled away, he softly flicked out his tongue, and it went straight to Noah's cock.

Holy fuck. So unfair.

Noah barely refrained from sighing. "Yeah, just like that, you bastard."

Will laughed and kissed his palm again, apparently enjoying tormenting him.

But Noah had to admit, pretending or not, it felt pretty damned good.

10

WILL

Will had texted his mom to let her know he'd arrived safely, and she messaged back that she was doing fine as well. He took a deep breath and shut his eyes, letting the sun lull him into a short nap. Noah did the same, even though it seemed to take him a bit to get settled.

But as the afternoon wore on, it became obvious how much Noah was not enjoying simply lying in a chair beneath the sun—at least not in a sweaty shirt—so Will asked if he'd like to walk on the beach.

As they strolled along the sand near the shore, Noah pointed down the beach a ways to where his family had once spent their summers. He explained all of it in a blasé manner, as if his emotions were tethered down and barely recognizable to even himself. And now apparently his parents owned a more modest property in Cherry Grove, but mostly rented it out on weekends during the season. He got the impression that the family didn't spend much time together anymore, and Will wondered what had caused that change.

The cool water touching their toes provided instant relief, and they fell into a comfortable silence; at least, Will hoped it was. "You feeling better about me being here?"

Surprise flitted through Noah's gaze. "Yeah, sure. I still can't wrap my head around the fact that I decided to hire someone to act as my—" He shook his head. "Do you feel okay being here?"

"I'm good," Will assured him and then added, "I've been in this scenario before, remember?"

"That's right," Noah replied through a clenched jaw, and it occurred to Will that Noah didn't like hearing that. Either it reminded him Will was a pretend boyfriend, or that Will spent plenty of time in intimate scenarios with other dates. Will had experienced jealousy from his clients every now and again, but this felt different somehow. Noah was a contradiction in all sorts of ways. Naive at times and worldly at others, he definitely intrigued Will. The endearingly innocent way he shut his eyes when Will kissed his palm at the poolside made his stomach feel unsettled.

"You're different out here." Will hadn't meant to say it out loud, but it slipped effortlessly from his mouth.

Noah stopped suddenly and dropped the seashell he had picked up to examine. "What do you mean?"

"Don't know exactly," Will replied, attempting to explain. "It's like, at work you...shine. You're super confident about how painlessly you bring in sales."

"Guess it's what I'm good at," Noah muttered as he stopped to pick up another shell.

"You are," Will admitted. "And I guess I always thought you were over-the-top and almost cocky about it."

"Seriously?" Noah asked in a defensive voice.

"But now I have some perspective," he supplied. "And honestly, who am *I* to judge?" He quirked an eyebrow, and Noah chuckled.

"But why did you think I'm different here?" Noah asked,

motioning to the beach house, which looked like a spec on the horizon now.

"You've been quiet...reserved, almost detached from your surroundings."

Noah nodded. "Guess we switched roles, then."

"Huh?" Will asked as he toed a colorful stone.

"You're hard to get to know at work," Noah replied as he kicked over an empty crab shell. "You keep a barrier up, and I guess I have some perspective now too, but I always wondered if you were just biding your time until something else came along."

"Isn't everyone?" Will mumbled.

"Not me," Noah replied with some verve. "I actually love what I do. Maybe someday I'll manage a store of my own, but for now, working at Home and Hearth really suits me."

That made a lot of sense, come to think of it. He'd probably be promoted someday, based on his tenacity and hard work alone.

"I actually think that's cool. You're great at it," Will replied with a smile, and he could tell by the way Noah's eyes glittered that he enjoyed the compliment. He was proud of his work ethic, that much was evident. "For me retail provides more steady hours, and I need that because..." Will shook his head. No way was he going to go there with his mom and her entire history. "Just because. Want to head back?"

Noah stared at him a moment longer before he nodded and started trekking along the sand.

As they headed up the walkway to the pool area, Will placed his hand on Noah's waist as they slipped through the gate. He felt Noah stiffen, and he didn't know if it was because of him or because of how his skin felt rough and uneven beneath the material. Christ, he wanted to ask, but he didn't have the right.

"Would you rather I didn't touch you when we're around your friends?" he whispered.

"Don't stop," Noah muttered over his shoulder. "I promise it's getting easier."

Will didn't think Noah realized just how much he was throwing him for a loop.

He generally didn't have to ask; his customers were usually explicit with their requests. Either they'd have their hands all over him by the end of the night, or they'd whisper in his ear exactly what they wanted. Not that the evenings always worked out that way. If he wasn't feeling it, he let them know in no uncertain terms, generous tip or not. Though he'd admit the money was enticing, especially when there was an end goal in mind.

Of course, it would be best for Noah and him to be mostly hands-off if they wanted their future encounters at work to be less awkward. But there was just something in Noah's vulnerability that made Will want to prove to him that he was enjoyable to be around. Christ, the guy saw himself as some pariah in the sea of all these attractive men, and if there was one thing Will had learned, it was that having someone to talk to, laugh with, and hold at night was really the most important thing. Fuck, look at all his lonely clients who simply yearned for human contact.

He knew that wasn't the only reason Noah had hired him, but if Noah could admit to himself that what he really wanted—what most people did—was for someone to be in it with him, someone to feel present...then if there was one thing Will was going to do this weekend, it was to show Noah that he was there for him, money or not.

Except when they stepped inside the house, Noah stopped short and his whole body tensed. "Mom, Dad, what are you doing here?"

On the other side of the kitchen island stood a couple Noah certainly bore some resemblance to. The copper-brown hair, the fair skin; his dad even had the same color eyes.

"As soon as we heard they were on the island, we invited them over for a drink," Tony's mom replied. "It's been so long, and so nice to catch up."

Noah blinked repeatedly. "Oh, did you return early from your trip?"

"We got back yesterday and decided last second to come up for the night since the renters won't be here until tomorrow," Mrs. Dixon responded. "Feels almost like old times."

Will could tell they were trying their best not to seem forced in a public setting. This was a family that didn't communicate easily.

"Play nice," Tony whispered as he moved by them. "It's only a couple of hours."

Noah seemed to gather himself as he pasted on a fake smile. "Great. Can I make you some margaritas?"

"They're really delicious, especially in this heat," Will added to try and break the tension.

Mrs. Dixon raised her eyebrows. "I don't think we've had the pleasure of meeting."

"I'm Max," Will said, extending his hand. "Noah invited me."

Mr. Dixon stretched forward to greet him as well. "Are the two of you—"

"Together? Absolutely," Will supplied, thinking it was probably the right response, even though he didn't really understand their family dynamics.

"Well, that's surprising news," Mrs. Dixon said with what looked to be a genuine smile.

He turned it up a notch by reaching out to knot his fingers with Noah's. Noah's cheeks pinked as Will gave his hand a squeeze, and then he broke contact to retrieve the blender from where he'd stored it in the fridge.

Will was used to schmoozing with the rich, and this wasn't much different, except he felt a momentary pang of compassion for Noah. He almost wished he didn't have to act for his parents, who seemed rather bowled over that their son had a boyfriend. Maybe he should've let Noah take the lead in telling his parents he was dating someone new, but Will had a feeling if he left it up to him, he would've balked, and Will would be left holding the bag. So he needed to put his money where his mouth was.

11

NOAH

Noah's heart rate escalated. It was just his luck that on the one weekend he hired a fucking escort, his parents happened to be on the island. The last he'd spoken to them, he certainly didn't divulge he was dating someone new. And though their relationship wasn't what it once was, there was a part of him that still sought their approval. He imagined their shock if they ever found out who Will really was. They would think it disreputable, and knowing his parents, too *risky*—what if he was put in harm's way again?

And then other memories washed over him. All the surgeries and skin grafts and months spent convalescing.

"*Your son is lucky to be alive. But the recovery will take years.*"

"*I will never look normal again, and I need to come to terms with that. So do you.*"

"*You can't keep me in protective wrap my whole life.*"

Noah poured the margaritas for his parents, and his fingers clenched tightly around the glass as he listened to his mother excitedly ask Will how they met. Will launched into the same story from earlier; Noah felt his heat as Will moved closer and then a warm slide of lips against his cheek. He made a noise in the back of his throat as the kiss left a stinging sensation on his skin. The intimate action made his stomach buzz but soothed him as well, even though he knew it was all an act.

Maybe it wouldn't be such a bad idea to soak up any affection he could get from such a gorgeous man. Besides, what did it matter? His services were already paid for, and afterward, they'd part ways and go on with their lives.

Still, he wasn't quite as smooth as Will when it came to pretending. It took practice to get out of his head, so when Will wound their fingers together again, his shoulders automatically stiffened.

"Relax or your parents will think you don't even like me," Will murmured in his ear.

"Fuck," Noah muttered and then attempted to make up for it by placing a chaste kiss against his cheek.

Will smiled warmly at him. "That's more like it."

He wished he had Will's confidence in these types of social situations. The only time he was good at this sort of thing was at work, when he had to sell the design, not himself.

Except having Will there as a buffer between him and his parents made it almost tolerable.

Noah listened as his mom and dad reminisced with Tony's parents about summers spent on the island and caught up on each other's lives.

"I love the renovations," his mother cooed.

He wondered what Will thought of all the talk about expensive restorations, square footage, the stock market, and charity fundraisers. But Will listened attentively, and when the conversation turned to him, he didn't even flinch.

"So you work in a bagel shop?" his father asked, and Noah picked up on the underlying dig. Noah felt that same wash of disappointment from his father, who'd wanted so much more from him. Status, money, living the good life—as long as he kept Noah in their perfect little bubble. His mother was an attorney, his father a corporate controller for a large accounting firm, and there was no way Noah would've followed in either footsteps, no matter how much of a leg up he might've gotten. He'd always had an interest in design and merchandising.

The memory of one summer hit him squarely in the gut right then. There was a family who'd rented the beach house beside theirs, and the instant he saw the daughter's two-story doll house, he'd latched on. They played for hours, arranging furniture and acting out characters, and Noah was in all his glory until the mom sent them outside to a group of kids throwing balls and wielding swords.

"That's right. But I, uh…" Will's hesitation broke Noah out of his thoughts. "I have a Fine Arts degree, so I've worked on a few Off-Broadway shows and auditioned like crazy, but the competition is fierce, quite honestly."

Noah noticed the tic in his dad's jaw, his immediate disapproval of Will giving up so easily, even if he thought acting was a career to be frowned upon. And to work in a bagel shop, of all places. But he could tell his mom was charmed by Will, even though she shared his father's tenacity. Unfortunately, it was that same tenacity that ultimately drove Noah away.

"You shouldn't give up," she said, patting his hand. "You never know, we might see your name in lights someday."

"We'll see." Will's mouth split into a grin, but the smile didn't quite reach his eyes.

His father wasn't finished with his inquisition, and now Noah regretted getting cornered in the kitchen with them. "And what do your parents do?"

Noah noticed how Will lost his composure for one millisecond before pulling himself together, so he decided to come to his rescue.

"Geez, Dad, what's with the third degree?" Noah asked, and his mother winced.

Tony threw him an apologetic look, but Noah shrugged it off.

Love Me Louder

"It's okay," Will replied and then turned to Noah's dad. "It's just my mom and me. We live on the Lower East Side."

Noah didn't think that part was made up either, and he wondered why Will decided to tell the truth when he embellished other things so well earlier. Why not just lie about all of it? He'd never meet Noah's parents again anyway.

But maybe there were certain things Will needed to keep close enough to the truth because it kept him firmly planted in reality. Or maybe Noah was just reading too much into it.

The conversation turned to reminiscing about the Pines and how the area had changed over the years, bringing a younger, rowdier generation. *Kids these days.* The fact that property values had skyrocketed and that his parents hadn't needed all that space once Noah had graduated. The couple who'd purchased the beach house had also done some amazing renovations.

But Noah was good at reading between the lines. What they weren't saying was how being at the beach house had become too difficult for all of them after the accident. Besides, their condo in Brooklyn was closer to the hospital and doctor's office. Noah held in a shiver, recalling all those visits, procedures, and inpatient stays. He'd knock on wood if he could that he was mostly healthy now and had been able to avoid waiting rooms.

After another pitcher of drinks and more small talk, his parents announced they were leaving. "It was so nice to visit with you," his father said to Tony and his parents.

"I'll walk you out," Noah said distractedly as they wished Matt a happy birthday.

"Well, this was a surprise," his father said as soon as they got outside.

"Sure was," he agreed. "How is Amanda?"

"Oh, as happy as ever. They are trying for baby number two."

"Cool," Noah replied. "I'll be sure to message her soon."

"It was nice to see our son." His mom lowered her voice as if someone would overhear. "Sure wish we saw more of him."

Noah cringed, and just as he was drumming up some way to respond, his father chimed in to keep the peace. "Let's do dinner in the city sometime soon."

"And invite Max," his mother added. "Nice catch, by the way. He's very handsome."

He bristled at the implication—as if he had to do the catching and not the other way around. But he also knew it was a sore spot that got poked from time to time, and it was his issue to overcome. His mom didn't mean anything by it; in fact, she looked proud. It was what she always wanted for him. Someone to love.

"Yeah, sure, sounds good."

It wasn't that he tried to avoid them; it was more that they kept falling back into the same old patterns that drove them apart in the first place.

When he made his way back inside, he noticed that Will got pulled into a conversation with a very attractive guy in a blue Speedo, who was obviously flirting heavily with him. Noah wondered if Will was kicking himself for not being off the clock, so to speak.

Noah realized his feathers were still a bit ruffled by his parents, so he took a minute to himself by stepping outside. He leaned against the railing and stared out at the ocean, lost in his own head.

Suddenly he felt arms wind around him and warm lips at his nape. By now he'd become accustomed to Will's scent, and he almost groaned aloud.

"What are you...doing?" he asked with some effort, still not allowing himself to just live in the moment.

"I figure if you're not going to claim me as yours in front of all these single men, I'm going to claim you," Will said against his neck, causing a shiver to race through him. It was the opposite side of his scars but close enough that he had the urge to pull away. "Isn't that why you brought me—to show that you're not here alone?"

"Yeah, of course," Noah replied in a breathless whisper. Will's groin sank flush against Noah's ass, the heat between their bodies making him tingle all over. "But I bet you're regretting—"

"Turn around, Noah," Will snapped.

Noah blinked. "What?"

Will took a step back to allow him room. "I said, turn around."

The gruffness in his voice made all the hairs on Noah's arms stand on end. His pulse was thundering in his ears as he swung himself around to face him.

Will's hand grasped his neck. "I need you to stop second-guessing my every move. I'm here with you. Only you. Nobody else is figuring into the equation, okay?"

Noah's shoulders dropped, and he nodded, feeling ridiculous about trying to question his every intention. Sure, this wasn't real, it was an arrangement. But Will wasn't acting like he was having a horrible time either. He hoped he could tell if Will was super uncomfortable or something.

"Sorry about the third degree from my parents," he mumbled. "They can be..."

Will shrugged. "Eh, that's what parents do."

Will's warm hand was still gripping his neck as he stared into Noah's eyes.

I could get used to this, Noah thought before he cast the idea aside.

Will's thumb pressed against his bottom lip, making his mouth prickle from the contact. "You could at least pretend you're into me."

If only Will knew that Noah was totally into him and fighting his body all the way.

Noah's tongue slipped out, and he licked the pad of Will's thumb. He heard the all too authentic groan in the back of Will's throat, and Noah's cock stirred to life. *Holy shit.*

"That's hot," Will whispered as he watched Noah's tongue flick against his skin again.

Encouraged, Noah hollowed his cheeks and sucked Will's thumb into his mouth. He increased pressure as he circled with his tongue before releasing it with a pop.

He arched an eyebrow. "How was that?"

"Nicely done." Will's gaze was hungry, and Noah liked that he could surprise him. "Had you kept going, I would be hard as a fucking stone."

Damn. Will was so incredibly sexy.

Noah bit his lip and batted his eyelashes. He could play along too.

Will tore his gaze away from his eyes, and as it slid down to his mouth, for a split second Noah thought Will might kiss him. His pulse spiked as he admitted to himself that he would want that. So fucking much.

Noah cleared his throat. "Anybody watching us?"

Will glanced around the party. "Definitely."

He grinned. "Good."

12
WILL

As the sun was setting, they were joined by Tony and Matt at the pool. It was such a pretty sight that the entire party seemed to go on mute as they watched the beauty of the colors painting the surface of the ocean.

Will kept his hand lightly on Noah's waist as he stood behind him, not only because he was trying to show that they were together, but the way Noah had shivered, he could tell he enjoyed the contact, and truth be told, so did Will.

His thumb still prickled from when Noah sucked on it. The way Noah's eyes stayed glued to his as he so boldly flicked out his tongue was hot as fuck, and the triumphant grin on his lips nearly disarming. Will's heart thumped hard against his chest.

When had Will ever thought Noah plain? When he smiled like that, he was mesmerizing.

"What's on tap for tonight?" asked one of the other guests once the ball of light disappeared beyond the horizon.

"Matt's performing at Verve for amateur night, if anyone wants to tag along," Tony said, rubbing his boyfriend's shoulders as if he needed to gear him up. But given the excitement flickering in Matt's eyes, that was definitely not the case.

Will threw Noah a questioning glance, and Noah explained that it was drag night and there was a contest for best amateur performance.

"Sounds like fun," Will said, thinking about the shows he'd seen at various bars in the city. They were always a good time.

"Have you ever?" Noah asked, twisting toward him. "You know, dressed in drag?"

"Yeah, sure. I mean, for productions. It was ultimately a lot of work—the hair, the clothes, the makeup."

"That's the best part," Matt quipped.

Will chuckled. "You be going all out for tonight?"

Matt shrugged. "I take some shortcuts, but generally yes."

"He's good at it," Tony said, and then gave Will a once-over. "Bet you would be too, with your theater background and all."

"You should do it with me," Matt said, but Will was already shaking his head. The idea of getting in costume... It was too much work. But performing onstage sounded good.

"Think about it. They provide the costumes and makeup, and a couple of drag queens even volunteer to help us look our best." He nudged him playfully in the ribs. "Bet Noah would love it."

Matt winked at Noah, and it seemed as though there was an inside joke there. Either Noah once fell for a drag queen or thought they were sexy. Now Will's interest was piqued.

IN ANOTHER HOUR, A LARGE GROUP OF THEM HEADED UP TO VERVE and stepped inside to a full bar and thumping pop music. The vibe in the club was energetic and playful, and Will found that a bubble of happiness rose inside him, which was unusual for him when he was on the clock. He certainly didn't feel like this was work, but needed to keep reminding himself of that fact.

Except so far, he just felt like he was out with a new group of acquaintances. Normally he would count down the hours until it was time to call it a night, or would have to constantly talk himself through dates with customers, reminding himself of the end result.

But not only did Noah keep him intrigued, he also made him smile. There was something quite endearing about him, and his friends were pretty cool as well as entertaining.

"You sure you don't want to join me?" Matt asked Will as he turned toward the back room to get ready for the show. "It'll be a blast. Your stage name can be *Maxine*."

Will barked out a laugh and found that he was actually considering it. It did sound like fun and definitely appealed to his love of theater. He glanced at Noah, who was standing beside Tony near the bar. "Would you mind?"

"Hell no," Noah said with an arched eyebrow. "Especially not when you look like that."

Will's brow furrowed. "Like what?"

"Your face totally lit up, bright as the sun, so maybe you miss the stage more than you realize," Noah replied, seeking his fingers for the first time on his own. Noah gave his hand a quick squeeze of support, and it made Will's stomach flood with warmth. "I think you should go for it."

"Told you so," Matt quipped as he gripped his arm and led him to the dressing room.

13

NOAH

"He seems like a great guy," Tony said, handing him his drink from the bar. Noah nodded, feeling guilty yet again that this entire weekend was one big sham. He was an idiot. Why hadn't he realized that bringing a random date might complicate things, especially a guy as charming and interesting as Will? "But something seems different about you."

"What do you mean?" Noah asked after a long sip of his gin and tonic.

"I don't know," Tony replied, studying his friend. "Sort of like you're holding back."

Noah's stomach clenched tight. "Holding back?"

"Like either you're unsure of Max, or you don't want to let yourself feel too much."

Christ, how had he not remembered how perceptive his friend could be? They'd known each other since childhood. Besides, Tony had helped see him through the lowest period of his life. He once filled an entire notebook with silly pictures and riddles and sent them to him when he was recovering in the hospital. After that he'd call or visit him regularly enough for two friends who only saw each other every summer. But they had forged a bond to last them to adulthood, and since they both moved to the city, they stayed in touch.

"So, am I right?" Tony asked, leaning in. "Is there something about this guy you don't like?"

If only—might make this a hell of a lot easier. Truth was, he really enjoyed spending time with Will. He was easy to be around, and as a result, Noah was feeling more comfortable with this whole arrangement. "No, that's not it. I'm just being...*careful*."

"That I can understand. You've had your share of assholes," he agreed as they watched the first drag performers take the stage, a trio in glittery dresses, belting out an old-school Britney song to whoops and hollers from the crowd. Tony spoke against his ear so Noah could hear him. "But Max seems pretty into you."

Noah's head snapped back. "He does?"

"Why does that surprise you?" Tony asked around a chuckle. "You've always been that way, so unsure of yourself. It would be nice to finally see you..."

Noah bit his lip and glanced back at his friend as the crowd seemed to surge toward the stage. "See me what?"

"Feel good about yourself for a change," Tony replied, clapping his back. "You're such a good person, and anyone should be proud to date you."

Noah's cheeks flushed, and his gaze turned toward the performance. Damn, he didn't expect to have a heart-to-heart with his best friend in the middle of a drag bar.

"You all set for tomorrow?" Noah yelled over the music. "Nervous at all?"

A huge smile stretched across his friend's face. "Hell yes, I'm nervous. But I'm so ready to make him my fiancé." A momentary look of fear flitted through his eyes. "If he says *yes*."

"Of course he'll say yes." Noah chuckled and thumped his friend's shoulder. "Anything I can help you with?"

"I'll let you know," he replied. "But for now, I'm all set."

They turned back to the show and watched as a new set of

drag queens catwalked onstage. Matt came out first, in a getup Noah had seen him wear before. He loved the platinum-blonde wig and stilettos, and Tony whistled loudly through his fingers as they pushed their way closer to the stage.

Noah's heart practically stopped when he spotted Will. Holy shit. He almost didn't recognize him. If he thought he was pretty as a man, he was gorgeous as a drag queen.

He wore a black wig with fringy bangs, bright-red lipstick, lashes a mile long, and some fishnet stockings beneath a formfitting silver dress. Christ, fishnets always did something for him. Not that he'd ever choose to wear them, but there was just something so damned sexy about seeing a man let his feminine side shine.

The song changed to "You Can Leave Your Hat On," and a cheer rose from the crowd. As soon as Will spotted Noah, he pointed his way and winked. The two drag queens expertly played the crowd, and Noah couldn't help but be completely riveted by Will—or was it Maxine?

As Maxine strutted across the stage, mouthing the words to the song, he could totally picture Will stealing the show in some Broadway production. He felt almost melancholy that Will couldn't follow his dream, even if he'd admitted he was disillusioned by it.

At the end of the song, Matt announced it was his birthday, so the DJ began playing "In Da Club" by 50 Cent as the crowd chanted the familiar "it's your birthday" line. Matt motioned for Tony to come toward the stage, and then he sang to him while Tony joined in and danced seductively in front of him. Noah hated being the center of attention, so he moved to the side and watched his friends from a distance.

Maxine walked down the steps and into the crowd in dramatic fashion as the music flipped to the next song, which was "Come to My Window" by Melissa Etheridge. Noah's pulse raced as he watched Maxine stroll toward him and reach out her hand.

"You look incredible," Noah remarked as Maxine wound their fingers together.

"You like it?" Maxine asked as she kissed Noah's cheek and nuzzled into his neck.

Noah nodded numbly, scarcely believing that this stunning man dressed in drag was paying him any attention at all. "The fishnets especially."

"Yeah?" Maxine shimmied her skirt up her thighs to reveal more of her legs, and that's when Noah spotted the black lace garter belt. *Fuck.*

"*Hot,*" Noah mouthed to him as Maxine belted out the song. This close up, Noah could also hear that Will had a great voice. He couldn't help feeling like his talent was being wasted, but who was he to judge? His parents thought he was wasting his life in retail, after all.

Maxine lifted her gloved hand to Noah's chin and ran a finger across his jaw. Noah could feel his neck and cheeks flushing hot. Damn, Maxine was sexy as fuck.

Maxine leaned forward, and her ruby lips found his ear. "Just go with it, okay?"

Noah drew back, a bit confused as to what Maxine meant, even as a ripple of awareness traveled through his body. When her gloved hand cupped his nape and dragged him forward, he didn't realize how a person's touch could reduce his whole world to a singular sensation of smooth fingertips on his skin. Their mouths met in a searing kiss, and the rasp of stubble against his cheek made him moan deep in his throat. He could hear the crowd cheering them on, but his knees felt weak as Maxine's tongue brushed across the seam of his lips.

He pulled away to catch his breath as his heart thundered in his ears. His hands wound around the silky waistline of Maxine's dress, and suddenly everything else in the room fell away. What was happening in that moment seemed far better and truer than any other experience in recent memory. Their eyes met a moment before their mouths reconnected in a fierce kiss.

The tip of Will's tongue flicked out, seeking entrance, and Noah remotely considered ending the showy kiss, knowing this was only to play to the audience. But Noah wanted it so badly. To feel Will's lips, to taste his tongue, even if it only lasted until the song ended.

So he parted his lips, and Will's tongue slid past his teeth, soft and tentative at first, searching for something. When Noah's tongue met and wound with his in response, a groan tore from Will's mouth, which totally threw Noah for a loop.

Could he be enjoying the kiss as much as him? Or only the attention?

When Will broke the kiss, Noah swayed, feeling almost drunk. Noah's fingers reached up absently to swipe at his mouth, like he'd been burned or branded by the one and only Maxine.

Will chuckled as he steadied him, tapping his mouth to Noah's lips one last time. "I got lipstick on your mouth. But I like it. You should leave it."

Noah nodded and grinned. "For the record, you know how to kiss."

Will arched an eyebrow. "Not too much tongue?" he asked, referring to their earlier conversation, which now felt eons ago. Noah laughed and shook his head.

The song ended, and Will's time was up. Matt motioned for him to take the stage with the other drag queens so a winner could be chosen. When Matt's name was called, Noah figured it was for being the birthday boy, but he might've also been a bit biased toward another drag queen who stood beside him, clapping madly.

After the drag queens made their way off the stage and back to the dressing room, Noah got plenty of thumps on the back from bar patrons as well as the group that had come from the beach house. Noah's cheeks heated from all the unwarranted scrutiny.

Tony chuckled as he made his way toward him.

"You okay?" he asked, pretending to steady him, or maybe he really did look like he was going to fall over. "Well, you *do* like your men in drag."

14

WILL

Well, *hot damn*, that kiss. He didn't know what had come over him, he was so in the moment. But the way Noah was looking at him, like he wanted to eat him with a spoon, was just too tempting. And to feel him tremble from his touch was way too heady. He needed to pull himself back, or he might feel more conflicted than he already was.

"That was a blast. Thank you," Will said as he scrubbed off the makeup.

"You were awesome," Matt said, and they high-fived. "We should do it again sometime."

Will felt a momentary stab of regret that the possibility was unlikely.

After he grabbed his clothes, he changed back into his jeans and T-shirt behind the large screen they had set up, making sure to leave the tight dress and heels as he found them.

He thought again of the look on Noah's face. That dreamy innocence along with that sated smile, and he wanted to put it back on his face again. He wasn't sure why, except maybe it was because Noah actually let down his guard and allowed him in—and that was not something he'd often seen. He certainly saw hints of it from clients who simply wanted his company. Someone to sit with them in a pub or hotel room. But he had never felt it so deep in his gut like he did with Noah—that longing and utter wonder that came from being on the receiving end of it.

Maybe Will would regret the kiss when they were back in the city, back at their jobs where Noah possessed in droves the overt confidence he seemed to lack here, but Will didn't think so. He also didn't think he'd forget the sounds Noah made when their mouths were fused, his velvety tongue entwined with his, and the fire in his eyes when he saw the fishnets. Maybe there was a side to Noah that was just waiting to break free?

And damn if he didn't want to be the one to see it happen. To see Noah let loose and completely lose himself in a moment of lust. Except, he was pretty tightly wound, and Will was certain it was for good reason. It made Will want to protect him and challenge him all at once, and that couldn't be good. Not when he was here as hired help. And from listening to Noah's parents' conversation earlier in the evening, that was exactly what he'd be to them. Christ, to even imagine owning property of his own someday, let alone on a picturesque island.

Once ready, he and Matt joined the large group near the bar. Matt and Tony decided to head back to start the traditional bonfire on the beach, while a few others wanted to walk down the block to another club.

"Let's just go for a little while," Will suggested, and Noah agreed, though Will saw the trepidation in his eyes.

"We'll see you later," Tony said over his shoulder as they waved goodbye. "Have fun."

Once inside the dance club, the loud thumping music made his head spin, and Will noticed how Noah seemed to shrink into the shadows like some delicate wallflower while the others took to the dance floor.

As he glanced over the large space, he could almost hear the cogs turning inside Noah's head. The club was wall-to-wall gorgeous, half-naked men with glistening skin and muscled bodies. Muscles weren't necessarily Will's thing, and frankly, some men went overboard. He certainly kept himself fit; it helped to be in good physical condition when he was performing, and it probably helped at the escort service as well. But they were all carefully placed layers to hide what was beneath the surface—the bald anxiety and fear about his future; that familiar worry about whether he'd someday end up like his mother; or worse, that she'd end up dead. Those worries eclipsed his fear of being evicted or in over their heads financially.

Shoving those thoughts aside, Will sought Noah out and reached for his hand.

"What are you doing?" Noah shouted in his direction.

"Dancing with you." He tugged on his hand.

Noah attempted to stand his ground. "No way. I can't—"

"Sure you can," Will said, pulling him to the edge of the floor. "Just stand by me and shuffle your feet."

Noah reluctantly joined Will in the fray of bodies. Once they found his friends, Will scooted up behind Noah, placing his hands on his hips and swaying in time to the music. After a couple of minutes, he could feel the shift in Noah's posture as he seemed to get into the beat. He unclenched his jaw, his shoulders unwound. Soon enough, he raised his arms, his hips rocking in time, as if allowing the music to wash over him. It was beautiful to watch.

"Look how sexy you are," Will crooned against his ear, and in response Noah ground back against him, making him instantly hard. Holy fuck. They stayed that close, sweating in a sea of bodies, dancing and singing their lungs out to familiar songs. It was the most fun Will had had in a long while.

After another hour, they were dripping wet, Noah's hair curling at his temples, and both agreed it was time to head back.

As soon as the cool night air hit their skin, making the walk more pleasant, they sighed in relief.

"That was a blast. I haven't danced that much..."

"In ever," Noah finished, red dotting his cheeks, and Will got the impression that was Noah's way of thanking him for making the suggestion.

When they got back to the house it was close to midnight, but there was a blazing bonfire on the beach. They grabbed a couple of beers and stood around the fire for a little while, mesmerized by flames and listening to Tony telling a story about a yearly sandcastle competition. Will reached for Noah's hand and asked if he wanted to walk along the shore, where it was cooler.

They walked away from the group hand in hand, and even when it became deserted and dark, with only the moon as their guidepost, Will didn't let go.

As if Noah suddenly realized they were completely alone, he dragged his hand from Will's grasp. "We don't need to pretend out here."

The words felt like a strike against his skin, reminding him the reason he was on the island in the first place.

"What if I'm not pretending?" he asked through a tight jaw.

"What?" Noah seemed guarded again as well as perplexed.

"I just mean..." Will sighed. "I'm having fun with you, so I'm just going with it. I was hoping it was the same for you?"

Noah stared at him as if unable to register Will's sincerity. "Well, yeah. It's been great. Plus, seems like people are pretty much buying that we're together."

"And that was the purpose of having me here? So your friends think you have a boyfriend?" Will asked, attempting to get more clarification, even though there was no reason for it. He was there because of a transaction, plain and simple.

Noah folded his arms as if placing a barrier between them. "Why are you questioning me?"

Will shook his head. *Fuck.* "I'm not. Sorry. Only trying to understand." When Noah simply blinked at him, he continued. "When we first discussed this arrangement, you said you hated being out here alone. That it was for beautiful people. And I get that; I see it all around me. But your friends don't seem to rag on you for anything. They seem pretty cool, actually. So again, just trying to understand."

Noah stopped walking suddenly and turned toward Will. He took a deep breath as if he was trying to make a decision of some sort. He looked around, likely checking that they were still alone, and then grabbed the hem of his shirt. Will saw Noah swallow roughly before slamming his eyes shut and lifting his shirt over his head. Will staggered back for one brief second, thrown for a damn loop.

Noah was showing Will what looked like massive scarring on his torso, and Will held in his gasp out of respect because *fuck*. Thick, angry, discolored, mismatched patches of skin covered the entire front of his chest and traveled in different directions. The lines and blotches in the center of his chest appeared red and raw. They extended toward his rib cage as well as across his collarbones, encompassing one shoulder, and up the side of his neck to right below his ear.

"Noah," Will whispered as he moved toward him just as Noah opened his eyes, stared at a point somewhere beyond his shoulder, and started talking.

"One summer—the year I turned thirteen—the kids around here gathered outside after a wicked storm to jump in the warm puddles." As he spoke, he pulled his shirt back over his head and slid it down his torso. But Will kept his gaze glued to Noah's face, needing to hear his story more than anything. "We continued an ongoing game from that morning with tree branches as swords. But not me. I had to be fancy and make mine out of aluminum. I was always doing stuff like that—taking the time to create something to set the mood or make it look realistic."

Noah swallowed several times in a row, and Will knew something pretty heavy was coming. He held his breath to take the brunt of the blow.

"Then I had to touch that fancy sword to a live wire that had fallen on the ground from the storm," he explained in a remote voice that didn't match his sorrowful gaze. "To this day, I don't know why I did it. My dad said I was always naturally curious about things, but I was old enough to know better."

This time Will couldn't hold in his gasp. He stretched forward and squeezed Noah's stiff hand.

"I could've died on the spot, and I'm so grateful. I definitely am." He took a shuddering breath. "I immediately fell unconscious from the jolt to my system and woke up in the hospital, having suffered an electrical burn over most of my torso."

"Holy fuck." Now the color and texture of his skin made sense. It must've been excruciating. Will's stomach convulsed.

"Months of rehab, years of skin grafts, and my parents hovering over every single decision, like I was made of glass. My life was exhausting. By the time I got through college, I needed to break away, strike on my own, become my own person." Noah finally looked at him, and it was like having the sun shining on him after a month of darkness. "But dating has not been fun, to say the least."

Will swallowed and stepped closer to Noah, still holding his hand, which now felt warm and inviting. "Thank you for telling me."

"I wasn't going to. Fuck, I don't even know why I did, but I'm glad it's out there now." He bit his lip and looked down at their feet. "And...well, I know we have a paid arrangement...but thank you for not looking at me like I'm a leper. For not thinking I'm ugly—at least not saying it out loud."

Will's heart dropped to his feet. "Wait, are you saying there have been guys who—"

Noah laughed grimly. "Like I said, it hasn't been easy. I've had some pretty horrible situations. And I get it; it's a lot to take on.

You have to look at me every time you want sex, so... I suppose it's like unwrapping a piece of chocolate that looked reasonably tasty on the outside and then finding out it's rotten on the inside."

"Goddamn, how fucking shallow." Will clenched his fists. He wanted to fucking scream. This amazing guy, who'd been through such an ordeal, also had to deal with jackasses who couldn't see beyond the scars on someone's skin? "It makes me want to throat-punch someone."

"Believe me, I've been there." Noah smirked. "You've made this weekend bearable so far."

"You've made it bearable for me too," Will replied. When Noah arched an eyebrow, he said, "My life isn't all roses either."

"Yeah right, look at you." He stretched out their linked hands. "You're beautiful. I know you haven't been able to make it in theater, but what could you possibly—"

"I escort to pay my mother's hospital bills. She's...sick, and visits to manage her meds are expensive." He let out a heavy breath. "And honestly, I might even remind you of your parents. Hovering over her, checking her every move, but fuck, it's been scary. But if I don't do it, she might...one day..." Will drew away and turned toward the ocean, trying to get his emotions under control. He felt Noah behind him, and then Noah's hand squeezed his shoulder.

"For the record, I don't do this—go away for weekends. That fact along with what I do for a living is why I can't have any sort of relationship right now." He turned back to Noah. "But this... arrangement would help pay off a good chunk of our bills, so... Damn, this is some heavy shit."

Will shut his eyes and gulped in mouthfuls of air. This conversation left him feeling so...*raw*.

"Damn it, Will." Suddenly Noah was cradling his face and peppering kisses on his cheeks and chin and lips. "Is this okay?"

He meant because nobody was around. *Fuck*, this man. It took Will a second, and then he lifted his hand and gripped Noah's neck. His other arm encircled his waist as he dragged Noah against him. The kiss was desperate and clumsy as their mouths mashed together, yet still perfect. His tongue slid inside Noah's mouth, and he kissed him long and deep until their lips felt bruised and the water lapping at their feet was the only other sound they heard.

"Well, this went a whole different direction," Noah said in a breathless whisper as their foreheads pressed together.

Will chuckled and then pecked his cheek. "What do you say we quit questioning every damn thing and just make the most of it?"

Noah smiled in that open and real way that made Will's stomach swoop for no logical reason at all. "Deal."

15

NOAH

When they returned to the party, the bonfire had died down to embers and most of the guests had retired to their rentals or hotel rooms. Noah and Will helped Tony and Matt pick up any trash scattered on the beach as well as in the pool area.

"Going to bed," Tony mumbled around a yawn as Matt tied up a garbage bag. "See you in the morning."

Noah and Will headed up the stairs and down the hall. Noah froze once they stepped inside the room and he remembered there was only the one bed between them. It seemed so long since that morning when they first had the discussion about where they would sleep.

As if sensing the change in Noah, Will stepped up behind him. "I could easily sleep on that couch and be fine tonight."

Noah glanced at the tan cushions across the room, and though they looked cozy enough, he was being ridiculous. If anyone, it should be him hunkering down on the couch. Besides, he had just attacked Will's mouth on the beach after an emotional conversation. And now he was nervous about them sharing a bed?

"I'm thinking too hard about this—as usual," Noah muttered. "It's a king-size bed, so there's plenty of room."

"If you're sure," Will replied, and Noah nodded. "If you change your mind, just let me know."

Noah dug his pajamas out of the suitcase and motioned toward the bathroom. "Okay with you if I..."

"Yeah, sure. All yours," Will replied, already searching through his own bag. "I'm just going to change and zonk out."

Noah closed the door behind him and splashed water on his face. He wasn't one to sleep in the nude, and he certainly hoped Will wasn't either. Although, Christ, seeing him like that would be...more than he could handle for one night. A shiver raced through him as he slipped on an old T-shirt and pajama bottoms.

He gathered his clothes in a bunch and pushed through the door, hitting the light as he went. Will was hunched near the bed, in the middle of kicking his jeans off.

A gasp escaped Noah's mouth. "Wait, what the hell... Are those—"

Will's legs were still covered in the fishnets from his performance, and his head was bent as he scrambled to pick up his jeans, his cheeks flushed a deep crimson.

"It was a stupid idea," he muttered, stooping over farther to cover himself. "I knew you liked them, so Matt said it was cool to keep them."

Noah's cheeks burned at the thought of Matt knowing Will might wear them for him.

Will made a motion to tug them off his legs, and suddenly Noah's mouth was pushing out the words. "Wait," he said in a throaty voice. "I...I want to see you."

Will shot a surprised glance over his shoulder. He straightened to full height, and...fuck all of everything. He was shirtless with only a pair of skimpy trunks and the fishnets.

Noah swallowed hard. "Damn, that's..."

"You *do* like them," Will said with a smirk, relief evident in his eyes. He played it up by stretching one of his legs so Noah could get a full view of his thigh.

"Fuck. You're like a fantasy come to life."

"Damn it, Noah," Will murmured, stepping closer to him. "First that sexy kiss on the beach, and now...how lit up these make you. You are certainly full of surprises."

"Well, you said to make the most of it, right?" Noah replied, his throat working to swallow.

"Absolutely. Have a seat, and I'll give you a little show."

Noah felt his entire body flush, but he did as Will asked, planting himself on the couch. As Will strutted in front of the bed, Noah's gaze raked greedily over the silky fishnet material that elongated his toned legs.

"Are you hard from watching me?" Will's gruff tone was a stark contrast to the frilly garter belt that showcased his bulging shaft.

Noah licked his dry lips and nodded, not wanting his voice to betray him. Truth was, he was stiff as a board, his cock pushing painfully against his pajama bottoms.

"Pull your cock out," Will said in a commanding tone, and Noah gasped. "Show me how you stroke yourself."

His heartbeat thundered in his ears. "No, I..."

"Don't be embarrassed." Will's voice softened as he stepped toward him, his gaze focusing on the bulge in his bottoms. "It's just you and me, and you look so hot right now."

Noah huffed out a breath. "I... I do?"

"Fuck yes, and look how hard I am." His fingers slipped inside the front of his underwear to palm his cock, and Noah's mouth ran dry. "Show me, Noah."

Noah's heartbeat thundered in his ears as he folded down the front of his pajamas, exposing his cock and fisting it. He slanted his head back to a more comfortable position, completely lost in the sensation. Will was like a wet dream standing before him, and if he didn't get some semblance of control, he would nut all over himself in two seconds flat.

Will strutted toward the couch and planted one of his legs on the cushion. He ran his fingers up his thigh to his cotton trunks and palmed his impressive cock. Noah only took his gaze off Will's cock for a split second to look into his eyes and was taken aback by the raw lust he saw there. Will was completely turned on, which probably only meant he liked putting on a show and not that watching Noah was cranking him up.

Noah suddenly felt emboldened. "Turn around for me."

Will quirked an eyebrow in his direction as he twisted toward the balcony and palmed his cheeks, the material outlining his crease. Noah's balls drew up tight.

"Holy fuck, Will." That had done it. Noah stroked faster, that familiar heavy feeling searing his balls and stealing his breath as he arched his back and moaned. As Will turned to face him, thick cock in his fist, Noah came with a deep groan, jizz spurting over his hand.

He hadn't orgasmed that hard in a long time.

As he slumped against the cushion, he felt Will move over him like a larger-than-life shadow—in fishnets.

"Fuck, that was hot." Will's voice sounded wrecked as he stroked his shaft. "Tell me what else you like."

Noah could scarcely believe that this gorgeous guy's cock was fucking hard as steel and leaking from the tip. Even after Noah revealed himself on the beach, Will still wanted to be near him. He let Noah kiss him before they walked back to the beach house as well. He had the urge to lean forward and lick him, taste his come, make him lose his mind.

"I, uh..." Noah watched as Will's hand expertly twisted at the wrist, as Will bit down on his bottom lip, on the verge of losing control. "I love giving head."

Will arched his neck toward the ceiling and groaned. Damn, he was sexy.

"And I, um...love being pounded senseless. From behind."

"Jesus." Will's eyes shut as his chest flushed a rosy shade and his cock seemed to grow even stiffer. A simple flick of the wrist and Will came with a string of curses, his come sliding down his fingers as his knee shook.

"Holy shit, that was the hottest fucking thing I've ever seen," Noah murmured, nearly melting into the cushion as he watched Will twitch and shudder.

After another long second, Will seemed to gather himself enough to walk to the bathroom. He heard the faucet turn on, and then Will returned with a towel. He reached for Noah's hand and dabbed at the come.

"Thanks," Noah slurred as he used it to wipe his groin and the front of his pajamas. "Fuck, so tired."

"Go to bed. I'll be there in a minute," Will said over his shoulder as he shut the bathroom door behind him.

Noah stood on shaky legs, liking the sound of that.

The last thing he remembered was sliding inside the covers and falling fast asleep.

16

WILL

Somehow Noah and Will had still gravitated toward each other in the giant bed even though Will had tried hard not to crowd him or freak him out since they had jacked off in front of each other last night. Will loved seeing how lit up Noah got over the fishnets, and he wondered how much he'd been able to act out any of his fantasies over the years.

And now in the sunlit room with the sound of the ocean just a stone's throw away, Noah felt warm and soft in Will's arms. Will probably shouldn't revel in it, but he did anyway because he actually enjoyed cuddling. His last relationship had ended more than a year ago, and he didn't do sleepovers with hookups, not only because they were temporary, but because he really needed to be there for his mom.

He'd held both men and women while on the clock with the escort service, but none had ever stirred him the way Noah did. When he nuzzled his neck, the man practically purred in his sleep, and it made Will feel lighter. He knew Noah was self-conscious about his body and placed people at arm's length because of shitty reactions over the years. But after seeing his battered skin—and having guys in his own life judge his relationship with his mother—he understood why.

What an awful ordeal Noah and his family had gone through. He could've died or damaged major organs. Fuck, he'd been lucky to survive, and he needed someone who appreciated all he'd been through and loved him because of it.

But Noah wasn't fragile like a sandcastle on the beach. His fragility was more like a bomb—devastating enough to turn someone's world upside down.

Suddenly Will's phone lit up with a message on the side table. He quietly checked the screen and saw the text was from his mom.

Hope you're being careful this weekend. You never know who's watching.

He shot up in bed, his stomach sinking like a stone as he disentangled himself from Noah's sleeping form as quietly as possible. He rolled out of the sheets, thankful he'd thrown on some gym shorts to sleep in the night before.

Will headed straight out the door and down the stairs, past Tony and a couple of other people near the coffee machine in the kitchen.

"Have to make a call," he muttered as he slid open the glass door and headed toward the beach, where the waves crashing against the shore would muffle his voice.

Once his mother answered the phone, he paced back and forth along the sand as he listened to her ramble about any number of things—she sounded agitated and out of sorts.

Was it because he was gone?

He knew he shouldn't have come this weekend. Why did he leave her? She was used to him being there, or at least a train stop away most nights.

Fuck, if this new combo of meds didn't work, he didn't know what the next option would be for her. They had already poured so much time and money into different treatments.

"Mom, what day is today?"

That seemed to snap her to attention. "It's the weekend—Saturday. You said you're gone for the weekend."

He breathed a deep sigh. "Yes, I'll be home tomorrow. And what year is it?"

He went through the standard reality questions he always did, and when she answered them all correctly, he nearly sobbed, he was so relieved.

"Did you skip any doses?"

"Just one, yesterday morning," she replied, and the guilt was like a lash against his skin. "I...promise it was a mistake. I didn't hear the alarm on my phone, and I..."

"No, it's okay," he replied. At least she was trying, she wasn't refusing them this time, which could happen especially if she thought they were poisoned or whatever else her brain came up with. It was a fucked-up disease for sure. "Won't your respite worker be there soon?"

"Yes," she replied, and just as she said the words, he heard the familiar buzz of the lobby door. "That would be her. Today it's Denise."

Respite was a service essentially geared toward giving family members who had to care for special-needs kids or adults a reprieve from their schedule. He wouldn't have even signed up, had one of the counselors not mentioned it. But it had become a godsend for them. It got her out of the house as well as her routine, and it made Will feel less drained during bad weeks.

"I'll hang on while you let Denise inside, and then I'd like to speak with her," he said, and he could hear her place the phone down while she answered the door.

He thought about how Noah said his parents had hovered over him during and after his recovery, but he swept that aside. This was different. This was life or death.

But maybe Noah's parents had thought so too.

Once Denise got on the phone, he explained that she'd sent

him a paranoid-sounding text that morning. Denise assured him that she would make sure all was okay during their visit. She was taking her to the grocery store and to the movies, which was plenty of opportunity to see how she was functioning. She promised to call if anything seemed amiss.

After he hung up, he was overcome with such sudden relief that he doubled over and caught his breath. That was when he noticed what a beautiful morning it was. The sand was warm beneath his feet, the sun wasn't quite beating down yet, and the breeze coming off the ocean helped soothe his jangled nerves.

When he spotted Noah walking down the beach, holding a cup of coffee, his face split into a giant grin. Wasn't he a sight for sore eyes. Then he remembered what happened last night, and his skin prickled.

"Thank you," he said as Noah handed him the cup, and he took a grateful sip. He marveled that Noah remembered how he took it from their one-time meeting at Starbucks, unless it was only a lucky guess. Regardless, the warm liquid felt good going down and cleared his head temporarily.

"Is everything okay?" Noah asked in an uncertain voice, and Will knew he meant more than rushing out of bed to find a private place to speak to his mom.

When their eyes met, his hand reached out to paint Noah's jaw. "It will be."

"Tony said you had to make a call...so I wanted to be sure..." He toed the sand.

"Yeah, sorry about that. I didn't want to get out of bed, but it was real important," he replied, wanting to assure him it had nothing to do with him or what happened last night. "It's all cool now."

But Noah's eyes were still creased with concern, so Will fished his phone out of his pocket, swiped the screen, and pulled up his mother's text. He flipped the cell so Noah could read his mother's random suspicious message from just an hour ago. He figured that would help in his explanation. Not that he needed to give one, but for some reason he wanted to. It felt easy with Noah, and besides, Noah had shared plenty of himself last night.

When Noah read the text, his face went through a series of reactions. His eyes became cartoonish wide before his eyebrows knit together as if attempting to understand exactly what Will was showing him. Without warning, a laugh bubbled up inside Will. There was always such a thin line between sorrow and hilarity, and in times like these, when his mind played any number of cruel tricks on him in a matter of minutes, he couldn't help the snicker that burst from his lips.

Noah turned his puzzled gaze on him, which only opened the floodgates. Will let loose a good, hearty laugh, and then all bets were off. He couldn't stop himself as his shoulders shook and his stomach hurt from holding it in. He laughed so hard, tears sprung to his eyes. It was a mix of relief and wonder at the peculiarity of his life.

It must have been infectious because suddenly Noah was chuckling right along with him and wiping at his eyes. "What the hell are we doing?"

Noah's face lit up, his eyes crinkled at the corners, and damn it all to hell. Noah was never *average*; he was always a stunning human being hiding in plain sight.

"Fuck, I'm sorry. It's really no laughing matter. At all. Sometimes I think I must be going...mad." Will whispered that last part as the gravity of his words slammed over him, and he quickly pulled himself together. Christ, he was a mess sometimes, emotions all over the place, and normally he could tamp it down, especially with clients. But Noah didn't feel like a client anymore; he felt more like a friend. And he could certainly use a friend right then. "My mom...she suffers from schizophrenia."

Noah sobered immediately, his breath catching in the back of his throat. "Is that why you live with her? Does she need..."

"Just easier and helps cut down on the bills," he explained.

"But it's a disease that's not always simple to live with, that's for sure."

Noah seemed to consider the diagnosis, maybe conjuring up the definition in his brain.

"People get it mixed up a lot, even in the media," Will blurted out. "They think it means dissociative identity disorder or even bipolar."

"When it actually means some delusions and breaks from reality?" Noah supplied.

Will inhaled sharply through his nose. "Yeah, how do you…"

"I, uh, suffered from panic attacks and PTSD after the accident, and I did a ton of reading when I was laid up in bed, trying to figure out what was happening to me. I remember that one. I actually asked the psychiatrist about it."

"What do you mean?" Will asked, marveling at all the aftereffects Noah has had to suffer through from one mistake, however huge. It had cost him so much.

"I kept reliving the accident and having what I thought were hallucinations when in reality they were like, flashbacks," Noah said, toeing the edge of the foamy water. "But damn, they felt so real."

"Do you still have them?" Will asked. "The flashbacks?"

"No. Not in a long while." Noah shook his head. "But every now and again something will trigger my symptoms—usually a bad storm—and I'll just *panic*."

Will conjured up a memory of Noah claiming to have to stay after hours at the store one night when there was a wicked storm raging outside. *"You go ahead, I'll lock up,"* he'd said, but his skin had looked all clammy, and Will vaguely remembered speculating if Noah was coming down with something. Damn, now it all made sense, and he lamented the fact that they'd never been friends, not that they would be after this weekend. But in this moment, he was glad to have gotten to know Noah, for what it was worth.

They fell silent, staring out at the ocean as seagulls hovered on the surface of the water.

"Will you need to get back home?" Noah asked tentatively. "It's totally cool if you do. I can help you pack, and we can walk back to the ferry. The guys would understand that you have a family emergency."

Will could've taken the out right then. Said his goodbyes and got the hell off the island and back to his life. His mom would be gone practically all day with Denise, but at least he'd be there when she got home. He could explain to Gotham City what happened, and they would prorate the fee for Noah. At this point, it felt wrong taking his money, but he needed to stop that line of thought in its tracks. He was doing what he had to for his family.

Was that why the idea of leaving gave him pause? The fact that he still needed the money? Or did it have to do with the beautiful surroundings as well as the good company, which provided a welcome reprieve from his hectic life?

"Actually, I checked in with my mom, and looks like it'll all be cool."

"Yeah?" Noah asked, and as his shoulders unwound, he seemed relieved, which made Will's chest feel tight, though he really couldn't explain why. "Are you sure?"

"She missed a dose, which happens from time to time, but she's still grounded in reality," Will explained, which was unlike him, especially to a client. He normally kept the details of their life under wraps. But with Noah, he was letting it all hang out—well, a decent amount at least—and he hoped it didn't come back to bite him in the ass. "I spoke to her worker, and I feel better about everything. Besides, I have my phone if they need to get ahold of me."

Noah breathed out. "I'm glad. Truly. And thank you for telling me."

Will swallowed roughly at the emotion on Noah's face, the

empathy, and almost spilled it all right then. Everything. All his fears and heartache.

That could end up being a grave mistake, so he needed to snap out of it and remember the real reason he was here in the first place.

17

NOAH

The rest of the morning they lay on lawn chairs on the pool deck, soaking up the sun. Noah still wasn't brave enough to take off his shirt, not even in front of Will. Besides, it had been dark on the beach last night, and who knew how closely anything had registered for him. Logically, he knew he was being ridiculous because after all, he was paying Will to be here, and no way would Will do anything intentionally to ruin that, maybe not even recoiling from Noah when he felt compelled to.

Will nearly had to leave on the next ferry—the thought had to have sat heavily in his mind at least—but he decided to stay. Was it for the money? It obviously had to figure in, given his family situation.

Will's mother suffered from a serious mental illness, and hadn't that thrown Noah for a loop. The man was way more complicated than he'd given him credit for. And wasn't Noah the hypocrite, insisting there was way more beyond a pretty face yet not expecting much out of Will.

But some of his own fear figured into the equation as well. Fear of Will being disinterested or even worse, disgusted by him.

Except he wore those fishnets just for him last night and then got completely turned on and jizzed while standing over him, so Noah didn't know what to think anymore.

Fearful his cock would stir just from the sensual memory, he thrust it from his thoughts and focused on the hot sun beating down on them. He fidgeted uncomfortably on the chair, his forearm over his eyes.

"Want to go for a swim?" Will asked suddenly. He sat up and wiped his brow with his towel. "It's already freaking hot."

"Nah," he said without even thinking it through. It was Noah's standard answer in any situation involving taking off his shirt. "You go ahead."

When Will didn't respond, Noah shifted his arm and looked over at him.

"When's the last time you were even in a pool?" Will asked, staring down at him. "Swam for the simple act of feeling some cool water on your skin?"

He shrugged, wanting to avoid the conversation at all costs. "Dunno."

Truth was, Noah could not recall a time in recent years when he'd taken a dip in any body of water. It just wasn't enjoyable for him.

Will leaned closer to him. "There's hardly anyone up this early, and I want to have fun with you. I promise you it'll be all right."

Now Noah just felt stupid, like he was being stubborn for the sake of being stubborn, and that would not do. "It's not because of my body," he spouted. "I just don't like water."

A total bald-faced lie. When he was a kid, he loved the water. Swam like a fish.

"Oh, okay," Will said in a nonchalant tone, even though Noah knew he was calling bullshit. "Because last night I heard Tony telling a story at the bonfire about you guys as kids building sandcastles and swimming in the ocean."

Cheeks enflamed, Noah suddenly stood up, pissed off at himself more than anything, not only for allowing Will to bait him, but for always taking the easy way out. He gripped the bottom of his shirt with trembling fingers before lifting it straight off and flinging it on the chair. Refusing to make eye contact with anyone, and certainly not Will, he walked to the edge of the pool and dived straight into the deep end.

The water was fucking cold and burned his lungs. When he sprang out, he shivered from more than just the chill of the wind on his skin. *Damn.* He'd actually done it. Got in the fucking pool for the first time in years, as if he'd been delivered a challenge and rose to the occasion.

Will was standing near the edge of the pool, and when their eyes met, he wore an adorable smirk-filled smile that warmed Noah all over. Like he was onto him. He knew he had pushed his buttons and was patting himself on the back. *Fucker.*

Without another word, Will dived into the deep end and swam underwater toward Noah, like a shark seeking its prey. It made Noah tremble and plump up. Damn, he was pathetic. As Will broke the surface, his arms slid around Noah's waist and pulled him under.

It turned into a splashing and dunking match, and Noah couldn't remember the last time he had so much innocent fun in a body of water. Christ, he needed to get over himself.

After they caught their breath, grinning at each other across the short distance, Noah noticed for the first time that the deck had filled up with not only people who had slept over the night before, but newcomers from the early morning ferry. Some he recognized, others he didn't. But more beautiful men were on display everywhere. Well, not everywhere, but close enough. In Noah's warped mind, that was all he could see for miles. Along with eyes gawking at him, at his patched-up skin, which made him move closer to the nearest edge of the pool so his torso would be covered. Fuck, it never ended.

As if Will could sense his change in mood, he waded closer, wrapped his arms around his waist from behind, and his lips found his ear, making a shiver quake through him. "For the record, I wish you could be more comfortable in your own skin. Because I think you're beautiful."

Noah couldn't catch his breath, his heart fluttering and flapping in his chest.

"But I know it's a struggle for you, and that's why having someone here this weekend was important." Will's fingers skimmed across his rib cage, and Noah quivered, hypersensitive to the sensation. "You deserve so much more, Noah. And one day there will be somebody worthy of you."

The words made his eyes sting with tears. *Fuck.* He tilted his head to glance at Will. He wanted to say so many things right then, but he couldn't trust his own heart. It had played tricks on him before.

"You're good at this," he mumbled, his eyes cast downward. "Your customers must love you."

Will's body became motionless, and Noah felt like shit for deflecting. He nearly apologized, but then Will pecked his cheek. "If that's what you want to tell yourself."

He backed away and waded to the edge, where he planted his hands and pulled himself out of the water. Now Noah was all alone in the pool, and he supposed he deserved it after being a jackass to him.

He watched as Will stood up, water rivulets running down his chest. He strode to his chair, grabbed a towel to wrap around his waist, then lifted the one Noah had been lying on, and walked back toward the edge.

He sat down and let his feet dangle in the water before locking eyes with Noah. He patted the concrete beside him and held open the towel. "Let me get you warm."

Noah's heart rose to his throat. Fuck, he was good. And kind.

And attuned to Noah's insecurities. A dangerous combination for sure. Noah would have to be on top of his game, or he would be in trouble.

18

WILL

The rest of the afternoon was spent helping Tony with preparations for the party. After they showered, Will and Noah strolled down the boardwalk to pick up some balloons, as well as a chocolate cake with buttercream frosting—Matt's favorite—from a popular bakery on the island.

On the way back he received a text from his mom, so he switched the bundle of blue and red balloons to the other hand and swiped the screen to read the message as his pulse thumped in anticipation of what he would find.

I'm feeling better, William. Please don't worry. I'm having a good day.

Will smiled to himself as he sent a quick reply back.

Love you, Mom. Call if you need me.

"Everything okay?" Noah asked. When Will nodded, Noah playfully nudged him with his shoulder, and all felt right in the world. At least in that moment.

Things seemed different between them since their time in the pool that morning, though he feared Noah would have regrets about allowing Will to persuade him to get in the water. But then he remembered that dazzling smile when they were dunking each other and messing around and the way Noah shivered when Will whispered in his ear, and he knew he'd made the right decision, even if Noah continued to remind him at every turn that this was a monetary arrangement between them. Noah was keeping a level head and placing Will at arm's length, and that was likely best for both of them. Soon enough their weekend would end and they'd be back in the city, living their separate lives.

After helping Tony's mom arrange the balloons in various locations around the property, Will joined Noah in the kitchen, where he was putting the finishing touches on a cheese tray Matt continuously tried to steal from.

"I could snack on this stuff all day long," Matt said, popping an olive in his mouth.

"That's why I asked for Max's help and not yours," Tony replied, wielding his chopping knife as he added more tomatoes to his guacamole. "It also means you can't complain when you have to do extra sit-ups on Monday."

"He could use the added calories. You both could. The gym is not missing you this weekend," Noah remarked with an eye roll as he swiped a piece of cheese for himself from the tray.

It was the most relaxed he'd seen Noah all weekend, and as he watched him interact with his friends, he couldn't help imagining what the man would've been like had the accident not happened.

Would he be as buff and calorie-conscious as his friends, strutting around in skimpy Speedos and hooking up with whomever he wanted every weekend? Somehow the idea of it soured Will's stomach. No matter how awful and traumatic the accident had been for Noah—and still was—there was no doubt it made him the person he was today. The person Will was completely enjoying getting to know this weekend. And he hoped that outside of the bumps along the way, Noah could truly be happy with the life he'd created for himself.

And perhaps it was the same for Will, where his mother was

concerned. She had a debilitating illness, and despite all the ups and downs, there was no question she had made his world richer. It was just the two of them, and though some days it felt like they were hanging on by a thread, he couldn't imagine not having her around, not caring for her in the way he had for so many years. Sure, it meant there was little room for anything else in his life—or *anyone* else either. Not that it mattered.

He wasn't sure why he was suddenly plagued by all these thoughts, except maybe it had to do with his present company and being on the island all weekend. Not that he felt stuck or anything. But he'd certainly never had an experience like this before while on the clock, and it was almost too close for comfort. Sure, acting came easy for him, but Will realized that his performance had taken too real a turn at some point last night. Maybe when he made the decision to wear the fishnets for Noah. Or when his dick got so fucking hard, watching Noah stroke himself. Or possibly when he crossed the line during the drag show and kissed him.

Noah probably thought most or even all of it was part of an act, and that also did not sit well with him. He was wading in dangerous waters, his emotions getting all tangled up, and that was not good. Not good at all. So getting paid handsomely and then getting back to his life in the city sounded more than enticing right then. After tomorrow, he could put all this behind him.

"Max, can I borrow you a minute?" Tony asked, breaking him out of his thoughts. He glanced over to where Noah was helping Matt arrange more seating around the large dining table.

He followed Tony to a back room, which ended up being the master suite. Damn, everything about this place was gorgeous. This room had a warm decor, posh canopy bed, plush white bedding, and modern artwork on every wall.

"I can't get over how amazing this view is," he remarked, staring out at the ocean through the floor-to-ceiling windows. It was a stark reminder that he would never own a place like this. It wasn't that it left a bad taste in his mouth, but more that it served to help him remember the vast differences between him and Tony as far as status and wealth were concerned.

He could've also placed Noah in that category if he didn't lead a seemingly modest life in the city. His parents could have probably set him up very nicely, but according to everything Noah had told him last night, he'd decided to break away from any of their influence.

"So...tell me what you think," Tony said from behind him, and when he whirled around, Tony was holding a black velvet box that no doubt contained an engagement ring. "Be honest. Although it's too late now, so maybe don't be too harsh if you—"

"Deep breaths." Will placed his hand on Tony's arm when he realized the guy was trembling. "I'm sure it's great. You have good taste. That much is evident."

"Thanks," Tony replied and inhaled sharply as he opened the lid. There was a brushed silver band with one diamond embedded in the center. As Will bent his head to get a closer look, he felt like more of a fraud than he had all weekend. Unquestionably he was here for Noah—his *client* Noah. And Tony, who was Noah's closest friend, assumed Will was in a relationship with Noah and was now taking him into his confidence. *Fuck.*

"It's really gorgeous." Will stared at the pricey band, feeling so many emotions swirling through him at once. Would this ever be his reality? He doubted it, so in a lot of ways even having this conversation felt foreign to him. "Bet it's a bit nerve-racking, huh?"

"Totally," Tony replied with a huff. "I just want it to be special. And well, I suppose there's always a chance he could say no."

Will's eyes snapped to his. "You're serious? You guys seem made for each other."

Tony bit his lip as he closed the box and carefully placed it back in the drawer he'd pulled it from. "You think?"

"Definitely," Will replied. "I know I've only just met you this weekend, but the way you look at each other says it all."

He blew out a breath. "Thanks, Max. That means a lot." Will nearly cringed at hearing his fake name used after such an honest conversation. He almost had the urge to blurt everything out. But not only would that prove fruitless, it would ruin everything. Will imagined Noah's mortified expression, so he immediately shoved the thought away.

Besides, after this weekend, he would probably never see Tony or Matt again.

That same heavy pit formed in his stomach.

"Wish me luck," Tony said, heading toward the door. "I'm going to propose after the cake is served."

"It'll be great. But yeah, good luck." *Break a leg*, he wanted to say because the old theater term seemed to fit so well in this scenario. Go figure.

"And, Max?" Tony turned with his hand on the doorknob. "I'm not sure what's happening between you and Noah, but he seems..." He paused as if searching for the right words. "He seems relaxed and...happy. I haven't seen that in quite a while."

Will smiled despite himself. "Glad to hear it."

"Everything changed after the accident, you know?" he said in a far-off voice. "It's a day none of us will ever forget." Will felt the urge to shiver. It had only just occurred to him that Tony had been there throughout Noah's recovery and into adulthood. What a history they shared. He couldn't say he had a friend like that, not even from his theater crowd. "He's been so different lately, like he's shut himself down, and I can tell he doesn't like coming out here anymore. So thanks for, um, making him smile again."

Fuck. He blinked rapidly as his eyes began to sting.

"Of course. He deserves to be happy."

And never had a statement resonated so deeply with him before.

Will could feel Tony studying him intently, and when their eyes met again, Tony cleared his throat. "So I hope your intentions are true. I'll be so fucking bummed if they're not."

Will gasped as Tony pushed past him and out the door. When they got out into the hall, Tony turned to him with a sheepish smile. "Sorry, had to say it. He's my oldest friend."

"Understood," Will mumbled behind him.

When he stepped back into the kitchen, Noah was standing at the counter, making a pitcher of sangria.

"What's up?" Noah asked with a puzzled glance between Will and his best friend.

Will kissed his cheek even though he felt caught between sweeping him into his arms to hold him close and catching the next ferry back to Long Island.

"I think he's just looking out for his friend," Will said, then popped into his mouth a strawberry that was lying on a tray with the other fruit Noah had chopped.

Noah's eyes widened. "Did he threaten you?"

Will laughed. "Nothing like that. Why...would he?"

Noah glanced over at his friend affectionately, as if remembering something from their past. "Depends, I guess. He can be protective of me, which definitely drove me insane when we were kids. Always trying to fight my battles."

"That's what good friends do," Will said as he glanced around the room. He noticed more guests had shown up for the celebration.

"True. No matter what a pain in the ass he can be." Noah reached for two glasses and filled them with his newest concoction. "Tony's dad is starting a bonfire on the beach. Want to make sure he doesn't need any help?"

"Sounds perfect," he said as he took his proffered drink and followed Noah through the pool deck to the steps leading to the beach.

And it *was* perfect. This time, when he reached for Noah's hand, Noah didn't even try to fight him.

19

NOAH

His palm tingled as Will walked hand in hand with him toward the blaze on the beach, where many of the newest partygoers had gathered. He stopped briefly to say hello to Tony's father as he stoked the flames and to a couple of new arrivals he remembered from past events. He noticed how many were giving Will the once-over, as well as their clasped fingers, and it made a secret thrill shoot through him that he was on the arm of such a gorgeous man.

Hypocritical, he knew, since there was nothing real about it, but all the same, it was so freaking nice not to be alone. It felt like a comfort to have Will with him this weekend, no matter the circumstances. Except the usual guilt creeped in about Tony grilling Will and being protective of him. It made him wonder yet again what would happen after he and Will parted ways. He'd definitely need to explain to his friends and family that they had broken up, and they'd probably probe him about the reason. But he didn't need to focus on that tonight. He figured he'd worry about it on the train ride home. Maybe Will would even help him conjure up a plan.

Damn it, why the hell couldn't Will have been just some

random dude he'd found on an escort site? Someone he could've walked away from free and clear and never seen again. He certainly hoped things wouldn't become too awkward between them at work.

But life had always felt complicated to him. Which was why he'd made some recent changes even though it had put a strain on his relationship with his parents. And yet as a result, he was mostly happy. Or so he thought.

"Do you like s'mores?" Will asked after taking another sip of his sangria.

Noah glanced toward the bonfire and the small table near it, which was loaded with all the ingredients, including skewers in a box next to the cooler.

When Noah nodded, Will pulled him along toward the table. "Want to share one?"

His stomach flipped at those simple words. *Want to share one?* It was something a regular couple might say to one another, so coming from Will made it feel almost intimate. That was the whole purpose of this weekend, after all—to act like he wasn't single anymore. But tonight felt like a different vibe between them altogether. As if they'd finally gotten over their initial awkwardness or perhaps they were actually becoming friends? It might be nice to have Will as more than an acquaintance at work, since the past few months they had only been painfully polite. He was enjoying this Will better than the one who showed up at the store all reserved and tight-lipped. Obviously, retail wasn't Will's dream job, and from what he'd learned about Will's situation with his mother, the escort business wasn't either.

But it was Will's current reality, and he desperately needed the money. That wasn't going to change anytime soon. Will even mentioned that relationships weren't something he bargained for, which made a ton of sense now. Not that he'd want to explore anything further with Will. But he definitely wanted him to be happy, whatever that meant.

It certainly made him feel guilty that he could turn down his parents' money to strike out on his own, and if his mother had been the one afflicted with a serious mental illness, his family would've been able to afford the help. But he knew Will would never want his pity—that was something they had in common, so it only renewed his respect for him.

Will reached for the bag of marshmallows while Noah grabbed a skewer. A guy he vaguely remembered from other beach parties asked Will a question as he passed him the open bag. While Noah slid the two marshmallows Will had retrieved onto the stick, Will threw his head back and laughed at something the guy said, and Noah's gut squeezed tight.

Will was too goddamn charming for his own good.

He tried to pay attention to making the s'more as he stepped toward the blaze and placed the skewer a distance above the flame. Noah had always been mesmerized by bonfires even though his skin had been charred by second and third-degree burns. But that had involved electricity and a live wire, not wood and kindling. Still, he always kept a safe distance. The warmth made him anxious and uncomfortable. But it was thunderstorms that kept him up most nights, especially the year after the accident.

Just the hum of the electric current slashing through the sky made him tremble and hide. It had taken him years to climb out of his shell, to feel his normal self again, though he never would completely—not with his scars always so prevalent. Breaking from his parents had helped, and so did living in the city and getting a job he was interested in.

He thought about what Will had said about Noah's persona at work and how different he seemed out here. Work was a place where Noah thrived, and maybe that was exactly what Will was doing now. He was good at acting—pretending—and the idea turned to acid in his gut.

Was this all an act? Or just the parts when they were in a

crowd? He felt like he couldn't tell the difference anymore. Maybe he never could.

He turned his head and watched Will as he focused on the guy's story, leaning toward him, keeping eye contact. A real charmer for sure. Noah wasn't the only one who couldn't take his eyes off his fake boyfriend.

Will glanced briefly toward him, and his brows drew together. "What?"

Noah just shrugged and smiled, and Will's eyes softened in a way that made Noah's chest tighten. The man thumped Will's shoulder and walked away.

"You're going to burn our marshmallows," Will pointed out as he stepped closer to Noah, holding a graham cracker and a large piece of chocolate.

"Shit." Noah immediately drew the stick away from the flames and blew out the part that had blackened.

"All ready for you." Will placed the chocolate on top of the graham cracker and held it out to Noah. He slid the warm marshmallows off the skewer and onto the graham cracker, where it immediately began softening the chocolate. By the time Will placed the other half of the graham cracker on top to make a sandwich, Noah's mouth was watering.

He held out the sweet dessert to Will. "You first."

Will drew his wrist toward him and took a hearty bite.

"Mmmm," he said with his mouth full, and Noah chuckled.

When Noah took his own bite, he nearly moaned out loud. He hadn't had a s'more in years, and it tasted pretty close to heaven.

"Good?" Will asked, and since Noah was still chewing, he simply nodded.

Will's thumb traced Noah's chin. "You've got some marshmallow bits... Here, let me help."

Will's hand clasped Noah's jaw. Instead of using his finger to wipe the mess away, his tongue darted out to lick at the dripping confection.

Noah gasped at the warm, slick sensation, but before he could pull away, Will planted a kiss on him that made his knees turn to mush. He knew they must've been making a scene, but then Will's tongue slid past his lips, and he had this uncanny ability to make the entire beach melt away. Noah focused on the sensation of their mouths molding together, Will's thumb tracing his earlobe as his heart went crazy in his chest.

When Noah drew back to catch his breath, Will's eyes looked dreamy even as his mouth quirked up. "Now there's no question you're with me tonight."

"Good job," Noah said absently as he tried to get his head together. Will had pulled that stunt for his benefit, not because he was just as desperate to taste his lips again. Noah's stomach clenched. *Damn it, Will.* "Now I'll be sure to get questions from newcomers."

"Let them ask. I'm ready," Will said with a chuckle.

"With your corny coffee story?" Noah quipped as he licked his finger and then fed the last bite to Will. Two could play this game. Even though it didn't even feel much like a game anymore.

"Shit. Wish I would've known you weren't a coffee drinker," Will replied as he licked his lips, chasing a stray crumb.

Noah quirked an eyebrow. "If you were friendlier at work, you could've figured it out."

"I'll try harder," Will said in a serious tone. "Now that I know you better."

"Good. I will too," Noah replied with a nod. "I totally don't want this to become awkward between us."

"Me neither," Will said, reaching for his hand and twining their fingers together. It seemed to come naturally to him, at least this weekend, and it made Noah's stomach flutter every time. "I'm glad you said something. I think we can have a good time tonight without it being weird."

He squeezed their palms together. "What happens on Fire Island stays on Fire Island?"

Will chuckled. "Sounds good to me."

There was a brief flash of heat in Will's eyes that held some sort of promise, and Noah felt his entire body flush as he recalled what happened between them last night.

He could roll with it, no matter what happened. Or didn't happen, for that matter. Though the idea of not feeling Will's lips on him at least one last time left him feeling...unsettled. Like an itch right beneath his skin he couldn't satisfy. Regardless, this weekend turned out way better than he could have ever envisioned, and it was all due to the gorgeous man pretending to be into him. It made his breath catch; he could scarcely believe it. Even though it was all an act. He deserved a standing ovation for that.

"So about this coffee thing..." When Will kissed his knuckles, goose bumps lined his arm. Had it really been only yesterday that they discussed his perfect kind of kiss? Will had passed with flying colors—unfortunately.

"Guess I'm just perky all on my own," Noah explained. "Caffeine gives me the jitters."

"Tea?" Will offered.

"Nope." Noah laughed at Will's incredulous expression. "Just lemonade. The owner makes it fresh daily."

"Regular or pink?" he asked, tilting his head.

"Just plain old regular."

"There's nothing *regular* about you," Will said as he tugged on his hand and enfolded him in his arms. Noah sank against his chest, holding back a deep sigh. They watched the embers burn, while another sort of fire smoldered inside his chest.

20

WILL

Will found some sort of comfort in keeping Noah close. It somehow felt simpler touching the man than not, which made no sense at all. But for the life of him, he couldn't keep from running his hands soothingly across his shoulders. Even his lips were drawn to his cheek or his throat, which always made the man shiver.

As they waited for the cake to be carried from the kitchen to the dining table by Matt's parents, Will leaned against the wall with his arms wound around Noah's waist, and the man sagged against him as if he found the same kind of relief at their closeness. He realized he was playing with fire, but he couldn't resist touching him every chance he got. The rough patches on Noah's torso were becoming familiar to him, even through the material of his shirt.

Earlier by the fire, his fingertips had inched beneath the hem to lightly brush over his rib cage. He could feel Noah holding his breath as he trembled, which made him even more appealing. Maybe Noah expected him to flinch when his fingers dragged over his scars. Or possibly be disgusted or even frightened. It only made him want to redouble his efforts. Someone needed to show him that he was revered. Fuck anyone who told him otherwise. If it took a paid escort to break through that barrier with him, so be it.

Will pushed aside the little voice in his head telling him he'd confuse things even more between them. But he was inexplicably drawn to the man, whether through duty or compassion. Or maybe just plain old longing mixed with lust. He'd never have thought in a million years that he and Noah would even kiss, let alone hook up. Yet here they were in their own little cocoon against the wall, and the further Noah sank against him, the more Will's cock hardened and his heart unfurled.

After the room sang a rousing rendition of "Happy Birthday" to Matt, Tony playfully fed him some frosting from his finger before dropping to his knee. Will could see Tony's nerves brimming right below the surface, leading up to this moment, and he swallowed the lump in his throat. Noah's body stiffened, his fists clenched in expectation as he watched his best friend propose to his boyfriend, who absolutely said yes.

As Tony and Matt wiped tears from their eyes and the room erupted in cheers and shouts of good wishes, Will leaned forward and whispered in Noah's ear. "Congrats to your friends."

He felt Noah shiver, and he loved that his touch brought about such a response from him. How innocent he was, even though he seemed jaded most of the time.

Tony's parents opened the bubbly and began passing flutes around with a splash of liquid gold to toast to the happy couple. Noah stepped up to help pass glasses around and then grabbed a couple for the two of them.

"Can you see that for yourself someday?" Will asked him after they toasted to the happy couple and sipped from their flutes.

"Nah, not really," Noah replied and turned to watch his friends make their way around the room to speak to their guests, who offered pats on the back, handshakes, and kisses.

"Why not?" he persisted, though he wasn't sure why. It wasn't like he thought about the possibility for himself either. But for some reason he wanted Noah to expect more from his life. To dream bigger.

"I don't think it's in the cards," he replied absently. "And that's totally okay with me."

"If it's okay, then why all this?" he asked, tightening his grip on Noah's waist. "Why make it a point that you have someone in your life?"

"I told you," Noah replied through a clenched jaw. "Being out here doesn't feel like me anymore, and I wouldn't have even come if it wasn't for this—the party and the engagement. This is their life, not mine."

"And what exactly is your life?" Will murmured in his ear as he dragged Noah closer. His skin was warm and flushed, and he felt Noah's body melt against him as if all his tension was draining away. For some warped reason, he was glad he could produce that effect.

"Believe it or not, I love living in the city," he replied. "My apartment, my job. Maybe a different company or location would be cool someday. But working in retail is what I want, no matter what anyone else says."

He must've meant his parents. He had pulled away from them, and maybe they didn't approve of his career choice. Supposed it made sense, given their upscale professions and lifestyle.

"Good for you," Will responded just as Tony and Matt headed toward them.

Noah stepped forward to hug his friends, while Will clapped them on the back, offering his good wishes.

"Did you know about this?" Matt asked Noah as he flashed him his ring.

"Maybe," Noah replied with a wink. "So happy for you!"

As Tony and Matt moved on to thank other guests for coming,

Noah turned toward Will and clinked their champagne glasses together.

"So how about you?" Noah asked as he anchored his shoulder against the wall.

"What about me?"

"You asked about my life, so now let's put you on the hot seat," Noah said after tipping his glass for the last drop of champagne. "The way I see it, you've made sacrifices to provide a decent life for your mom."

"It's what I had to do. It all falls on my shoulders," Will replied, feeling his skin prickle as Noah scrutinized him. "I can't ignore my responsibilities."

Will hoped he didn't sound bitter because that was not his intention. Maybe he'd felt a bit cynical at the beginning of this arrangement, but after discovering everything Noah had endured in his life, his feelings had evolved.

"You take care of people," he replied, and Will's eyebrows drew together. "That's what you do."

"No, I..."

"You take care of your mom, as well as customers—in retail and in your escort business—am I right?"

Will had never thought of himself that way. It took him another moment to gather his thoughts. "You're making me sound more generous than I actually am. There are days when I despise the disease that took my mother from me," he admitted with a shaky voice. Why did this guy's opinion affect him so much? "And...and I only see the money when I'm an escort. I help fill a void for mostly lonely clients, but when it comes down to it, it's only a stupid job."

Even with his neediest clients, he wanted to get the fuck out of the room. He couldn't take the stark loneliness—it somehow mirrored his own, and it was too painful seeing himself that way. His sole purpose had become to make fast money, pay his mother's hospital bills, and get his family on more stable ground.

Noah grew silent, his eyes shuttering closed as he locked himself down. Fuck, Will had downright insulted him. Had essentially stripped him down to monetary value, or to an object he merely tolerated.

"Damn it, Noah. I didn't mean..."

Noah straightened, his body arching away from Will's touch. "No, it's okay. I...I shouldn't be trying to understand you or your motivations. That was stupid on my part. We were never friends to begin with." Noah stepped forward and got lost in the swell of people entering the kitchen from the deck.

Will tried to swallow the huge lump in his throat as he blinked repeatedly and looked around the room, trying to rein in his swirling thoughts. He downed his champagne and placed the glass on a side table.

Will searched around the room as the same man from the bonfire pulled him into a conversation with another guy near the kitchen island. They were friends of Matt's from Queens, but he barely paid attention as he tried to spot where Noah might've disappeared to. Had he gone upstairs to their room?

Excusing himself from the conversation, he took the stairs two at a time. His chest ached, and he hoped to find him and explain...apologize...but for what exactly? Everything he said was true. At least it had always been true until now. As an escort, he had never once felt something for a client. Sure, he'd been turned on a few times, which was a purely physical reaction to someone flattering him or worshipping his cock.

But this thing with Noah...it somehow cut deeper.

He had this visceral need to care for Noah, to find ways to make him smile. Noah thought he was ugly and unlovable, but he didn't see what Will did, and Will couldn't understand how someone else hadn't seen it either. Because Noah deserved someone special. Someone to make his eyes flash with surprise or lust. Someone proud enough of him to kiss him in front of the fire. Those were the things that mattered. Not the scars on your skin, but the depths of your soul.

When Will didn't find him in the room, his shoulders deflated. He stepped toward the window and stared out at the dark night. He realized in that moment how much Noah's moods affected him. He felt a thrill every time Noah sent shy glances his way when their eyes met across the room, when his smile lingered or grew brighter. When he sighed into Will's kiss, his pulse fluttering at his neck. That stern line that appeared between his eyebrows when he was discerning or puzzled about something. How his fingers would curl into fists when he was nervous or angry.

How Noah's skin felt warm and smelled clean with a hint of sweat and spice. He might've put his arms around Noah for show at the beginning of this weekend, but now he realized how much it anchored him too.

His gaze narrowed to the bonfire, which was still burning but less vibrant now. And as his eyes drifted to the waves lapping against the shore, that was when he spotted a lone figure standing at the water's edge.

21

NOAH

"Noah..." He heard his name being called from somewhere behind him on the beach.

"Don't... It's okay." Noah turned briefly to look at him. He had no right to make Will feel bad. Will was doing him a favor. "I'm sorry that I keep forgetting."

"Forgetting what?" Will asked as he stepped up beside him, his breaths ragged as if he'd run from the house to find him. Noah squashed down the buoyant feeling it gave him.

"That this is a job, a transaction between us," he muttered, cursing himself for starting to care. "That we've never been... friends. I think it's because I already know you. But don't worry, it won't happen again."

He felt Will's heat as he moved closer, and Noah fisted his palms, nervous he'd touch him again, and then it would all be over. His willpower was weakened around Will, that much was evident.

"The idea that I was paid for this weekend actually makes me nauseated," Will said in nearly a whisper.

"Wait, what?" Noah's head whipped around to stare at him,

unsure where the exchange was headed. Was Will going to tell him he had regrets?

"Because I feel like I would've come anyway"—Will explained, digging his toe into the sand—"had we been *friends* and you'd asked me. Because I'm enjoying myself out here...with you."

Noah's pulse quickened at his kind words. "I'm enjoying myself too. And honestly, knowing that money is going to help pay for your mom's bills and stuff..."

Will cringed. "Can we not? Everything feels too mixed up right now."

Noah stared at him for a long minute, seeing the confusion in his eyes. Maybe they were more alike than he realized. Maybe Will was affected by their time together just as much as he was. "Yeah, okay."

Damn it, he didn't want their last night together to be so awkward. He had been hoping that they had finally crossed the line to friendship, but he had gone and ruined it by trying to figure Will out. How stupid of him.

After another minute of tense silence, Will dipped his toes in the water. "The ocean calms you."

"Huh?" he asked, confused at the turn of conversation.

"You said you don't like being out here, but you like the ocean. You like standing here and thinking. You're drawn to it."

The fact that Will could be so perceptive was messing with his brain, because he was right—Noah was drawn to it. He even kept on his bedroom dresser a box of shells he'd collected over the years, and he'd painted his walls a soothing ocean blue.

Noah shrugged. "It's the only thing I miss. We had good times out here, until everything changed."

"Maybe it's about creating happy memories again," Will suggested, but the idea soured immediately in Noah's stomach. Too many parties, too many lonely memories the past few years.

"Maybe," he said, just to agree and change the topic. He

turned toward Will. "Let's just go back to the party and have a good time. We'll be leaving tomorrow, so we should make the most of it, like you said."

"Sounds like a plan." Will smiled, but it didn't quite reach his eyes. He seemed melancholy, but Noah didn't want to ask. Look what happened when he questioned him last time.

They hung on the deck the rest of the night, sitting near Tony and Matt, who relived their engagement story several times as various people approached to congratulate them. Things felt more relaxed between him and Will, but not quite as comfortable as before. In fact, there was still a slight tension that Noah didn't like. But he supposed it didn't matter, since their time together was almost over.

A couple of people Noah hadn't seen since childhood sidled over to say hello and meet his boyfriend. He figured it was curiosity more than anything. After all, Will was a gorgeous guy, and they had never really seen Noah with anybody, not like this, with Will so close and attentive. Even though Will was hands-off this time around, Noah still felt his pulse jump in his throat every time their arms would brush. And when Will told the story of how they met in true animated style and threw him an adorable crooked grin when the word *lemonade* was mentioned, Noah couldn't help smiling from ear to ear.

Will made him feel lighter this weekend, and for that he'd always be grateful. When Will got up to pour them a couple more drinks, Tony sat down in Will's place, looking happy and sated and sweet.

"You did good tonight," Noah said.

"I sure did," Tony replied dreamily as his eyes roved over Matt's form across the pool, where he stood talking to his parents, who were about to depart for the night. Tony's mom and dad had said their goodbyes just an hour before.

"And how about you?" Tony asked, his tone suddenly serious. "You still having a good time?"

"Yeah, sure," he replied cautiously. "Why do you ask?"

But he already knew that Tony could sense something was off between him and Will since they walked back from the beach, more than likely because they weren't touching. How stupid of him to think he could get away with an arrangement like this and not have it come back to bite him in the ass.

This could've been his chance to give Tony a heads-up that things between him and Will might be headed south. Wasn't like it hadn't happened a million times before. He just wished that his friends didn't seem to have such a vested interest this time.

Normally, in the past, Tony showed his protective instinct when it came to the guys Noah hooked up with. *"He's just using you,"* or *"he's a player."* And even though Noah did indeed have a discussion with Will about their relationship earlier in the day, he could tell that his best friend was rooting for them. *Figured.*

As if Will could sense the direction of the conversation between him and Tony, he returned with their drinks and placed them on the side table. Before Tony could get up and offer Will his seat back, Will plopped down on Noah's chair and wormed his way between his legs.

Noah felt a rush of warmth and affection as Will leaned back against him and sank into his arms as if it were the most natural thing in the world. Too bad it felt that way for Noah too. It was one of the reasons he was struggling so much with this arrangement. Will felt too good, too perfect.

"What are you doing?" Noah murmured into his neck, out of earshot of Tony.

Will lifted his head to kiss him on the lips. "Just go with it," he whispered.

Just like he'd said at the drag show right before he kissed him, which now felt worlds away. Had Will really worn fishnets home for him?

Damn, his cock perked to life at that thought, and Will

noticed immediately, as he playfully wiggled his ass into his groin.

"You guys are too adorable for your own good," Matt said with a laugh as he returned from walking his parents out. Noah's cheeks reddened as he met Tony's eyes.

Seemingly satisfied that everything was okay between them, Tony smiled and nodded his approval as Matt pulled him up from his seat and delivered a sweet kiss of his own.

As they walked hand in hand through the sliding glass doors to the kitchen, Noah noted that the mood of the party seemed to have shifted. The parents were gone, the music had been turned down to a tolerable level. And they weren't the only ones coupled up on lawn chairs. There was kissing, touching, and grinding going on. This was normally the time Noah would've excused himself and made his way up to bed. Even if he had a hookup, it was always over so quickly, it barely even registered for anyone, let alone him.

Just as he was about to nudge Will off to remind him that their audience had left, Will flipped over onto his stomach and nuzzled into his neck. Their bodies were now connected from chest to groin, and fuck if he didn't love feeling Will's weight on top of him. It seemed to ground him, make him feel...*real*. Like he had substance.

"Are we ready for bed?" Will murmured into his neck, making gooseflesh rise along his arms and legs.

And instead of feeling flustered and his cheeks flushing from the visual, a flicker of fire roared to life in Noah's body, lighting up all his nerve endings.

Will sucked on a spot at the hollow of his throat, and Noah groaned in response.

"You like that?" Will asked as his mouth brushed along his jawline and feathered up to his lips. When their mouths connected in a hot and searing kiss and he could feel Will's stiff shaft rubbing against his own, he thought he might combust right on the spot.

Will certainly knew how to push all the right buttons. Noah batted away the dark thoughts about Will being skilled at this sort of thing. That he acted this way with all his clients.

He desperately needed to feel special—*wanted*—if only for one night.

He drew away to catch his breath, and as his chest heaved, he stared into Will's eyes under the glow of moonlight. Noah could've sworn he saw raw emotions in his gaze—affection and unfathomable longing—but it could've just been his own reflection.

"I want to taste you," Will whispered as he dragged his lips across Noah's earlobe and sucked the tender skin into his mouth, making him shudder.

"Damn, the things you say," Noah mumbled into Will's shoulder.

They light me up. You light me up.

Noah threw a look over Will's shoulder, suddenly remembering they were in plain view on the deck. But they weren't doing anything scandalous compared to the two men grinding in the corner. Still, they were on full display, which compelled Noah to remember what this weekend had been all about.

"I want you, Noah. So fucking much," Will growled as he reached for his chin, forcing Noah to look at him. The sound reverberated beneath his skin. "I want to taste your skin, and make you come again, but this time in my mouth."

Noah trembled beneath him. *Holy fuck.* "Will, I..."

"Let's go upstairs so I can show you," Will continued with pleading eyes. His fingers snaked between their bodies to where their groins met. "Your cock is as hard as mine. You're so fucking sexy, and you don't even realize it."

Noah moaned as Will took his mouth in a fierce kiss that he

felt deep in his bones. He melted into the seat and reveled in the full weight of Will's body as well as the kiss.

At least he'd have a hell of a good memory to play back in his head about this weekend.

Will dragged his mouth away, his breath releasing in soft pants against his lips. "Unless you want to stay out here and give somebody an eyeful. But I'd prefer to devour you in private."

After another minute, Will slid off the chair, and Noah immediately missed his heat. He held out his hand to help Noah up. He felt unsteady on his feet, wishing he could feel Will's weight on him for longer. "Let's go."

22

WILL

As soon as they shut the bedroom door behind them, Will had Noah up against the wall, his hands pinned on either side of him. His mouth was everywhere at once—lips, neck, ears—devouring him whole, and the noises bursting from Noah's throat only urged him on more. Will had no idea what had come over him, but he had this burning desire not only to see Noah come undone, but to satisfy his own desires for the man as well.

Noah drew back, his breaths rough and uneven, his eyes bleary, his lips glistening.

"You can..." He looked over Will's shoulder as if getting acclimated to his surroundings, his mouth curving into a gloomy little frown. "You can slow down. We don't have an audience anymore, so..."

A flash of anger spiked hot inside Will's chest. Noah was accusing him of putting on a performance downstairs, and maybe it had started out that way, when it became obvious Tony was questioning Noah about Will. But holy fuck, did he actually think he was some sort of robot that could switch his desires on and off at a moment's notice?

"Are you fucking kidding me?" He took a step back, allowing for space to clear his head.

When Noah didn't respond, Will tugged at his hand and slid it against his ample crotch. "You think this is all an act? That whatever happened downstairs was all for show?"

"Well, no," Noah stuttered and drew his hand away. "I get it... We were rubbing up against each other, and anyone would've had a physical reaction to that."

"Seriously?" Will huffed out an exasperated breath. He was running on raw emotion and pure instinct as he paced back and forth like a caged animal. "Maybe I need to show you just how fucking much you turn me on."

In one second flat, he had his pants unzipped and his hard shaft in his hand. Noah's eyes sparked with a frisson of heat as he stared openly at Will's cock, the head flushed with blood.

"Not sure how you don't see it," Will said in a low murmur. He nearly groaned out loud at the way Noah was watching him, the longing evident on his face. "You're so fucking sexy...and you deserve someone who's going to make sure you know it."

"Christ, Will." Noah's chest was heaving from his heavy panting. "I can't even... You make me feel so..." He shook his head, either overwhelmed or unable to find the right words.

"What, Noah?" he asked, closing the distance between them. "Tell me."

"You make me feel like I matter," Noah murmured, and Will's heart nearly cracked into a million pieces.

Will reached for him, wanting to pull him solidly to his chest and enclose him in his arms. But instead, Noah dropped to his knees and stared openly at his dripping shaft. "Please let me taste you."

"Fucking hell," he groaned, his head tilted to the ceiling. And before Will could explain that it was supposed to be the other way around, that what he had planned when he got the man up here was to devour him, Noah's tongue darted out and swiped at his slit, collecting the beads of precome that had gathered there.

Knees nearly buckling, he grasped Noah's shoulder for leverage. Noah glanced up at him with those beautiful doe eyes that looked both innocent and devilish as he leaned forward and grazed at the tip again.

A groan ripping from his throat, Will fisted his shaft and fed his cock to Noah's willing mouth. As Noah tenderly suckled the crown, Will's eyes nearly rolled back in his head.

He brushed the bangs out of Noah's face so he could watch his shaft disappearing between those plump, shiny lips. Noah groaned and increased pressure, his cheeks flushing a warm crimson color. The heat and the pressure were so fucking perfect, Will could barely hold himself together.

After all the pent-up tension from touching him today and then thinking he'd probably never get another chance, Will was sure to blow his load in another minute. But he wasn't done with Noah—not before he convinced the man of how much he wanted him.

He grasped Noah's jaw and gently tugged his sensitive shaft from his mouth. When he pulled Noah to his feet, his eyebrows knit together in confusion. "Get on the bed. I want my own taste."

When Noah muttered in protest, he kicked out of his jeans and underwear, then walked Noah backward toward the bed. His calves hit the mattress, and he sank down in the sheets.

"Let me see you, Noah. No second-guessing, no excuses. Just you and me—here and now," he growled, and Noah's eyes lit up. He liked when Will was sure-handed with him. He needed to remember that.

Except, there wouldn't be another time. He shook the thought away, which was like a jagged spike in his chest. Tugging his shirt over his shoulders, he tossed it on the floor.

Noah's gaze catalogued every inch of his naked torso, making his blood boil in his veins. The worshipful way he looked him over made his cock even harder.

"You're stunning," Noah murmured as their gazes clashed.

Will placed his knee on the mattress, driving Noah back onto his elbows. "Let me see you," he repeated, not willing to wait a moment longer. "Please."

Noah bit his lip and with shaky fingers, pulled his shirt off and tossed it behind him. Noah averted his eyes as Will glanced down at his raw and battered skin. He had the sudden impulse to kiss all Noah's insecurities away.

Afraid Noah would have another moment of self-consciousness, Will bent down and licked one of his nipples. "Unffff," Noah groaned, his body trembling beneath him. Will wondered just how many men had paid his chest any attention, so he planned to fix that tonight. When Will touched the tip of his tongue to the other nipple, it swelled in response. Noah hissed and shuddered as if he'd been stung.

His tongue divided its attention between both nipples as he tenderly licked around each areola, because even broken things needed love and attention. Noah gripped the sheets on either side of him as his body squirmed, stiff cock poking from the top of his waistband. Deep gasps rumbled from his chest, and Will paused, momentarily wondering if he was providing too much stimulation at once.

Will's fingers danced across his chin and drew his gaze to him. "This okay?"

Noah swiped at his glossy eyes, looking equally blissed and overwhelmed. He opened his mouth to speak but nodded instead. He watched as Will lowered his head and carefully feathered his mouth over the reddened, tender skin down the center of his stomach, his abdomen convulsing from his touch.

He licked at the rough patches along his rib cage down to his darkened hip bone that almost looked stained. When he glanced up, he watched as Noah closed his eyes as if in relief.

And fuck if that wasn't his undoing right then.

All the man wanted was to be pampered—valued—and hell if Will wasn't going to be the one to give that to him.

It reminded him of something his mom had said after one of her episodes, and it'd stuck with him all this time. *Sometimes it takes total darkness to dream in color.*

As Will's tongue teased inside Noah's belly button, his hands dragged along his waistband, dipping his fingers inside to the wetness leaking from his cock. He carefully unfastened his pants and lowered them past his knees to his ankles and then tugged them off his feet.

When his hot breath washed over his shaft, his cock pulsed and jumped.

"Nobody's ever…done…" Noah's breath stuttered out. "Your mouth is doing magical things to me."

"I'm glad," he replied as his palm encircled his cock. "I want to make you feel good."

Noah shivered at either Will's words or his firm touch. Resuming his ministrations, Will licked at the sensitive skin all around his shaft, teasing him relentlessly until he finally took the first swipe with the flat surface of his tongue. Noah nearly sprang off the bed. He continued probing the red tip and collecting his seed as he gently fondled his balls. He could feel them tightening and pulling up as he circled around the crown.

A ragged moan released from Noah's mouth. "Please. I want to touch you too."

Will encouraged Noah to turn on his side, and then he lay down opposite him so they could provide mutual satisfaction.

Noah hungrily attacked his cock, and as soon as he felt his warm mouth surrounding his shaft, Will shivered. It was so hard to concentrate because Noah was performing sensual tricks with his tongue, licking up and down the vein and then circling the head. Will was squirming, the hairs on his nape standing at attention as Noah sucked him into submission. "Jesus. Feels fucking amazing."

Redoubling his efforts, Will leaned forward and inhaled his scent by shoving his nose in the coarse patch of hair at Noah's groin. He licked at the crease where his thigh met his torso, noticing that the burns did not extend any lower. He studied his cock, the long curve, the thickness, the weeping head, and was grateful that the accident hadn't been much worse.

He licked at his slit once more before finally sucking his cock into his mouth. As Noah shuddered, he could already taste the come on his tongue. He knew Noah wouldn't last long, and given the treatment Will was receiving, neither would he.

Breathing through his nose, he took Noah farther inside his mouth by relaxing his throat. Noah thrust his hips toward his mouth, enjoying the sensation.

Releasing his shaft, Will positioned his head farther back, pulling the wrinkled scrotum between his lips and then sucking on each of his balls. Will was enjoying the different noises Noah was making and joined him with his own deep groan as Noah took him all the way to the back of his throat.

Will's fingers explored the crease of Noah's ass, discovering the softer hair around his hole. Resting his chin behind his balls, he spread his cheeks apart with his thumbs, and Noah moaned.

He lapped at the area just behind his scrotum before licking a wet stripe across his wrinkled entrance. Noah's hips shot forward as he released a groan from deep in his chest. He smelled like the ocean—musk and sand—and tasted like salt, and Will found he couldn't get enough as his tongue painted circles around his hole.

"You're going to make me come." Noah's cock was resting snuggly against his neck and leaking down his collarbone. Will's thumb replaced his tongue as his hand gripped Noah's shaft, and he enveloped his straining cock inside his mouth.

"Holy fuck, Will." Noah's entire body stilled before he cried out and coated Will's mouth with ribbons of come, and he worked his throat to swallow it all down.

Will hummed around Noah's shaft as his own orgasm rolled over him in long, languid waves, the sparks intensifying like a fireworks finale as his groin jolted forward in Noah's mouth.

He could feel Noah's shallow breaths against his shaft as he softened against his lips. Will licked his slit one last time before he sat up, drowsy and completely sated.

Will reached for Noah so they could slide their tongues together in a long, deep kiss that lasted for what felt like minutes. Warm hands moved over him in tender strokes as he opened his eyes and met Noah's adoring gaze.

"That was incredible," he said against Noah's mouth. "Thank you."

He pulled Noah into another soft and tender kiss before collapsing to the mattress, dragging Noah with him. After another minute of catching their runaway breaths, he encircled Noah in his arms and held him for as long as the night would allow.

23

NOAH

Noah woke at dawn, the silent darkness pressing at him like fingers. Will's body was firmly planted against his back, and his soft breaths washed along his neck. His hand was wound around his middle, and Noah tried to hold in the shiver when he thought about how Will had looked at him last night and took his time with his body—his skin—as if he could see beyond the scars.

It felt like a mesmerizing dream, and thinking about it as anything else was wading in dangerous territory. Removing himself emotionally from this situation was best. After all, Will was a paid escort, and he'd move on to his other clients, showering them with the same sort of attention. His stomach revolted, but he locked the memories from last night into their own special vault in his heart because soon enough reality would come crashing back down on them.

But for now, for another hour at least, he wanted to sleep in Will's warmth and pretend. Pretend that guys like Will actually existed. Three-dimensional men who didn't keep their distance once they saw his scars. It was no fun having to explain himself all over again. It was a bit like coming out, which happened with every new person you met. And that got old fast.

Working in retail had certainly helped bring him out of his shell. He could still feel customers' eyes on him at times, and though he was good at hiding most of his scars—collared shirts helped—he knew people were just naturally curious creatures.

Noah fell back asleep in the cocoon of Will's embrace and awoke to loud voices from the pool area. When he blinked open his eyes, he noticed that Will was lying awake, staring at the ceiling.

"Hey, sleepyhead," Will said in a croaky voice.

"Hey, yourself." Noah shifted to his back, and when he remembered they were nude under the covers, a blush spread across his cheeks.

"What?" Will asked in an amused tone.

"Nothing." Noah cleared his throat and sat up, taking the sheet with him. It was one thing to reveal your body in the heat of the moment, but something altogether different in the bright daylight.

He felt strong arms encircle his shoulders as Will dragged him back down.

"What the hell are you doing?" he asked as he burrowed his face in Will's neck.

"Just checking with you," he said against his ear. "Making sure you don't have any regrets."

"About last night?" Noah asked as he tilted his head toward Will. "No, I'll never have regrets. That was…" A shiver wracked him.

"For me too." When Noah glanced at him skeptically, Will reached for his chin, forcing him to look him in the eye. "That's the truth."

"Okay," Noah replied, needing to get away from his scrutiny. But his stomach buzzed with relief. He reached for his phone on the nightstand to look at the time. "We can catch the next ferry back in an hour. Sound okay to you?"

It took Will a long moment to respond. "Sure, sounds good."

Noah rolled out of bed before he caved again, then strode to the bathroom with the sheet wrapped around him. He was being ridiculous, but old habits were hard to break. "Jumping in the shower. I'll be quick."

As the water blasted down on him, he remembered all the places Will touched him last night, and his cock plumped up. Damn it.

He heard the door open, then Will's voice. "Taking a leak."

"No problem." A minute later the shower curtain rustled, and Will stepped inside completely nude, his cock fully erect. Holy damn, he was gorgeous. So much skin, Noah didn't know where to look first.

"Do you mind?" he asked with a smirk. "It'll save time. Plus, it's still technically the weekend."

Noah's breath caught as Will stepped under the warm spray.

"You've got a point," he muttered as his pulse went crazy. He passed Will the soap, and after only a moment of awkwardness, shy smiles passing between them, they began washing each other in a perfunctory way even though they both had raging hard-ons.

Soon enough slippery fingers were touching balls, grasping cocks, wet mouths fusing together as they jacked each other off, groaning into each other's necks.

Will reached for one of the towels first, and before he stepped out, he twisted to look back at Noah. "In case you had doubts, I still think you're beautiful. Inside and out."

Noah gripped the wall for leverage as he bit his lip hard. His eyes stung, and he blinked tears away. Will wrapped the towel around his waist and left the room, not giving him a backward glance. As soon as Noah trusted his legs enough to leave the shower and towel off, he noticed that Will was already dressed and had his bag packed.

"I'll meet you downstairs. Gonna grab a coffee for the road."

Noah swiftly changed into clean shorts and was shoving the clothes he'd discarded last night into his knapsack when something caught his eye. He dug to the bottom and pulled the fishnets out. Will had stuffed them in his bag—maybe as a joke, maybe for memory's sake—and Noah couldn't stop smiling.

As he made his way downstairs, he spotted Will sitting at the kitchen island, sipping coffee with Tony and Matt. When Will caught his eye, he offered him a disarming, lopsided grin that caused his heart to trip over itself.

"Thanks for everything." Tony stood up to walk them out. "I'll text you in a few days."

"Max, it was so good to meet you," Matt said. "You're welcome back anytime."

And just like that reality slammed back into Noah. He could tell Will was just as affected by hearing the name *Max* as well as the open invitation. His shoulders remained tight and rigid as they walked along the boardwalk.

Reining in his galloping breaths, Noah collected his thoughts. He'd paid Will to accompany him to the island. And they had a great time, in more ways than one. That was all this was. Noah would thank him properly when they parted ways in the city, and all this would come to an end. The way it was meant to be.

So why couldn't he swallow past the lump in his throat even as they boarded the ferry, their elbows touching on the upper deck as they sailed away from the beach? He felt their parting like a cold punch to his chest. But it was only one weekend. Several scattered hours together. How was it possible for one person to wind his way around his rib cage and plant shallow roots inside his chest in such a brief period of time? He'd feel better once he got home where everything was familiar.

Except Will had become familiar too. His scent, his arms, his smile.

His heart.
Noah was truly fucked.

24

WILL

"Ma, I'm home," Will announced as he pushed through the door to their apartment. Even though they'd texted that morning and the respite worker assured him yesterday she was doing fine, he could never shake the cold sweat that passed over his body every time he crossed over the landing. There had been too many times when he'd found her either inconsolable or paranoid to the point that she even questioned his motives, her own child.

"In here," she called in a chipper voice. That was reassuring.

He found his mother in the kitchen with the table covered in flour, a worn cookbook opened to a dessert page as she attempted to make some sort of pastry that involved dough and sugar.

"What is going on?" he asked with a laugh, his heart suddenly lighter.

"Pull up a chair," she replied, straightening her apron. "I'm attempting to make cinnamon sugar knots from your grandmother's recipe."

His grandmother was no longer alive, having succumbed to heart disease when his father was still around in the early years. Will and his mom had both lost two important people in the span of five years, which might explain why they clung to each other so much.

"She made the best sweets. I still remember her chocolate chip cookies." Will slid into a chair at the table and watched his mom work.

"She was a good cook," his mother added wistfully. There was also a hint of guilt in her gaze as she looked down at her rolling pin. She'd tried her best after his father left, but truth be told, they ate a lot of canned soups and TV dinners. He'd never fault her for that—at least he always knew he was loved. "Unfortunately, she never really wrote anything down. It was a pinch of this or a dash of that. So I'm trying to get some help from one of her cookbooks."

He reached forward to brush some flour from her nose and gave her a good once-over. She was dressed and had combed her hair. "You look good, Mom."

"I know you're worried, William," she said with a smile as she spread cinnamon sugar over the top of her knotted dough. "You're such a good son."

Once he washed his hands and helped her line up all the dough on a greased cookie sheet, she handed him the dishtowel that had been draped over her shoulder. "I know there was a little blip yesterday, but I think they got the med combination right this time."

"Sure hope so," he replied as he held open the oven door, and she slipped the pan inside. "If not, we'll figure it out. We always do."

He tried sounding more confident than he felt, even though his stomach quivered at the thought of paying for another hospital stay. She hated the state-run hospitals, which was completely understandable, but a more private setting had waiting lists and a higher price tag. Regardless, he knew the kind of care she deserved, so he'd do anything to help her stay well. Including becoming a paid escort.

Immediately his thoughts flashed to his weekend with Noah on Fire Island. The ride home on the ferry had been sobering, to say the least. Neither spoke very much, each lost in their own thoughts. Will would admit he felt a bit melancholy when the ferry pulled into port. And though they caught the same train back to the city before parting ways, Will felt like their time was already over the minute they said goodbye to Noah's friends at the beach house.

The most mortifying part had been when Noah pulled out a wad of fives and tens to offer him as a tip before their stop at Penn Station. Apparently, the Gotham City representative who arranged Will's services had told Noah clients tipped regularly if they felt the escorts' duties went *above and beyond*. And while that was certainly true, Noah offering it to him made him feel like a prostitute, even though he knew he didn't mean it that way.

"Fuck, Noah. Keep it," Will had said as the train doors opened. "*I'll see you around.*"

And without another glance back, he'd pushed through the crowd at the doors and pretended to get lost in the sea of people heading up the stairs.

Except he still felt in his bones that they'd shared something more profound than he'd even shared with most men he'd dated. He had the urge to hold Noah on the ferry ride, to reiterate that he had an amazing time, but that would've only dragged it out, and he'd said everything he wanted to the night before. And then the next morning in the shower. A smile lined his lips.

Will and his mom talked at the kitchen table about their weekends until the pastry was pulled from the oven and cooled enough to eat. And after he put away his bag and checked his messages, they turned on *Shark Tank*, one of his mom's favorite shows to binge watch. Per usual, she made the offhanded comment that she needed an invention to make her a millionaire, this time adding, "To buy us one of those beach houses you described on Fire Island," and then they rattled off some ridiculous ideas and laughed themselves silly.

"Love you, Mom," he said, kissing her cheek before he retired to bed early.

He considered knocking on the super's door to thank them for keeping an extra eye out, but it was late. No doubt they would've called him immediately if they noticed something was off with his mom. Satisfied that everything would be cool, at least for the time being, he finally let himself relax.

By the time he lay down in his sheets, he was beat. Sleeping in his own bed was nice, though he immediately noted the difference in mattress comfort as well as thread count as compared to the beach house. But the hum of their faulty refrigerator and the noise of the city down below him always felt like a familiar comfort, lulling him to sleep.

Before passing out, he thought about Noah's scars, how he shivered at the simplest touch, and how his smile would linger on him when he wasn't hiding himself. Will had the urge to text him something to make him grin. But that wasn't the type of relationship this was going to be. At least, they hadn't established that.

It could certainly get awkward when he saw Noah at the store for the first time, but he had to admit he sort of looked forward to it as well. He now had a completely different view of Noah. Whereas before he saw him as an overly enthusiastic sales associate, now he could hear the earnestness in his voice when he told him how much he enjoyed working there. How he didn't really aim to do anything else, and that in itself was admirable. In this city, practically everyone he knew was aspiring to be someone else.

Noah was refreshingly just himself.

Will fell asleep on that thought, and when he woke in the morning, he felt recharged and ready for his week. He opened a few bills that he was able to pay off, checked his work schedules, and noticed he had a new client tomorrow through the escort service as well as an afternoon shift at Home and Hearth.

On his way to the gym on Tuesday, he stopped at the corner coffee shop and spotted his friend Oren working today. After he placed his order, he moved down the line to wait for his latte.

"So what's up?" Oren asked as he placed the cup under the machine to make his drink.

"Same old, same old," Will replied in a neutral voice. "Been busy."

"Yeah?" Oren asked, studying him closely. "You hear there's an open call for that new Bronstein production on the Upper West Side?"

Will got that same feeling in his gut he always did—that urge to be part of something creative. But then he remembered the hours, the shitty pay, the fierce competition, and he wasn't exactly sorry that he'd walked away last year.

"You going to audition?" Will asked instead of answering him.

"Thinking about it," he replied, and Will saw the same sort of dreaminess in his eyes. "You ever miss it, Will?"

"Sure, every now and again," Will explained. "Until I remember all the bogus stuff."

"Tell me about it," Oren replied as he handed him his steaming cup. "Is the other gig going okay for you, though?"

Will glanced around to be sure nobody was in earshot. "Yeah. Actually, just got back from a weekend on Fire Island."

"Sweet." Oren whistled. "You seem to have made it through in one piece, so it wasn't too much of a hardship?"

It was a discreet question about the client. Oren was the one who'd warned him that some situations could get hairy. But also that the pay was good. And as a whole, his advice had been sound.

"No, he was cool, and it was actually really nice." Will cleared his throat before he gave himself away.

"Sounds like you're still thinking about this guy." Oren arched an eyebrow. "That good-looking?"

He sighed. Noah was right in that regard. Why did it always come down to physical attributes? Still, he played along because it was the truth. "Gorgeous," he replied and then headed for the door.

In every single way.

After his workout, he helped his mom clean the apartment and then got ready for work. He felt nervous as he walked up the subway stairs to street level and then walked across to Home and Hearth.

As he pushed through the door, Noah and Samantha were on their way out, so obviously they were on opposite shifts.

"Oh, hey," Will said in as casual a voice as he could muster as he held the door open for them. "Um, have a good night."

Samantha smiled and passed through first, and as Noah walked past, he stopped briefly and turned to Will. He looked as anxious as Will did as his gaze shifted around the store and then out to the sidewalk to make sure his coworker was an ample distance away. She looked back once with some confusion on her face but then kept going.

Fuck, this was awkward.

"I wanted to text you the other night, but then I thought..." Noah shook his head, and the ache in Will's chest eased. He had been thinking the same thing. "I wanted to ask how your mom was doing, but I didn't know if... I didn't want to pry."

"She's doing good," he said with a smile. "I actually found her in the kitchen when I got home, baking up a storm. I mean, because she normally doesn't... Never mind."

Now he was rambling and blocking the doorway for a customer trying to get out.

"No, I get it...I think," he said, his eyes now diverted to his shoes. "Glad to hear it. Well, catch you later."

"Noah?" Will said as he swept partially through the door

behind a woman carrying a Home and Hearth shopping bag. His chest felt tight again, his hands clammy. He wanted to say more or just be in the same room again or something so they could get over this initial awkwardness.

"Yeah?" Noah asked as he swung around on the sidewalk to look at Will. He bit his bottom lip and clenched his hands, and damn, he looked so adorable.

Will reluctantly shook his head. "Nothing... just...good night."

25

NOAH

It'd been a couple of weeks since Tony and Matt's engagement, and Noah had only been on schedule with Will a handful of shifts. Every time they were in the same room, the tension between them would crackle—at least on Noah's end.

Even tonight he'd caught Will watching him from across the room more than once, but then he'd look away. Sometimes he'd smile, and Noah would remember how Will told him he was different at work. But Noah had said much the same about Will, and it might've been Noah's imagination, but he noticed a slight difference in him—like he was trying a bit harder to be more open with coworkers. Noah couldn't help feeling smug that he possibly influenced that decision.

It was certainly hard not to want to ask him about personal stuff in his life, like his mom's health and well-being. Then he'd see him hightailing it out of the store and remember that he was an escort and probably had a client. It made acid burn in his stomach as an unfamiliar yet fragile ball of jealousy took root in his gut. But what could he possibly do? Will didn't owe him anything. Besides, he needed the money, and Noah certainly couldn't begrudge him that.

He wasn't sure if Will was having the same struggle of constantly reliving moments of their weekend together. Imagining their arms around each other, their mouths locked in an all-consuming kiss. He'd stuffed the fishnets in the back of his underwear drawer and would sometimes run his fingers over them when getting dressed. He'd never had anybody make his body buzz that way, and he wasn't sure if he'd ever experience it again. And that made a certain kind of melancholy hang over him like a storm cloud. Because he was never more aware of how lonely he was than in the days after he'd shared a bed with Will.

"Noah, can we speak to you?" Rick, the regional manager, had come from the back room with his manager Kara in tow. She threw him a quick smile, which reassured him that he wasn't in trouble or being fired. Rick had come to the store to discuss the plan for the new location on Columbus Circle. So more than likely, they were going to be asking some staff members if they were interested in a transfer. And Noah certainly thought he should consider it because it was difficult seeing Will like this after they'd shared so much. He didn't know what he'd expected, but it wasn't this miserable longing to simply engage in a conversation with the man—even though nothing was ever that simple.

But maybe his need would lessen over a few weeks' time, and they'd go back to pre-Fire Island days when they all but ignored each other. But damn, that didn't sit well with him either.

He entered the office through the back room, and Kara asked him to take a seat.

"How's it going?" Rick asked as he slid into the chair behind the modest desk. Kara spent ample time back here at the computer, but mostly she seemed to be out on the floor with the employees and customers.

"Good," he replied, and for some reason his hands were shaking. He wasn't sure what to expect, and to think about voluntarily leaving this store simply because he got too involved with a coworker was unsettling.

Would it really be the worst thing to ask Will if he wanted to hang out sometime—as friends? There was nothing wrong with that, and it might help dispel the tension between them. As silly as it sounded because it was only one weekend, he missed Will. It was tough to go from being so intimate to avoiding each other at work.

"We've been getting good feedback on the sales you bring in, and your customer service is always impeccable," Rick stated while Kara smiled.

Noah sat up straighter; he hadn't been expecting that praise. "Thank you."

If there was anything he could feel proud of, it was that. His work ethic.

"We'd like to offer you the manager position at this location," Rick continued. "Kara will be transferring to the new store, and you come highly recommended to step into her shoes."

Holy shit. Noah covered his mouth in surprise and felt completely bowled over.

Rick told him about the pay raise, Kara training him, and the fact that his schedule might change slightly, but that was just background noise; he would've taken the position regardless.

"I accept your offer."

"Fantastic." Rick reached over the desk to shake his hand. "Congratulations."

"I'm thrilled," Kara said, stepping up to hug him. "We'll announce it in our staff roundup tonight."

There was a bounce in his step as he strode back onto the floor. He felt like he was floating in the first bit of good news he'd gotten in a while. A management position was something he'd been aspiring to the last couple of years, but he hadn't expected it to come to fruition this soon.

When his eyes met Will's, who was helping a customer with a throw rug, Noah positively beamed.

Will's eyebrows wove together before a smirk lined his lips in amusement. Probably because it was the first genuine smile they'd shared in their otherwise timid exchanges. He wished he could tell Will the news, but he'd hear about it soon enough.

At the end of the night, the doors were locked and the staff began their ritual of straightening, cleaning, and cashing out. When they were called to the middle of the floor by the managers, his palms began sweating. Had he really been promoted?

Kara and Rick went through a couple of announcements about their store. "If there are any employees who'd prefer to transfer to the new location, see me or Kara privately," Rick said. "The grand opening will be in two weeks, and though we've already hired enough employees, there would be room for one or two more."

Will's gaze met Noah's across the semicircle the employees had formed. He offered him a half shrug as if maybe he'd been considering it. Little did Will know, Noah had been pondering it before he was offered Kara's job. He would've liked to talk to Will about it—he certainly didn't want him to feel like he had to transfer, but he also wondered if it wouldn't be for the best.

"One more announcement before we send you on your way," Kara said, and Noah's throat felt thick. He wondered what the reaction would be, not only from the staff, but from Will. "I'll be transferring to the new store, and Noah Dixon will be promoted to my position at this location."

There was one silent moment when the sound seemed blotted out, and then reality came crashing back in. His coworkers were cheering and clapping him on the back.

"No surprise there," Samantha said. "You'll be great."

When he caught Will's eyes, they were crinkled in joy, and Noah blew out a breath.

They got back to closing up the store, and a few minutes later, as there was a swell of employees headed to the door, Samantha turned to him. "Let's head to Chauncey's for a celebratory drink. Everybody in?"

"Sounds good to me," Noah said. He could definitely use a drink.

As they spilled onto the sidewalk, his gaze briefly met Will's, and he could tell that he was about to beg off like he normally did. So maybe he had a customer or needed to get something else done. Noah tried to hide his disappointment as he turned away, awaiting Will's excuse.

To his utter amazement, Will did not descend the steps to the subway as the group trudged toward the bar. He followed behind. Maybe he could use a night out as well.

They entered the pub, where they pushed two tables together as well as some chairs, and somehow Will ended up sitting beside him. As they ordered pitchers of beer, Will leaned closer. "Congratulations. I know how much that means to you."

"Thank you." He felt a flush crawl across his cheeks. "And thanks for coming. I know you don't normally—"

"Don't sweat it," Will responded quickly before glancing around the table. The only person who seemed to notice was Samantha, and Noah shook his head to beg her off.

As the beers were served and his coworkers recounted their day, he could feel the heat of Will's thigh against his and had the urge to twine their fingers together like they did so many times over the weekend at Fire Island.

He noticed a blush dot Will's cheeks as he threw him a sidelong glance, unless he was imagining it.

"Does this promotion mean you can't cavort with your employees anymore?" Samantha asked with a pout.

Noah's beer stopped midway to his mouth. He hadn't considered that.

"He'll definitely have to draw a line in the sand and dock us when we're late and all that," Michelle replied.

"C'mon, I'm sure it won't be that bad," Noah replied, trying to brush it off. He'd have to ask Kara about that. Though it was true she rarely hung out with them after work. But she did have a toddler waiting at home.

"Why do you think Trish was transferred to the Brooklyn store?" Michelle asked with exaggerated hand motions, and a couple of his coworkers snickered. Trish was the manager before Kara, but he barely had time to interact with her before she relocated. Noah always thought it was because she lived closer to the other store.

"What do you mean?" Samantha asked. She started working at Home and Hearth a couple of months after Noah.

"I guess she hooked up with Keith one night, and then it became awkward because he wanted to date her," Michelle explained as she leaned toward the table conspiratorially. "Someone complained she was giving him *preferential* treatment."

"Seriously?" Noah asked. He was never close to Keith, but he did remember he'd also quit pretty quickly after Trish transferred.

"So unless you plan on hooking up with one of us, should be all cool to still hang out for a beer every once in a while," a coworker named Greg said, and everyone laughed.

Will made a noise in the back of his throat, and then he shifted in his seat. Noah didn't dare look in his direction, but he felt the heat from his thigh again, and his stomach tilted uncomfortably.

Maybe in the back of his mind he always thought maybe…maybe what?

He was being ridiculous. There was nothing between him and Will except that one weekend that he couldn't seem to shake.

And now they really couldn't be anything, not while they were working at the same store. Besides, could he really date someone who was a paid escort? Warm bile clawed up his throat, but he swallowed it down. Maybe he was just being delusional that he somehow felt Will was different with him.

"Anyone for some pool?" Greg asked, and a few of them got up to play near the back of the bar. That left only four of them at the table. Michelle and Samantha were involved in a conversation about another store, where there was some sort of drama they'd heard about.

"Noah," Will muttered in his direction, but Noah shook his head, afraid he'd say something that would be overheard. Noah noticed how Will glanced at the time on his phone, and he figured he was going to bolt any minute.

"Want to play a round of darts?" Noah blurted before Will could decide to leave the bar.

"Yeah, sure," Will replied with a measure of surprise in his eyes. Samantha and Michelle didn't appear to even notice them leaving the table as they walked to the edge of the bar where the two boards were located.

He picked up the darts and handed Will the three with blue tops. Will motioned for him to go first, and he aimed the red ones in a daze, only hitting the perimeter of the board.

"What were you going to say to me?" Noah asked in a lowered voice as Will took his turn.

"Dunno exactly," Will replied as Noah took his place and threw his own darts at the board again. "It was just...you seemed upset during a time you should be celebrating. So I'm considering transferring so it won't cause any more strife between us."

"But then that would be it," Noah said, his heart vaulting to his throat. "We wouldn't have any reason... Never mind..."

"Is that what you want?" Will asked, their hands brushing as they changed places. "A reason? I consider you a friend now, so if you ever need anything—"

"Yeah, okay. You too." Noah hated that he felt so jumbled up inside. "It's just...I'd hate for you to have to rearrange your life for..."

"It's just a different subway line, maybe some extra minutes. It's totally fine," Will replied. "You know this job is only temporary for me. It's more important that you get off on the right foot in your new position."

"Don't make any rash decision yet," Noah replied. "Just, let me get used to the idea of being a manager for a few days. Then if you still feel—"

"Yeah, okay," he responded as the coworkers who were done playing pool clapped Noah on his back with a final congrats on their way out the door. After another round of darts, they walked out with Samantha and Michelle, who split a taxi ride home. Will and Noah headed down the nearest subway steps even though they would be going in different directions.

After moving aside for a swell of people rushing through the turnstile to catch a train that had pulled up, Noah twisted back to say goodbye.

Suddenly Will backed him against the brick wall, and his mouth came down on Noah's in a desperate, needy kiss. Noah whimpered against his lips as his hands gripped the back of his shirt to anchor himself. Holy fuck, it felt good to hold him close and taste him again. He didn't know what had come over Will, especially since they were in public and had just left a celebration for his promotion, but he didn't even care.

Will groaned as he dragged his mouth away. "You're not technically my manager yet, so I figured I could still do that."

He leaned in to nuzzle his neck as Noah panted in a daze.

"That was all me, by the way," Will added, backing away. "Had nothing to do with a job or money."

Then he was gone, and all Noah could do was lick his lips to chase the flavor of that amazing kiss.

26

WILL

The following weekend, Will was trying hard to be in the moment instead of going through the motions with a new customer. The man had requested that *Max* meet him for dinner around the corner from his hotel. The older gentleman was in town for business and apparently traveled so much, he was lonely for some company.

After dinner he was invited back to his room, where they shared a nightcap, and the man requested to watch Max jerk himself off. The client placed a thick wad of cash on the nightstand as a generous tip, then sat on the bed, his hand against the front of his pants, nursing his stiff length.

Will hated the fact that the money taunted him and could make a dent in the bills. It was what ultimately made him stand in front of the man and unzip his pants. He glanced at his reward as the man's hungry gaze fixated on Will's cock as he pulled it from his jeans.

He was still limp, so he shut his eyes and imagined he was pleasuring his shaft in his own bed. With a twist of his wrist his cock hardened to a half chub just from the contact.

The man moaned from his front-row view, which broke Will

out of his concentration. He opened his eyes as his customer tugged his own dick out of his pants. Afraid he'd go soft again, Will racked his brain for some visual to hold on to as he stared at the swirling painting above the bed. His mind sifted through recent porn he'd watched, trying to latch on to a scene that made him shoot pretty fast—like that threesome from the other night.

When that didn't work, he thought about his kiss with Noah in the subway station, how Noah moaned against him, and his dick instantly grew stiffer. His mind sorted through their weekend at Fire Island and landed on the night after the drag show and how turned on Noah had been to see him in the fishnets. And then the next evening, when he shivered all over as Will kissed and licked the entire length of his torso.

Suddenly his cock became impossibly hard, and he stroked faster to work toward release. He heard the man's breathing change and knew he was close. When the client groaned and shot over his fist, Will shoved his cock back in his pants and hurried to the bathroom, pretending he had orgasmed as well. He straightened his clothes in the mirror and reached for a wad of tissues. Back in the room, he handed them to his client, whose cheeks were flushed as he tucked himself back in.

Afterward, Will sat with him, watching mindless television until the client was about to nod off, and then made his escape. He shoved the twenties from the nightstand in his pocket, feeling nearly hollowed out. As he caught the subway home, he had to refocus his energy on why he was doing all this. The bills. The hospital stays. The med changes.

The following evening, Will was glad not to be on schedule with Noah since he'd just fantasized about their intimate moments to get a client off. He'd have a hard enough time looking him in the eye after that.

He considered telling Kara right then and there that he wanted to transfer with her to the other store, but the idea of not seeing Noah on a regular basis made his stomach bottom out, even though it was completely torturous at the same time.

Just hearing him across the room, the way his voice pitched when excited about a sale, made him smile on more than one occasion, and listening to that throaty laugh got him through the shift. He understood the appeal now, why people seemed to gravitate toward him. His sense of humor, his sunny outlook and self-deprecation were like a magnet for customers coming through the door.

Tomorrow, he told himself. Tomorrow he'd consider a transfer.

The next day, when his mom seemed out of sorts and he felt terrified that she'd plunge into the abyss again, he thought about texting Noah just to have some sort of contact. Instead, he got her out of the apartment for a walk in the park, and afterward she seemed much better. Plagued with worry the rest of the night, he visited Oren for his tea concoction in order to get some decent sleep. Oren again encouraged him to audition for the new Bronstein production he'd mentioned last time, saying he'd heard a rumor that the budget was large.

The night after, he had just finished watching a documentary about aliens with his mom and both of them had shuffled off to bed, when he received a text from Noah.

I have a favor to ask.

His hands shook on the keys. **Go for it.**

Figuring it was a work-schedule change, Will wondered why he hadn't just waited to ask him at the store.

My parents are coming for dinner. I could go through your agency, but I thought I'd ask you first if I could hire you again… just for the night.

Will was struck dumb even as excitement coursed through him. But why would Noah want to follow through with such a ruse? Before he could even respond, his cell pinged with a follow-up text.

I know I should tell them that we broke up or whatever, but I'm struggling with that for a few reasons.

He replied in a flash. **No need to explain, unless you want to.**

I definitely do. Can I call?

Yeah, sure.

A minute later his cell rang, and he picked up.

"Hey, thanks for talking me through this."

"It's cool," Will replied, his skin buzzing just from hearing his voice. "You don't have to be so formal with me, though."

"It's, uh, hard to know how to act," Noah replied with a sigh. "I'm your manager now, which is why what I'm asking you is stepping over the line."

"Except we established this...*connection* before you became my manager."

"I know, but if anybody at work found out—"

"Nobody will. I wouldn't do that to you—or me."

"Yeah, I know. I'm just feeling strange. And I feel like Samantha keeps throwing me suspicious looks whenever we're on shift together, which is sort of freaking me out."

Will had actually noticed that as well, which was why he'd kept his distance even more. "Push comes to shove, she's your pal, right?"

"Work friend, yeah. But if Michelle gets wind of it... She loves gossip."

"It'll be okay. We can keep it under wraps."

"Yeah, let's hope so." He sighed, and it was a sweet sound. "Thanks for listening."

"It's cool. What else do we need to talk through?" Will asked as he got adjusted on the sheets.

"It's just... As you know, my relationship with my parents is strained." Will could hear the sounds of the wind along with city noise through the cell line, so he wondered if Noah had a balcony in his apartment. "Last time we talked I told them I got promoted, and now they want to celebrate."

"Are you meeting somewhere in the city?"

"No, I offered to cook at my place this Saturday night." It was definitely the balcony because he heard a sliding sound and then the noise was blotted out, so he must've gone back inside. "Believe it or not, that's something I enjoy. I just never… Anyway… So yeah, they're coming here."

"Okay," Will replied as he marveled at the things he was still learning about Noah. Him enjoying entertaining didn't surprise Will in the least. He'd always pictured Noah's life to be from some Williams-Sonoma catalog, after all.

"They said they hoped *Max* would be here. And I guess I could've said you were busy that night. But I had a harder time admitting we weren't together anymore." He inhaled a deep breath. "I know it's fucked up and hard to understand, but it's just… I know in the end, they mean well. And they want so badly to see that I'm happy, and I never have anyone to—"

"I get it, Noah," Will said in a rush. Noah certainly didn't need to explain. He could hear the strain in his voice, the heartache and embarrassment too. He'd do anything to make him feel lighter again. "And I'd definitely do it."

"Fuck, thank you." Noah breathed out in relief. "I promise next time I'll put an end to it."

"Well, gee, thanks," Will said with a laugh. "Break my heart, why don't you?"

That got a chuckle out of Noah, and Will loved hearing it.

"So tell me… How would you break up with me, anyway?" he asked, feeling playful. "Through a text message, perhaps? I've definitely had someone ditch me that way before. *Coward.* What was your most miserable breakup?"

"Christ, mine had to be a couple weeks into dating this guy, and we were finally going to get intimate," Noah said in a sober tone. Will's jaw tightened because he thought he knew what was coming and now he regretted asking the question. "Once he had my shirt off, he basically made up some ridiculous excuse and bolted out the door."

Will clenched his fists. "Bastard."

"Well, it would be a shock, even if I warned him," he replied, like it was an everyday occurrence, which made Will even more annoyed. "Can't really blame the guy."

"Don't make excuses for the asshat."

Noah's voice dropped down a register. "You were really cool about it, though. So thank you. I mean...you had an out, so that probably helped."

"Bullshit," Will replied. He hated when Noah put himself down. "I could've left the morning my mom texted me, but I didn't. Know why?"

Noah's tone turned hesitant. "Why?"

"Because of you. I enjoyed our weekend together. In case you needed me to spell it out again."

"Is that why you kissed me...in the subway?" he asked cautiously.

Will's heartbeat kicked up a notch. "I like kissing you." *Fucking loved it, was more like it.* "I enjoyed everything we did that weekend. I think about it some nights. Such a fun time."

He heard the small gasp in Noah's throat. "Yeah...me too."

There was a long pause, and Will didn't want to say anything that would let his deeper feelings show, not when he didn't know where it would even get them. Besides, nothing had changed. He was an escort, Noah was his manager, and here they were about to get themselves in deeper. Or maybe not. Maybe this time it would be obvious they needed to just cut contact.

"Well, um, cool. Thanks again. Guess I should hit the hay, since it's getting late," Noah said in a tentative voice. "So I'll just... contact Gotham City tomorrow and ask to schedule you Saturday night?"

He heard the regret in his voice, and Will definitely felt on edge that they were already back to business.

"No need. Just tell me the time and place, and I'll arrange it through my end," Will replied.

"Sounds good." Noah gave him his address on the Upper East Side and told him his parents were arriving at seven. "Can you come early? I can show you around my place so it seems like you're comfortable here."

"Absolutely. See you then," Will replied, and they ended the call, even though Will felt like he could've stayed on for longer. But it was just as well because they were right back where they started—with a business transaction.

27

NOAH

Noah was flustered as he stopped at the corner market and bought white begonias for the center of the table. It was one of the things he loved about his city—that you could purchase bouquets of fresh produce and flowers on nearly every neighborhood corner, which lent a small-town feel in the center of a large metropolis.

Why had he caved and invited Will to dinner? It was wrong on so many levels. Not only because he was pretending to have a boyfriend in front of his family and friends, but he had also just been promoted to Will's manager at Home and Hearth.

It felt like it could all crumble at his fingertips, but somehow when his mom mentioned Max, a warmth flooded him. Not only the idea of having him at his apartment—in his personal space— but of him providing a cushion between him and his parents.

Because ever since their weekend at Fire Island, he was trying to force his life back into patterns that actually made sense. He could've put himself out there again, on dating sites or in gay clubs, not that he had much time since his promotion. But it just felt too unnerving to meet anyone new and have to explain himself all over again. It was the exact problem that led him to seek out an escort in the first place.

Plus, he also wished that this thing between him and Will could in fact be real.

"I like kissing you." That couldn't really be true—could it? Was Will only trying to make Noah feel better about hiring him again?

He pushed all those negative self-doubts away before they became insidious.

Truth was, he actually cared about Will and felt a deepening affection for him. His stomach fluttered every time they were working together in the same room, and though he should've encouraged him to transfer to the other store during his training period with Kara, they never broached the subject again. Which was only playing with fire.

He also had this niggling fear that Will wouldn't show at all—that he'd ditch him and leave him holding the bag with his parents tonight. His payment to Gotham City hadn't posted yet, he'd checked that morning, so that either meant there was a bank delay or that perhaps Will decided against another date.

Noah was too chicken to ask him, to feel the sting of rejection.

"I enjoyed everything we did that weekend. I think about it some nights."

Yeah, Will. Me too. Big-time.

He traipsed back to his building, up the elevator to the fifth floor, and took in his apartment as he stepped inside. It was a small one-bedroom, but he'd made it his own. Walnut floors and furniture with taupe and teal accent pieces from Home and Hearth. He was proud of his decorating sense. He couldn't afford a place with a doorman, much to his parents' dismay, but the building was in a good neighborhood, which seemed to alleviate their fears.

He carefully arranged the flowers in a vase and placed them in the center of the table, which was already set with his favorite modern tableware. He had just placed a pan alongside the chicken on the counter when he heard the buzzer.

Relief instantly flooded his system. He made it.

He took a deep breath and glanced around one last time before he let Will up.

When he heard the elevator ding, he opened his door and saw Will standing in the hallway, holding a bottle of white wine. He wore dark jeans and a button-up shirt, sleeves rolled to the elbows. Damn, he was gorgeous. "Come on inside."

Will whistled as he crossed over the landing and took in his apartment in one swift glance. "I just knew you'd have a place like this."

"What do you mean?" Noah's cheeks reddened as he reached for the bottle of wine and shut the door behind him.

"It's a great space and...totally *you*," Will replied with a smile.

"Thanks." Noah couldn't help feeling some measure of pride. He had painstakingly decorated it to his liking. "Have a look around and then, um, make yourself comfortable."

Noah placed the wine on the counter and then watched for a couple minutes as Will walked around his apartment, taking in his furniture, his artwork, the table settings. "Christ. Everything could be a display from our store."

Noah bit his lip self-consciously. "Guess I sort of went over-the-top."

"That's not at all what I meant," he said over his shoulder as he stepped to the bathroom threshold, then glanced through the open door to his bedroom, which contained a queen bed and an upholstered headboard. His gaze landed solidly on his jar of seashells, then the teal-blue walls, and Noah knew the idea wasn't lost on him. *"The ocean calms you."*

"You made it cozy too," he noted. "Wish my place felt half as much."

"You don't like where you live?" Noah asked, trying to

remember conversations they might've had about the apartment he shared with his mother.

"I mean, it's clean and neat; my mom wouldn't have it any other way," he explained as he looked out the sliding glass doors to his tiny balcony. It wasn't the best view, but scoring any type of outdoor space in the city was a feat. Will hesitated as if he was going to add something else, but then decided against it. "But in the end, it's just a place to…lay our heads at night. Plus, the rent is affordable."

Noah had the urge to offer to make their apartment feel more like home, but he had to lock that idea down. That wasn't what this was about. This was another business arrangement between them, and even though it felt intimate to have him at his apartment, it was only because his parents were due to arrive any moment.

Will stepped up to Noah and squeezed his shoulders, which made his stomach fill with warmth. "I can tell you're nervous. Take a deep breath, and tell me what you're cooking."

Noah guided him to the kitchen and motioned for him to sit on a stool.

"I'm making chicken Alfredo," he said as he pulled the heavy cream and Parmesan cheese from the fridge. "Pretty simple recipe."

"If you say so," Will replied with an arched eyebrow. "I'm not much of a cook, but I love to eat."

Noah laughed as Will watched him brown the chicken and then make a sauce with the drippings from the pan. He liked the idea of feeding Will, and without his parents' presence, it sort of felt like a date.

"Can I help?" Will asked as Noah drained the pasta.

"Nope." Noah winked before he dug through his utensil drawer for a small cheese grater. "Unless you want to pour us a couple of glasses of wine before my parents arrive."

"Sounds like a great idea."

Noah allowed Will to fish around in his kitchen drawers and cupboards to familiarize himself with things in case he was called upon to retrieve something for his parents. In the process, Will found the wine opener and popped the cork on the bottle he'd brought over.

"That sauce smells amazing," Will remarked as he poured two glasses of wine and passed one to Noah.

Noah held his glass up in a toast. "For helping me out again."

"It's no hardship being your fake boyfriend," Will replied and then leaned closer. "Or your friend."

Noah's pulse thrummed in his veins, and just as he was about to respond in kind, the doorbell rang. Noah froze momentarily before wiping his hands on the nearest towel and placing the lid over the bubbling pan. "Here goes nothing."

He buzzed his parents up and welcomed them into the apartment.

"Honey, the door to the street level was propped open again," his mom said by way of greeting. "Last time you promised to talk to your super about fixing the latch."

Noah nearly rolled his eyes as Will smirked apologetically in his direction. Noah was relieved he'd shared what a struggle he'd had with his parents in the last few years. And at least they'd already met on one occasion.

"Noah has a guest, dear. Give him a moment to breathe," his father said, extending his hand to Will. "Max, good to see you again."

As Will led them into the living room, Noah noticed how effortless it seemed for him to slip back into the boyfriend role. But he forced the thorny thought away.

Acting as the ultimate cohost, Will poured Noah's parents some wine and then painlessly fell into a conversation with his father about their recent trip to London as well as his daughter, Amanda, while his mother helped set the garlic bread on a plate in the center of the table. He recalled all the entertaining his parents had done over the years for charity events or business relationships; he had definitely gotten his decorating gene from her.

As Noah turned off the burner and stirred the Alfredo in the pan, Will stepped behind him to reach for the Parmesan cheese he'd watched Noah grate earlier into a small bowl for the table. His hand wound around Noah's hip as he reached forward to kiss Noah's cheek. Noah nearly sighed out loud, it felt so good to be touched by him again.

After he spooned the pasta into a serving dish for the table, he saw his father staring up at the fire alarm above his kitchen island. He stiffened, thinking he was going to check the batteries like he'd done on other occasions, but surprisingly, he held himself back.

Will repeatedly patted Noah's knee or held his hand on top of the table in plain view of his parents. Their fingers felt like they fit together, like something he'd already gotten intimately acquainted with, which was why playing this game was too dangerous for his heart. But it was probably only because they had enough practice on the island.

He had a split-second thought of starting some sort of crazy argument with Will like he once saw in a romantic comedy and then requesting for Will to leave so his parents thought their relationship was on the rocks. But it was too easy to pretend he was happy with Will beside him, grasping his hand like he meant it, and Noah was too weak to resist the lure of playing make-believe for one more night.

"Congratulations on your promotion, son," his dad said once they sat down and he served them heaping plates of food. They lifted their glasses in a toast. "Maybe you'll even *own* your own business in the city one day. Doesn't even have to be retail."

Noah could feel a flush forming, hot on the back of his neck. "That's actually not a goal of mine, Dad."

"But it's definitely cool to be managing your own store," Will piped in and then leaned over to kiss his cheek. "So proud of you."

"Now make sure they don't have you working too many hours," his mother said after she dug into a forkful of penne pasta coated in Alfredo sauce. "You still need time to relax and enjoy yourself."

He clenched his fist in his lap as the same tension rolled through his shoulders. "Mom, you don't need to—"

"I can tell how much your parents worry about you," Will remarked as he lifted the basket of bread and offered it to Noah's father. "It reminds me of my mom."

"Oh?" his father replied, reaching for the garlic bread and placing a piece on his plate. Noah held his breath, unsure where Will was heading with this conversation.

"Yep. Except it's the other way around," Will explained. His parents waited as Will chewed a mouthful, their attention piqued. "My mom has lots of…health issues, and it's just the two of us. So I'm always double-checking everything before I leave the apartment, and I know I drive her crazy with my worry. But… it's totally out of love."

Noah's mother cleared her throat as she blinked repeatedly, her eyes growing misty. Noah had trouble swallowing past the boulder in his throat. Will had encapsulated the tension-laced dynamic between them in only a couple of sentences.

"It's definitely out of love," his mother murmured, and Noah's heart clenched.

"I can tell that you care about your son very much," Will replied as he glanced sympathetically at Noah. But Noah was too busy watching his mom as the layers were suddenly peeled away and he viewed her in an enhanced light.

"I'll try not to be such a pain," she said in a quiet voice as his father reached for her hand. "I just—"

"I know," Noah replied.

"I'll get more bread," Will said, jumping up from the table

with the empty basket as if he needed to give them a minute. Fuck, how the hell did he always know?

Noah and his parents continued to eat in silence as Will left the table. When he was out of earshot, his dad said, "To use your mother's words…I think he's a *keeper*."

Noah barked out a laugh at his father's modern turn of phrase, which made his mom snicker, and by the time Will walked back to the table, they were all grinning at each other.

After dinner, they all shared a glass of wine out on the balcony, and though the tension had abated some, Noah was drained and ready to show them the door.

"There's a storm brewing, Noah," his mother said, staring up at the gray clouds moving in off the water. "Make sure you close all your…"

His father placed his hand on her arm, and she immediately trailed off. Noah breathed out in relief. Old habits were hard to break. Though storms still bothered him, he was really only affected if he was stuck outside in one. Otherwise, he'd recently found some beauty in watching them indoors, from a safer distance.

A few minutes later, he hugged his mom and dad goodbye, they shook Will's hand, and he closed the door with a heavy sigh.

28

WILL

Noah looked spent by the time his parents left, so Will slipped behind him and began rubbing his shoulders. Noah groaned as he anchored his head against the door. "Well, that's over. I won't have to see them again for a couple months, and by then, you and I will have broken up."

For some reason, hearing those words had a strange effect on him, and he froze mid-massage. Noah noticed immediately and twisted around to catch his eye. "You okay?"

He quickly composed himself. "Yeah, sure. Let me help you clean up."

"No, that's all right," Noah protested, but Will had already walked to the kitchen. "You've done so much already."

Will knew he was talking about more than the meal prep, and he appreciated the sincerity in his voice.

He helped him load the dishwasher and wipe down the table. It felt a bit domesticated as they worked together to get his place back in order. It wasn't an unpleasant feeling, only a foreign one.

He'd become so hyperfocused on his mother's care the past year, what with appointments and new med management to keep her out of the hospital, that he didn't have time or interest in anything more than a hookup. Besides, explaining why he lived with his mom and that he also happened to work for Gotham City was not something he looked forward to. So no matter how much he liked the idea of being with Noah like this, it still boiled down to the fact that he had a job as an escort so he could pay his mom's medical bills. Plus, Noah was officially his new boss. Add all that up, and the cards were definitely stacked against them.

As they finished loading the last dish, thick bolts of lightning lashed across the sky, followed by intimidating rumbles of thunder. Noah's gaze swung warily toward the window before he seemed to shake it off. He thought of what Noah had shared with him on the beach that one night about being occasionally triggered by storms. And his mother still seemed concerned about his reaction to them—or perhaps they activated something in her as well even after all this time.

But he didn't want to call attention to the fact that it was raining bucketloads outside. Besides, Noah had been through dozens of storms in the years since his accident.

"Maybe you should wait out the storm," Noah said in a guarded voice as the wind and rain pounded against the windows. "Up to you."

"Sounds good to me." Will refilled their wineglasses, and they sat down on the comfortable sofa on opposite sides.

"So what do you do in your spare time, Noah?" Will asked, noticing the half-dozen design magazines on the coffee table.

"Outside of work, you mean?"

Will nodded.

"I work out some, but I'm not obsessed with it like some people," he responded, and Will knew he meant his friends at Fire Island. But Noah did have a nice build; Will definitely noticed that when they were naked together that one weekend.

"I'm also taking an online merchandising class for the heck of it, and I sort of have an obsession with home-renovation shows," he said, dipping his head in an adorable way. "Like that would surprise you."

"Not one bit," Will replied with a chuckle. "So does that mean you're thinking of getting into design?"

Noah's lips thinned, and Will recognized that look immediately. He had given it to his father earlier when he talked about his business aspirations. "Hey, I'm only making conversation. You asked me about theater not too long ago, so I figured it was fair game."

"Sorry, it's just a natural reaction," he replied, and then took a gulp of wine. "I appreciate your help with my parents earlier. Not that you were trying to help, exactly. It's just—it seemed pretty genuine."

Will scrunched up his face. "Pretty much everything I've shared with you has come from an honest place. I mean, outside of the ridiculous story I concocted about how we met."

Noah laughed, as if he'd already forgotten about that cheesy version of events.

A bolt of thunder lit up the sky, and Noah stiffened momentarily.

Will sipped his wine and waited for him to relax. "But honestly, it does seem like your parents mean well."

"I know they do." Noah sighed. "Just like you mean well with your mom. How is she, by the way?"

"She has her ups and downs, but pretty good in general. Thanks for asking." Will couldn't remember the last time someone had even inquired. Tonight he'd left her with a friend who stopped by with a bagful of yarn. His mom agreed to learn how to crochet so she could join the weekly group the woman belonged to. It was a nice gesture from an old friend, and she didn't have many who hung in there with her after all she'd been through. Neither did he, come to think of it. He tried to push the dark, heavy thoughts away. Fuck. They were always there, right at the surface.

"Hey, what's wrong?" Noah asked with a frown.

"It's nothing. Just stuff that creeps up on me every now and again."

"That I can understand," Noah replied in a soothing voice. "And just now it was like a dark shadow moved across your face."

Will stared at Noah from his end of the couch, his chest tightening like a screw. Noah added, "I'm a good listener."

Will's palms felt clammy, so he placed his glass down on the table before it slipped from his fingers. "Did you know that schizophrenia can be hereditary?"

"So it can be passed down to someone's kids?" Noah scooted forward and reached for Will's hand as if he knew he needed it.

"Yeah," he responded, linking their fingers together like it was the most natural thing in the world. "Apparently having one parent diagnosed increases your chances of developing the disorder by ten percent."

"But wouldn't you already have some symptoms?"

"Yeah, most start appearing in adolescence, some even earlier," Will explained, thinking back to the latest article he'd read about it. "It's an irrational fear, I know..."

"I'm the king of irrational fears, remember?" Noah remarked, and it made Will instantly feel better. He couldn't believe he admitted his anxieties out loud to Noah, but he supposed they had said so much between them already. Maybe that was what made it easier.

Their arrangement may have been secret and temporary, but damn, he trusted Noah. Felt safe with Noah. That was the most fucked-up part.

"Looks like the worst of the storm has passed," Will announced as he reluctantly glanced out the window. "Probably should get going."

"You don't have to," Noah muttered, his cheeks darkening.

"Would you like me to stay a bit longer?" Will asked, his pulse thumping wildly.

"Only if you want to," Noah replied, reaching for the remote. "It's...been a while since I've had somebody here like this."

Will scooted closer and wound his arm around Noah, the warmth of their bodies permeating each other. They flicked on the television and flipped to an older comedy that barely registered. Will was too cognizant of Noah's every move. Every breath. Like a current humming through the air, occupying the space between them.

At one point, he heard Noah sigh. "What's up?"

"I shouldn't want this," he whispered. "This closeness with you. But I do."

"I'm enjoying it too," Will crooned in his ear. "And we're already pretty used to each other, so it makes sense."

"That's the thing," Noah explained, adjusting his body so he leaned closer to Will. "You already know my baggage, and I... I feel comfortable around you."

A spike of longing jabbed at him, but he clamped it down. Noah was supposed to be his client tonight...and his boss tomorrow. Christ, this was so fucked up.

"Maybe we shouldn't examine it too hard," he suggested. "Just let me hold you for a while longer."

Noah relaxed against Will's chest, and soon enough he nodded off. He didn't want to move, but he'd need to if he was going to get home at a reasonable hour.

29

NOAH

Noah felt Will shift, and he blinked open his eyes, remembering they were still nestled on the couch in front of the television.

"You should get to bed," Will whispered, reaching for the remote and flipping off the television.

Noah unwrapped himself from Will's chest and flopped down on the cushion, stretching his hands over his head.

"You make a good pillow," he said around a yawn as Will stood and shook out his numbed arms and legs.

Will stared down at him with an adorable smirk, and as Noah blinked up at him, he thought he'd never seen a more beautiful sight. Will's hair was slightly mussed, his cheeks flushed, and his T-shirt wrinkled down the center where Noah had been nuzzling him.

Wordlessly, Noah reached for Will's hands, dragging him forward, and Will sank down easily. Winding his arms around Will's neck, he mashed their mouths together, their tongues tangling, giving in to that visceral connection that seemed so natural.

Tasting him, feeling his weight, their muscles pressed firmly together, Noah realized kissing Will had become one of his absolute favorite things. Something he craved all too often.

Soon enough they became a tangle of sweaty limbs, grinding against each other, sucking each other's tongues, hands groping wherever they could reach.

"Please, Will," Noah rasped as he writhed beneath him.

Will groaned as he thrust downward. "Tell me what you want."

"You, Will. I want you. I've been fantasizing—" He shook his thoughts away.

What the hell was he admitting to?

"Tell me," Will insisted as he grasped his jaw. "Maybe I have fantasies too."

That admission only stoked the fire inside him.

"I... I've thought about you fucking me."

"I have too."

"From behind and wearing those fishnets," Noah admitted, his fingers shielding his eyes as his cheeks burned. "Fuck."

"Don't hide from me." Will dragged his hands from his face. "You've got my dick so hard."

Noah groaned as Will held his hands above his head and thrust against him. "You still have them?"

"Yeah." Noah motioned toward his bedroom. "Dresser. Top drawer."

"Mmmm...so hot," Will murmured as his tongue lashed against his earlobe, making Noah tremble beneath his hot breath. "I'll fuck you, on one condition."

"What's that?" Noah asked, squirming. He was so turned on from Will's stiff cock rubbing against him, he wasn't even sure he'd make it to his bedroom.

"That you're sure about this, Noah," Will said, growing motionless as he stared down at him. "I came here tonight because you hired me to—"

"I'm sure," Noah said without hesitation. "I... I feel safe with you."

"Goddamn, when you say stuff like that...it makes me want..."

"Want what?" Noah asked in earnest as he looked from his eyes down to his mouth. He wanted to drag him forward and ravish him.

"Want to..." Will fumbled on the words before clearing his throat. "Want to make you feel good."

"You already do, and when you...*oooooh yeah*, just like that," he groaned as Will thrust against him.

Hot mouths clashed as Will pulled Noah from the couch, and they stumbled their way to his bedroom, tearing at each other's clothes and landing on the mattress with their bare groins rubbing together. Even though Will had already seen Noah's scars and could probably feel their roughness now, Noah felt braver with the lights off as hands groped skin.

Panting, Will urged Noah to flip onto his stomach. His fingers dragged down the center of his spine before he jerked forward and his dick slid against Noah's crease.

Noah whimpered, lifting onto his knees and pushing back against Will. "Condoms and lube are in the same drawer."

Will backed away, and Noah could hear him rustling around for the supplies before he threw a condom and lube on the mattress.

When he felt the softness of the fishnets against the back of his thighs, his knees shook in anticipation. Will dragged the material up his spine, making him shiver. The hosiery rounded his shoulder, and Will slid the lacy edge across Noah's lips before taking his mouth in a fierce kiss.

"So fucking hot," Will growled as his fingers gripped the meatiest part of his ass.

He appreciated that Will didn't treat him with kid gloves. He wasn't fragile or broken and didn't want him to hold back. He wanted to feel all of it, especially if this would be the one and only time.

Will extended his leg and pulled one stocking up at a time, giving Noah a sensual show that made him vibrate with need. "Goddamn, Will."

Will fisted his cock and stroked upward as Noah groaned and dragged his fingers down Will's thighs, appreciating the silky velvet feel over hard muscles.

Will offered him a brief kiss before moving behind him again, his hand gripping his hip tightly. Will leaned over him to feather his lips across his nape and then down the knobs of his spine. Noah shut his eyes in bliss. He wanted to feel every sensation while he had the chance.

"Damn, do you look good."

Noah moaned and swayed, wondering how long he was going to last at this rate.

He heard the lube bottle open, and in another instant Will knelt behind him, his cool finger rubbing against his hole. "I've imagined doing just this with you."

Holy fuck, Noah's balls drew up tight. He squirmed and bit out curses as Will circled and teased. "Now you're trying to kill me."

He heard a soft snicker as Will pushed a finger inside before nibbling at the tender skin on his thigh. Noah threw his head back and moaned, feeling like he was going to shoot. But when Will reached forward and encircled the base of his cock in a tight grip, his dick suddenly cooperated.

He didn't know how long Will fingered his asshole because he lost all track of time. He could only focus on the wet slicking noise and the feel of Will's hot breath on his skin. His legs were shaking, his heart hammering, and when Will added a second digit and curved it downward to rub against that spongy place inside him, his eyes crossed. "Ah, fuck. I'm going to come."

"Not yet. I need to be inside you," Will growled, dragging his fingers out, and Noah whimpered at the loss of fullness. He heard him grab the condom wrapper, tear it open, and sheath himself.

Once he had his dick slick with lube, he lined up with his hole, kissed his shoulder, and pushed his way inside. Noah sucked in a harsh breath. "Fuck, that's...oh, *Christ*."

A groan tore from Will's throat as he snapped his hips forward in shallow thrusts. "Jesus," he murmured through clenched teeth as if struggling to hold on. "So fucking tight."

Will's hands gripped his hips as he drove all the way to the hilt. When he was buried balls-deep, Noah could feel the fishnets rasping against his thighs, which made his balls draw up tight.

"More," Noah begged, and Will gave him what he wanted as their bodies slapped together, Will ramming his shaft inside in a punishing rhythm. Sweat slicked his nape and dripped down the small of his back. He dropped his head to his forearms and closed his eyes, reveling in his fantasy come to life.

A strong arm encircled his torso, Will dragged him up, panting into his nape, slick chest sliding against his back. Angling his chin, he took his mouth in a sloppy kiss as they moaned and their tongues tangled together.

Will pressed his lips to his shoulder before returning to fucking him, and Noah trembled from the intimate gesture.

Noah's balls grew heavy and tightened into uncomfortable fists as that familiar sensation traveled up his spine. Will reached up to grab his cock, but it was all just too much. He came as soon as he touched it, shooting all over his hand and stomach.

"Fuck. Ughnnn," Will mumbled incoherently as his thrusts turned chaotic and sloppy. He felt the exact moment that Will's orgasm peaked as his hips stiffened and his back bowed.

"Noah," he called out, and he could hear the ache, the utter longing in Will's voice, and it made his entire body shudder.

After Will came back to his senses, he carefully pulled his cock out and threw the condom in the trash can beside the bed. He collapsed to the sheets, dragging Noah down with him.

Noah played with the damp hair along his neckline and rubbed his back in a calming motion as Will hummed against his shoulder, their legs entwined and the fishnets soothing against his heated skin. After another minute, Will lifted his head and kissed him tenderly.

This meeting of lips was different somehow. Gentle, filled with affection. It felt like more than sex. It felt like vulnerability and yearning and a deeper connection. Will's hand encircled his nape, drawing their mouths more firmly together as he kissed him in a desperate sort of way that spoke to Noah's heart. The brush of Will's thumb against the base of his throat seemed more profoundly intimate than what they'd just shared with their bodies.

A noise that strangely sounded like a sob tore from Will's throat, and before he knew what was happening, Will was pulling away. "I'll grab a towel," he mumbled, retreating from the room.

Once he returned from the bathroom, the fishnets were gone; he bent down to reach for his boxers and slipped them up his legs. He sat on the edge of the bed, swiping at Noah's skin with the cloth while his fingers played with his hair.

"Thank you," Noah began, but Will shushed him, his eyes softening.

"Go to sleep..." Will cooed, lulling him into slumber as his fingers brushed his cheek, and eyebrow, and forehead.

Before he burst into hot, emotional tears, before he begged Will to stay, he swallowed roughly and shut his eyes, enjoying the hypnotic feel of Will's fingers on his skin.

The last thing he remembered was Will's ghost of a kiss against his forehead.

When he stirred a couple of hours later, Will was already gone, and Noah felt strangely hollow.

30

WILL

Will braced himself as he walked into Home and Hearth the following Tuesday because Noah was sure to be stewing about the other night. Will had expected at least a text over the weekend, but one never came.

Noah liked things spelled out, and this thing between them wasn't spelled out at all—it was messy and confusing and sexy and profound and one of the reasons he'd needed to leave Noah's apartment as soon as Noah fell asleep that night. It had gotten way too intense for him after he fucked the hell out of Noah and came so hard, his teeth rattled. He realized right then how easily he could fall for the man, and maybe he was already half in love with him anyway.

A conversation was nearly impossible, though, with an audience around them all night. Either customers or coworkers were always in their space, plus Rick, the regional manager, who was in the store to help after Kara's transition. But the tension between them was evident, and Samantha seemed to be watching them with interest. Unless it was only his imagination.

Besides, Noah could barely look him in the eye, and it only solidified Will's decision to ask for a transfer to the other store.

He knew something like this might happen the further they got in this little arrangement. And he wanted Noah to be on top of his game in his new position.

"Rick," Will said as he headed him off near the storage room. "Can I talk to you a minute?"

"Sure thing," Rick said and then looked out onto the floor before motioning for him to follow him to the office.

Will could feel Noah's gaze on him, burning a hole into the side of his head, but he refused to look in his direction.

"What's up?" Rick asked once they were alone and out of earshot.

"I wanted to let you know I'd be cool transferring to another store if I'm needed at a different location." There, he'd said it. It was long overdue.

Rick's eyebrows knit together. "Does this have anything to do with the recent change? With Kara leaving the store? Is there something you need to tell me about—"

"No, nothing like that." Well fuck, now Rick thought something was wrong with Noah being in charge of this store. That was absolutely not how Will had expected this to go. "I'm fine to stay here too. A couple of weeks ago you made the announcement about transfers, and I meant to ask sooner."

Rick studied him for a long moment before his brows evened out. "Okay, then. We're all set at the new location for now. But schedules are always changing, so I'll see if there's anything brewing at our two other stores."

"Cool," Will replied, feeling ridiculous that he'd said anything at all. Nevertheless, one of the locations was in Hoboken, and he wasn't about to traipse out to Jersey, unless he had to.

When they walked back onto the floor, he immediately felt scrutinized by his coworkers and even more like an outsider—not that he hadn't brought that on himself.

Fuck, this was so not going as planned.

Gratefully, the end of the shift arrived, and Will was relieved because his pulse had been erratic all evening. Not only that, he needed to get home to change because he had an escort job tonight with Louise at the Plaza Hotel. Some kind of fundraising shindig.

Ironically, he was fine taking payment for his services from other clients because their purpose was clear. They needed him as a front, much like Noah had—at least until feelings got involved.

After the door was locked, the register cashed out, and the store cleaned, Will could sense Noah behind him, heading onto the sidewalk. He scooted down the stairs to the train with his heart pounding in his throat. He just needed this torture with Noah to end.

"What did you say to Rick?" he heard Noah's voice behind him, and he realized Noah had followed him into the subway.

"I asked for a transfer," Will said over his shoulder, and when he turned, he noticed the sting of hurt in Noah's eyes. He immediately regretted the decision again. "I just thought it was time, and I figured you'd think so too. Besides, Samantha—"

"Yeah, I know," he replied with resignation in his voice. She was bound to ask Noah sooner or later, unless she already had. "Fuck, I'm no good at this... The other night was so...*damn*."

Noah kicked at a stray metro card on the filthy ground, and Will waited him out. As he got his thoughts together, Will braced himself for what he knew was coming. "I asked if you were willing to be hired again, even though it was risky with my new position. You agreed to arrange it from your end. But when I checked my bank statement, I was never billed by Gotham City."

Will knew he'd figure it out sooner or later. He half hoped his transfer to another location would be swift so he wouldn't have to explain.

But explain what? How fond he'd grown of Noah?

How could they figure out whatever this thing was between them if Noah was his boss? But that certainly wasn't the only opposing factor. The odds certainly didn't appear to be in their favor.

Noah balled his fists in what looked like anger. "Help me understand what the hell is going on. I told you I didn't want to be a charity case."

Fuck, Will had forgotten their very first conversation at the coffee shop. *A pity fuck*, Noah had said.

Damn it to hell. This was becoming way too complicated.

"You are not a charity case or a pity fuck," Will said as he nudged Noah against the wall to allow a mother and her two kids room to pass. "I didn't take your money because...I didn't want to."

Noah's eyebrows rose to his hairline. "Why? You said you need it to help with—"

"Damn it, Noah. You make me feel things." Will scrubbed his hand over his face. "Somehow in all this...you've became one of my favorite people."

Noah stiffened. "You mean favorite *customer*?"

Will shook his head. "You're not just a customer to me, Noah. And I know that goes against everything this arrangement was supposed to be, but it is what it is, and I'm not taking your damn money."

Noah's chest was heaving, a deep flush lining his cheeks.

"I want to kiss that confusion right off your fucking lips," Will murmured. "But I won't because that'll only muddy things more."

He ached to be with Noah. To pull him into his arms and feel his warm skin. But it would never work; too much was standing between them. How could he possibly ask Noah to understand that his escort job involved being behind closed doors with customers? After what happened between the two of them, it would always be in the back of Noah's mind. And that would totally suck.

He backed away and fished his MetroCard out of his pocket. "It's best we just...let things go."

WILL COULD BARELY CONCENTRATE AT THE FUNDRAISER THAT NIGHT with Louise. He definitely played the role like he always did, but in the quieter moments, his mind kept drifting to Noah. To how he looked right before Will walked away from him. His cheeks ruddy, his eyes wide in wonder. His lip plump from biting down on it.

For a brief moment, he imagined making a go of it with Noah —if he'd have him. How they'd make sweet love. How he'd kiss every part of his body Noah hated until he believed himself worthy. Show him enough adoration to chase away all his self-doubt. But he'd obviously met Noah at the wrong damn time in his life. And that was like a kick to the gut.

Just as he was stepping away from the open bar with two glasses of wine, he heard a vaguely familiar voice. "Max?"

He turned sharply, wondering who could possibly know him in this setting, unless it was someone from another event with Louise. When he came face-to-face with Tony and Matt, it felt like shrapnel had lodged in his throat.

"What are you doing here?" Tony asked as his eyes darted between him and Louise. From their perspective, they were probably an unlikely pairing—she in her designer gown and him in the tux she'd rented for him for such occasions—and Will felt hot under the collar.

"I, um..." He had no idea why he couldn't find the words he needed in that moment.

Suddenly Louise reached for his elbow. "Max is here as my date tonight. We've known each other for years."

Though he was thankful for Louise's save, he now felt obligated to introduce her to Noah's friends. They made small talk about their companies and charitable contributions, but Will wanted to fade into the crowd and disappear. Absently or perhaps not, Louise linked their hands together and squeezed reassuringly.

"Let's join our table, darling, shall we?" Louise asked, and when he nodded numbly, they excused themselves from Tony and Matt's intense scrutiny.

The rest of the evening, Will felt like he wanted to crawl out of his skin, especially during the dinner and auction portions when he could feel their eyes on him as he pretended to make small talk. They were only being protective of Noah, and they had every right, but it was still unnerving. As dessert was being served, he desperately needed air, so he got up to use the restroom. He washed his hands and patted his face with cold water, trying to get his head on straight.

Unsurprisingly, Tony was waiting for him outside the door, and he supposed now was as good a time as any.

"What's up?" he asked casually, but Tony narrowed his eyes.

"Listen, I'm a hired escort with a company here in the city. This is my side job." His shoulders dropped. "To help pay for my mother's medical bills," he added, as if that excused him from everything. But he'd done nothing wrong, so he shouldn't have needed any defense. But under Tony's inspection, he felt flayed open, his every insecurity coming to light.

"Does Noah know you're an escort?" The question struck him as funny until it dawned on him that they thought he and Noah were an actual couple.

"He knows," Will responded in a tight voice. "You should probably talk to *him* about it."

"Oh, I plan to," Tony replied through a clenched jaw.

"I'm sorry if this ruins things between us. I really enjoyed hanging out with you guys that weekend." Will didn't want to give any more away. It was Noah's story to tell now.

Tony sighed. "We did too. Matt even planned to invite you to his upcoming amateur drag show at Ruby Redd's."

"I know that place. In the West Village," Will said wistfully, again wishing things could be different. "He'll do great."

"Listen, I'm not judging you or your relationship." Tony winced. "This blindsided me, and I need to make sure my friend is happy."

Will wanted to explain more, to tell him that he wished he could be that guy for Noah, but it was better to leave it as a conversation between best friends. "I understand. I want that for him too."

There was nothing more to be said, so after they parted ways, he walked back to the table to play out the rest of his miserable night.

Louise didn't comment, but he was certain she could tell he was off his game no matter how much he tried to make conversation and smile. When the car service pulled up in front of her building, she didn't invite him up. Instead, she leaned over and kissed his cheek. "It sucks when real life gets in the way. Hope everything works out."

"Thanks," he mumbled, relieved she seemed to understand his mood.

THAT NIGHT AS HE LAY IN BED, HE CONSIDERED GIVING NOAH A heads-up. He'd hate for him to be caught unaware. He lifted his phone to call him and wondered if he'd even pick up.

As soon as Noah did, Will blurted, "I ran into Tony and Matt at a fundraiser tonight."

"Oh?" he replied in a tense voice.

"I was there with a female client—a regular customer," he explained even though he wasn't sure why.

He could hear Noah's breathing kick up during a long pause.

"So they think you're cheating on me? Fuck, I'm sorry."

"Tony confronted me outside the restroom, and I admitted I

was an escort." Will winced. "It was a split-second decision, but in hindsight maybe it would've been better to let them think I was a cheating asshole—that would be reason enough for you to break up with me."

"It's okay," Noah replied in a resigned tone. "I had a feeling it was going to come out one way or another." Another moment of heavy breathing. "So what did Tony say?"

"He asked if you knew I was an escort, and I said yes, but that he needed to talk to you about it. Sorry if I messed things up."

Noah laughed miserably. "So he thinks I'm cool with my boyfriend being an escort? I'm not sure which scenario is worse; both make me sound a bit desperate."

"Plenty of couples have open arrangements, you know that," he pointed out, thinking of other escorts he knew who were in long-term relationships.

"True. Guess I never saw myself in that sort of scenario," he replied, and that only served to squash any small sliver of hope Will harbored for them. "It would be tough—maybe even devastating—to know my boyfriend is—"

"Hey, I get it. *Really*," he replied, not wanting to hear any more, even though it was what he already expected.

Will could feel the tension through the phone as silence descended.

"Anyway, Tony's your best friend. Once you explain everything, he'll understand," he offered.

"Yeah, I know. Thanks for the heads-up," he said with some melancholy in his voice. "Sorry if it ruined your night with your client."

"Nah, she's pretty cool," he replied, thinking about how much worse it could've gone with anybody else. *Christ.*

"So…isn't it an early night for you?" Noah asked hesitantly. "What normally happens at the end— Sorry, none of my business."

Noah had never asked for any details about his clients, so

honestly, it felt like a bit of a relief that he didn't have to hide it. Not after Noah admitted there was no chance for them anyway.

"For the record, the last person I had sex with was you," he confessed as his heart vaulted to his throat. "And I wouldn't have it any other way."

31

NOAH

Noah took a deep breath as he spotted Tony and Matt walking into the restaurant. He'd received a text from Tony that morning, asking to meet them for lunch in the financial district.

"What's up?" Noah asked as his friends slid into the seats across from him. They looked handsome and smart in their suits, and the engagement ring on Matt's finger only added to his striking appearance. They didn't get together like this often during the week, but Noah knew Tony wouldn't want to discuss anything over the phone. Plus, Noah wasn't due into work for a few more hours.

"How about you tell us?" Tony replied with a huff.

"Don't start acting like a mother hen." Noah rolled his eyes. "Just get to the point."

After the server took their drink orders, Tony's gaze planted firmly on his friend. "We saw your boyfriend at a fundraiser event the other night."

"Yeah, I know." Noah sighed. He was glad for the heads-up from Will, even though that phone call with him had sounded so *final*. "He told me."

"So...you're okay with it? With him being an escort?"

Noah knew it was time to let go of the farce once and for all, yet doing that also meant letting go of Will—or at least the idea of him. But what did it even amount to? Damn good sex, that was for sure.

"And I wouldn't have it any other way." He nearly sighed out loud. Then he remembered the fishnets dragging across his lips, and he had to suppress a shudder.

He hadn't realized that something that felt so good and honest and true could turn his world entirely on its head. Now that he knew what it was like to want something—*someone*—so viscerally, he'd have to learn how to live with that longing deep inside him. And the world would continue on as if he had never stumbled across someone like Will Crossen.

"Don't judge until you've heard me out," he said pointedly as the server dropped off their drinks and then took their lunch orders.

Tony took a long sip of his iced tea. "Okay, go for it."

"So, *Max* actually works with me...*for* me at Home and Hearth." Whoa, that was a heady thought. The transition to manager had gone well, but it was also completely overwhelming trying to learn the ropes, and this stress added on top made him toss and turn for nights on end.

Tony's eyebrow rose, but his lips twitched as if he was barely keeping himself from launching into some lecture. No wonder he got on so well with Noah's parents.

Noah took a deep breath. "In a roundabout way last month, I found out he worked for an escort service, and it got me thinking about hiring one...for Matt's party."

"Why in the world would you do that?" Tony scoffed, as if he'd forgotten all the quieter conversations they'd shared throughout their years of friendship. Their early twenties were especially filled with angst and regrets.

"Let him finish, honey," Matt said, delivering a stern look.

Matt was always the more levelheaded of the two. They truly balanced each other out. And damn if he didn't long to have that with some amazing guy someday. When the image of Will holding the towel open for him at the pool sprang to mind, he stripped it away.

"It can be uncomfortable for me out there...not necessarily because of the accident, and not all the time, but like..." Noah motioned down at his torso, not wanting to say the words out loud. "You know what I mean."

"You don't give yourself enough credit for—"

"Are you shitting me right now?" Noah fired back, silencing him. He adjusted the collar on his button-down shirt, and for the first time in a long while, Tony seemed to zero in on the fact that he hid himself quite well. Maybe even well enough that Tony forgot sometimes. "Even hookups can get pretty awkward when it comes to the disrobing part."

"Noah—"

He put a hand up to still his friend. "Even my own parents—"

"They love you. They just don't know how to—"

"Stop worrying long enough to treat me like an adult? An adult who can make his own decisions, his own mistakes too?" he blurted out. "Not *all* my choices will end up in disaster."

At least not of the physical variety. Emotionally...that was a whole different ballgame.

Tony sat back and sighed. He couldn't dispute the obvious.

Matt looked between them as their lunch was served. Before he bit into his corned-beef sandwich, he said, "So you hired Max to be your escort the weekend of my party."

Noah nodded.

"Fuck, I would've never guessed. You guys seemed so..."

"Natural," Tony added. "Into each other."

Noah smiled wistfully at the memory; he couldn't help himself. But then a dark ball of doubt formed in the pit of his stomach.

"It was a good performance. When you saw him the other night..." Noah cringed. "You thought they were together too, right?"

Matt and Tony shared a look. "At first, sure," Matt admitted.

"But after closer inspection," Tony continued, "it was totally different. Almost forced."

Noah shook his head. "Don't say that for my benefit. I'm a big boy. I can handle—"

"We're not," Matt said, placing his hand on top of Noah's. "We honestly thought you guys were perfect together."

Noah dropped the sweet-potato fry onto his plate beside his burger. He didn't want to believe it, but at the time it did seem pretty perfect. Maybe too good to be true.

"I mean, is this any more different than what Joe had going with Lou and the porn studio?" Matt asked Tony. Joe was a friend of theirs from LA, who performed sex scenes for a living. "It's just a job, right?"

"Right. That's what he says," Noah replied. "His mom..." He shook his head. He wasn't about to get into Will's personal business.

"So then why not give it a shot?" Matt asked.

"Well, for one, there's the issue of me getting promoted," he responded. "I'm his boss now, which messes up our chances even further."

Though Will did ask for a transfer. Rick had told Noah the next shift, along with asking if there'd ever been any issues between them—*awkward*—but there weren't any openings at the moment. Even if there were, one issue down and two more to go.

Tony leaned in. "How do you feel about him?"

"Does it really matter?" he asked, playing with a sugar packet.

"Yeah, of course it does," Matt replied.

A small smile lined his lips. "I... Fuck, I really like being with him. He's smart and funny and completely adorable, not to mention hot. And he makes me feel like..."

"Like?" Tony asked with an arched eyebrow.

"Like I matter," he said with a heavy sigh.

His friends stared at him for a long moment. Tony reached over and gripped his fiancé's hand. "If there are mutual feelings, maybe it's something you should explore."

Noah shook his head. "Not a good idea. It's just too complicated. I'm his boss, he's an escort, and no way I'd feel comfortable knowing what he could be doing behind closed doors. I'm not built for that. I have a hard enough time all on my own."

Noah took the last bite of his burger, then pushed his plate away as his friends seemed to quietly consider his reasons. "Then there's the fact that I paid him to hang out with me for a whole weekend. I mean, he wouldn't accept it that last time at my apartment, but still."

"Wait, what?" Matt asked.

"The other night I made dinner for my parents, and they asked me to invite my boyfriend." Noah pushed the ketchup around his plate with his fork. "I caved and hired him again. Long story short, he refused the money and said he did it because he wanted to."

"You've become one of my favorite people."

"Seriously, Noah?" Tony asked in a hopeful tone.

"No, don't," Noah responded, feeling grim. "And by the way, his name is Will, not Max."

"Mind blown," Matt said, his hands fanning out like his head had exploded.

They fell silent as they finished their food and asked for the check.

"So Matt is doing an amateur contest at Ruby Redd's this Thursday. Winner gets to guest-perform at future special events," Tony said.

"*Tate* will be working that night," Matt said, and Noah smiled. Tate Sullivan—now there was a man who knew how to wear fishnets. His alter ego, Frieda Love, always put on an incredible show.

"Of course I'll be there," he replied.

"Maybe invite Max—I mean Will," Matt said as they left their table. "Just as friends."

Noah shrugged. "We'll see."

On the way home, Noah realized he was relieved the truth was out—except to his parents, of course, but he could deal with that later.

He went home to an empty apartment and flipped through some home-decor magazines before pulling out a pad of paper and sketching some ideas he had for Home and Hearth. His online class was in merchandising, and he knew customers loved looking at window displays—they'd been competing with the amazing exhibits across the street at Saks for years, and he wondered if they should step it up. There was nothing wrong with their displays now—if a tad boring—but he had long envisioned something magical. And now that he was manager, he could make these types of decisions.

He spent the next hour sketching his ideas and found they satisfied his creativity in a wholly different way. He considered telling Will, but he needed to shake that mindset. Samantha was a good person to bounce ideas off too, but she'd already asked him the other day if he was crushing on the mysterious Will Crossen, and when he denied it, explaining that they'd sort of become friends, she still appeared skeptical. Maybe one day, when they were officially out of each other's lives for good, it would make for good gossip.

On that somber note, he slipped into his shoes and headed out the door to work.

32

WILL

You're welcome to meet us at Ruby Redd's tomorrow night. Totally as friends this time because obviously the jig is up.

Will smiled to himself. It certainly was. Noah had explained everything to him in a quick and hushed chat on their way to the subway station after work last night.

Well darn, I was looking forward to some form of public breakup.

I could yell at you a couple of times if that would make you feel better.

Can you order me around too? That would be hot!

Will couldn't help flirting with Noah, except he might've gone too far.

There was a long gap, and Will could picture Noah's cheeks getting rosy from embarrassment or maybe irritation. He needed to tone it down.

You'd...like something like that? Noah asked.

He couldn't even take the adorableness, and wished that Noah was standing right in front of him so he could kiss his cheek or hold his hand. But he'd been friend-zoned, which he supposed was for the best—and better than nothing.

Sometimes, sure. I'm not stuck on any one way. He'd love to have Noah take charge in the bedroom someday, if he was ever given the chance. **Whatever works for the two people involved, right?**

A short pause this time. **I like that.** A smiley face at the end.

Will searched for something else to say that wouldn't come across as desperate. *Show me, fuck me, hire me again just so we can pretend to pretend.*

He settled on, **Maybe I'll see you at Ruby Redd's.**

NO WAY WOULDN'T WILL SHOW AT RUBY REDD'S. HE WANTED TO see Noah again in a social setting, not at Home and Hearth where there were only discreet but longing gazes exchanged across the store in front of suspicious eyes. Plus, he looked forward to seeing Noah's friends again, this time on better terms, as well as a good drag show. Anything theatrical really. He realized how much he missed it. The escort business was beginning to wear thin even though he was closer to paying off their major bills. If his mom stayed healthy, he could finally be in the clear and stop working so hard. Maybe even consider the theater industry again.

Except just this past week she'd seemed more out of sorts, more despondent, and one night he'd walked in on her rocking in the corner, staring at nothing, her knitting yarn thrown to the side.

Fear had skyrocketed inside him as he'd carefully removed the needles from her reach and urged her to talk to him. After more prodding, she'd finally confessed she'd been isolating herself again from friends, even turning down invitations. So he checked in with the psychiatrist and respite worker, hoping to get her through this rough period that occasionally resurfaced with the disorder.

Last night they walked to a new custard shop in the neighborhood, and she seemed lighter. Sometimes her moods materialized out of nowhere, and it was exhausting to always be on watch. But tonight she'd been invited to dinner by Mrs. Wilkens on the first floor, and Will had been relieved that she accepted. Still, he'd be sure to get home at a reasonable hour tonight.

Once he took the train to the West Village, walked down Christopher Street and through the crowded doorway of Ruby Redd's, he felt the energy of the crowd, the vibe of a show underway. He spotted Noah, Tony, and Matt near the far corner of the long bar and noticed how Noah's eyes lit up upon seeing him. It made his stomach swoop and his breath catch.

Tony stretched out his hand. "I feel like I need to introduce myself all over again. I'm Tony and you're *Will*."

"I am." Will grinned, and then he nodded at Tony's fiancé. "Matt. Good to see you."

He glanced sideways at Noah, who seemed momentarily embarrassed, but as soon as their eyes met, his shoulders seemed to unwind.

Will ordered a draft beer from the crowded bar and took a long sip, licking the foam from his top lip. The drink definitely felt good going down, and it felt equally as good being out with friends instead of with a client, even though he wished things could be different with a certain guy Will had trouble keeping his eyes off of. A stab of melancholy hit him, but he whisked it away.

"You okay?" Noah asked as the swell of the crowd forced him closer.

"I'm really glad to be here as myself," Will admitted. "But I sort of miss Max."

Noah's eyebrows drew together. "Why is that?"

Will leaned closer, keeping his hands to himself no matter how tempting it was to reach for Noah. "Because Max got to touch Noah even if it was only supposed to be pretending. Max and Noah could forget not only that they were boss/employee, but escort/client as well."

"I miss that part of it too," Noah whispered close to his ear, and the feel of his warm breath made the hair on Will's neck stand at attention.

"You guys are way too freaking adorable," Tony said, clapping his friend on the back. "Just look at you."

Will chuckled. "What do you mean?"

"You want so badly to be together, but you don't know how," Matt added from behind his shoulder.

"You know why we can't—" Noah began with narrowed eyes.

"If you want to be together, or at least give it a shot, you'll find a way to make it work," Tony offered.

"Ever the optimist," Noah grumbled. "If only it could be that easy."

Before it could get any more awkward, Matt clasped Will's arm. "Come help me get ready backstage, and you can meet Frieda Love."

"Frieda Love?" Will asked as he was pulled away. The name sounded familiar.

"You'll find out soon enough," Noah replied with a crooked grin.

As soon as they stepped into the room behind the stage, it was like being back on a production schedule. The flurry, the makeup, the costumes. The *divas*. It made Will's heart quicken with an excitement he had buried the past year. Matt wormed his way to an area in a corner beside a mirror and began changing into a slinky red dress, but not before he used duct tape to bind his dick and balls, which could not be comfortable. The show on the island was laxer, and they had both definitely swung free. He watched as Matt pulled the hose over his thighs and then slipped into black stilettos.

Will looked around, trying to guess amateur from professional drag queen, and the one difference he noticed immediately was self-confidence. It was the same with stage actors—they intimately became their characters once the costumes and makeup were on.

When he noticed Matt fumbling with his wig, he ordered him to sit on an empty chair so he could take over, sliding seamlessly into the role of backstage assistant, one he'd performed hundreds of times before. After he got his wig secured with hair tape and bobby pins, he expertly painted his eyes, cheeks, and lips with the makeup Matt had brought from home.

"Oh, honey, you are good at that," someone behind him remarked, and he turned to see a gorgeous guy with purple hair and a shirt that read: Make America Gay Again.

"Probably because I've been around the block a few times," Will replied with a grin and a shrug.

"Will has worked on a bunch of Off-Broadway productions," Matt added. "Will, meet my friend, Tate Sullivan, also known as Frieda Love."

So this was the infamous Frieda Love. And he could see why anybody, let alone Noah, would have a complete crush on the man, probably more so once the entire persona came to life. "Nice to meet you."

Will helped Matt put the finishing touches on his costume and kept him calm because he was starting to sweat bullets. This was definitely a larger venue than on Fire Island, but from the tidbits of info he'd collected in conversations with Matt and the other drag queens, he was performing in drag for the simple joy of it. It probably helped him blow off steam from his high-powered Wall Street job. He loved that Matt was putting himself out there regardless of the outcome.

Supposed he could learn a lesson or two from that.

"You'll do great! See you out there."

When he walked back out, a tall, dark, and very handsome

man in a crisp blue button-down had joined Tony and Noah in the corner of the bar.

"This is Sebastian, Tate's boyfriend," Tony said.

No sooner had they shook hands than the show started. And what a show it was.

Matt looked amazing prancing around with the other amateur drag queens as they belted out a couple of songs and played to the audience. At the amateur finale, he was chosen as a runner-up, which meant he'd be invited back for one or two guest appearances. He could see the pure joy on Matt's face as he strode into the audience and kissed his fiancé. Will was thrilled for him and felt like he had made some new friends, this time not under false pretenses.

By the time the headliner—Frieda Love—made her appearance, Will was already on his third drink and had yelled and whistled his lungs out.

He was having such a good time, and couldn't believe it was nearly midnight already. He discreetly fished his phone out of his pocket to make sure there were no missed messages.

"Is she okay?" Noah asked close to his ear, having noticed the small action.

Will breathed out in relief. "Seems so."

Frieda Love's fans watched with rapt attention, and it was no wonder because she was a complete showstopper, as well as hilariously funny—if you weren't on the receiving end of her jokes or intense scrutiny, that is. Any unassuming patrons who had only strolled in to get a simple drink at the bar were her primary targets as she strutted in dramatic fashion and called people out in between performing to sing-along pop songs.

"Who's screwing each other's brains out in this audience?" Frieda Love asked on one of her passes near their group. She stopped to skim her hand down Sebastian's shirt and mewled in his direction. "I mean, besides the two of us."

The audience went wild as she leaned forward to offer

Sebastian a surprisingly tender peck on the lips and Sebastian's hand landed possessively on her neck. Will could only imagine how combustible it was between the sheets for those two.

"How about you?" Frieda asked, turning on Will and offering him a wink. She definitely remembered him from the back room, but now all bets were off. "Who are *you* fucking?"

Will cleared his throat as she stretched the mic to his mouth. "No one currently."

"Who do you *want* to be fucking?" she purred, rubbing his shoulder.

Unfortunately, she didn't miss his slight glance in Noah's direction. The man flushed beet red as soon as she turned her laser-focus on him.

"Oooh, I detect something going on between these two," she announced, and everyone roared with laughter. "Let's hear the story. We want to hear it, don't we?"

Deafening cheers from the audience. Fuck.

"I mean, I cannot take the longing looks. Seriously," Frieda added, rolling her eyes.

"Right?" Matt said as if he were her sidekick, and Will wanted to strangle him.

Noah glanced at Will with pleading eyes, as well as a slight shake of his head. But Will knew that Frieda wouldn't drop it now that she'd latched on to something juicy.

"I'd definitely like to be with him," Will said in a show of honesty, and he heard the catch of Noah's breath. "But it's complicated."

"How complicated can it be?" Frieda said in a pitched voice, hand on her hip. "You don't look related. Now *that* would be complicated."

There were several uncomfortable titters from the people standing closest to them.

Will searched his brain for something to say that would be

tamer than the fact that he was an escort and Noah had once been a paying client. "Well, he *is* my boss."

Oooohs and *aaahs* blasted his ears from every direction.

"End of story," Will added and then took a step back, figuring the scrutiny was over.

"Oh no, child. You are not getting off so easy," Frieda drawled, stepping closer. Will wished there was an exit directly behind him he could slip out of instead of the cold edge of the bar digging into his back.

"Do you feel the same?" she asked Noah, and Will held his breath.

Noah shrugged, attempting to appear nonchalant, but Will noticed the tremor in his fingers as he reached for the mic handle. "*Yes.*"

Some shrieking in the back from someone who might've had one too many, but Will was too busy listening to his own heartbeat pounding in his ears.

"The plot thickens, audience," Frieda announced before she turned back to Noah and Will. "So...convince us. Show us what you want."

Will shook his head. "Not a good idea."

Except suddenly Noah was closing the distance between them. Their gazes clashed, and as if he'd gotten a burst of courage, Noah's fingers encircled Will's neck and yanked his head down to take his mouth in a scorching kiss.

The audience went absolutely berserk. Yelling, whistling, clapping.

Noah's mouth felt right against his own, as if their lips were meant to fit together. In fact, it had never felt wrong—only safe and sexy and so damned good.

"Mmmm-mmm-mmm, yesssss, that's what I'm talking about," Frieda Love said as she watched them make out like a couple of teenagers. "Let this be a lesson to you, audience. Sometimes people need you to love them a little *louder!*"

"Amen," Will heard Tony say in agreement.

With that she turned on her heel as a song was queued up and everyone joined in on a rendition of "Crazy in Love" by Beyoncé.

Will broke away to catch his breath but kept their foreheads joined. He chuckled. "Wow, what the heck came over you?"

Noah pulled back, his cheeks flushing as if he couldn't believe he'd attacked Will's mouth in front of an entire bar either. "Dunno. Maybe I needed you to know you're one of my favorite people too."

They grinned stupidly at each other before Will spun him around and pulled him against his chest. Noah sighed and sank against him as they watched the rest of Frieda Love's performance.

Will's lips found his ear. "So, what do we do now?"

Noah shrugged and glanced back at him. "Maybe talk it all through?"

"We could do that," Will purred against his shoulder. "Maybe when we're alone with no alcohol in sight. But for now, let's just enjoy the rest of the show."

"Deal," Noah said, so Will kissed his temple and reveled in the closeness.

33

NOAH

Noah hadn't seen Will in almost three days. And even though that was nothing new—they weren't always on the same schedule—it felt monumental after their night at Ruby Redd's.

He might've felt more unnerved if it wasn't for the fact that Will had called in sick due to *family stuff* the past two shifts. Noah knew that probably meant something was up with his mother, but when he reached out to him by text—**Everything okay?**—Will had only offered him a scant response hours later. **It will be.**

Noah barely made it all the way through the afternoon shift, glad the store closed early on Sundays, before searching the employee files for Will's address. Some vague part of him wondered if he was crossing a line, but another part had a visceral need to be there for him. Will had come through for Noah plenty by now.

Just as he stored the information in his phone, there was a bright flash outside the window, followed quickly by an angry rumble of thunder.

"Looks like a nasty storm is headed our way," Samantha noted as she twisted the lock on the door.

Noah sucked in a harsh breath but kept going through the motions of cashing out the register. He didn't have time for a freak-out right then, not when he wanted to offer support to Will so badly. In months past, he might've dragged his feet for as long as he could until the storm passed, but now he wanted the time to jump ahead so he could be on his way, rain or shine.

After the store was secured and he parted ways with his employees, who rushed down the subway stairs to avoid the rain, he half considered heading straight home and cocooning under his sheets until the showers passed.

It's only a storm. You've been through hundreds of them and will absolutely go through hundreds more in your lifetime.

He clenched his jaw, pushed through the turnstile, and headed the opposite direction of home on the downtown train. By the time he got off at the right stop and back up to street level, the storm had eased a bit but not enough to his liking. He pulled up the GPS on his phone again and stayed under storefront awnings as much as he could as he strode down 1st Avenue toward Will's apartment. By the time he got there, he was mostly soaked but still determined.

Locating the number on the building was a relief as he slipped inside the defective door to the musty-smelling hallway. But it was dry, and that was everything. A crack of thunder resounded behind him, and he held on to the wall for leverage as he panted through it.

You're safe. You made it.

As he climbed up the rickety stairwell, he could almost picture Will's embarrassment about his dilapidated building. *"It's just a place to...lay our heads at night."* But at least the hallway looked clean and decently maintained, if a bit shabby.

When he got to the door he raised his hand to knock but nearly faltered. What if Will was pissed that he showed up here? Maybe he just wanted to be left in peace.

He forged ahead anyway because the worst Will could do was turn him away, and at least he would have tried to be supportive.

Once he knocked, there was a long pause before he heard the latch slide, and then the door swung open. Will's mouth dropped open as shock registered. His clothes were crumpled, and bags lined his eyes as if he hadn't gotten much sleep. In fact, he looked downright exhausted.

"What are you doing here?" he asked in a shaky voice.

Loving you louder.

Will glanced warily over his shoulder as if he wasn't entirely sure he'd even consider letting Noah in.

"I care about you and want to support you no matter what." Noah could see a woman sprawled on the couch at the far end of the room, likely his mother.

A rumble of thunder made Noah's shoulders hunch to his ears.

"You came all the way here in the middle of a storm?"

"Yeah, of course, I—"

"Who is it, William?" the lady asked.

"It's…just a friend, Ma."

Noah nearly cringed from the sting of those words. But even though he felt like so much more than a friend, that was really all they were. Besides, Will's mother wouldn't have known who he was, unless Will talked about him. The idea warmed his stomach.

His parents didn't know the real Will either. For the most part.

"Well, don't be rude; let him inside."

Will winced before he opened the door wider. "Our place is not like yours…"

"Don't," Noah said as he passed by him. "It doesn't matter."

Noah tried not to glance around too much as he stepped inside. The small apartment looked lived in but clean. Second-hand furniture, worn rugs, a decent television.

"Hi, Ms. Crossen." Noah stepped toward Will's mother, taking in her nightgown and robe, her hair a bit mussed, her eyes glassy.

Noah had no idea if she had come down with a bug or something else was going on, but he figured she wouldn't have invited him inside to spread germs.

"Have we ever met before?" she asked in a confused voice before she shot a look at her son.

"No, you haven't," Will replied. "He's the friend I went with to Fire Island last month."

She squinted. "Fire Island?"

Noah speculated whether her memory was failing her, but it was none of his business unless Will chose to share it with him.

Will squeezed his eyes closed and took a deep breath. When he reopened his lids, Noah saw grief plain as day across his features, along with fatigue. "It's okay, Ma. I'll have to tell you about it again sometime."

"Offer your friend something to drink," she muttered absently as she turned back to her show, which looked like some type of reality wilderness program, and effectively zoned out.

Will led Noah to the kitchen, where he opened the fridge and presented him with a soda.

"Thanks," Noah replied, glad to have something to do with his hands.

Will pulled out a chair, Noah followed suit, and they both sat down at the table.

There was a long minute of awkward silence where Will fiddled with the tab on his soda and Noah attempted to think of something benign to say.

"Thank you for coming."

"Of course," Noah responded, hoping to catch his eye.

But Will kept his gaze firmly planted on his can of Coke as he spun it in place, then cleared his throat. "Thursday night, when I came back from Ruby Redd's, I found her in that chair in the corner. She wouldn't talk…or move."

Noah leaned forward to glance into the room, toward the chair Will was referring to near the window.

"It can happen with schizophrenia—they can lapse into a catatonic state. I've seen it before, so I recognized it immediately."

"Fuck," Noah whispered and reached for Will's hand across the table.

"They scheduled her for electroconvulsive therapy on Friday, which is an outpatient procedure," Will explained as his thumb moved absently against Noah's palm.

Noah tried to register that information. *Electroconvulsive.* "You mean like shock therapy?"

"It's not like what you've seen in the movies. That was a long time ago," Will replied in a lowered register, which also contained a hopeful lilt. "There are longer-term studies for the positive effects it has on depression, but it's also been used pretty successfully for schizophrenic patients."

Noah marveled at the science of it. The brain was a complicated thing. "That's good news, yeah?"

Will nodded. "And apparently it can help with paranoia and hallucinations. She'll still be on her newer medication, but the doctor was going for quality of life."

Will sagged against the seat and looked a decade older in that moment. Like he was the parent and his mom was the child. And Noah was suddenly thunderstruck by how very much Will had to deal with all on his own. He looked completely wrung out, and Noah had the urge to wrap him in his arms and soothe him, take care of him. Protect him.

Maybe like Will wanted to do for his mother.

And like Noah's parents wanted for him.

He could feel tears stinging his eyes, but he blinked them away.

Noah squeezed his hand, and Will offered a melancholy smile that made Noah's chest feel tight and funny. "The thing is, after treatments, the patient can have short-term memory loss."

"Amnesia?"

When Will nodded, that helped explain why his mother

didn't seem to remember something he'd told her only last month. Noah honestly wasn't sure how the hell Will could process all this, but given his appearance, he was barely hanging on.

"The procedure isn't as expensive as inpatient, but not completely covered by the insurance either."

Fuck, now he understood even more why Will was juggling two jobs.

"They recommended not leaving her alone for at least twenty-four hours after...so I wanted to stay with her through the weekend," he explained, "to make sure she didn't do anything to put herself in danger."

"I get it," Noah replied. Will was sure to stress over his missed shifts and try to double up somehow. The pressure had to feel enormous. "You're a good son."

"I'm trying." Will tipped his chair to glance at his mom in the other room. When Noah followed his gaze, he saw that she had fallen asleep curled up on the couch. "Good, she needed it."

Glancing toward the window, Noah noticed that the rain had eased a bit. Now that he had checked on Will, he wondered if he should head home and let him get some rest as well. But for the life of him, he couldn't muster the words. He didn't want to leave his side.

"Is it okay if I stay a bit longer?" he asked. "I know you must be exhausted, so don't feel obligated—"

"You'd want to stay?" Will blurted out and then dipped his head as a flush rose on his cheeks.

Noah smiled. "More than anything."

They tiptoed past his mother's sleeping form like a couple of teenagers sneaking around, so that Will could show him his bedroom down the hall.

"It's not much," he said with a shrug as he flipped on the light.

"It doesn't matter," Noah reiterated. There was only a bed and dresser along with a couple of boxes on the floor. He was taking care of his mom, paying all the bills, yet he was worried what Noah would think of his living arrangements. But now it made sense when he said early on that his life wasn't all roses, his relationships either.

One of the boxes on the floor was partially open, and Noah could see the corner of a colorful pamphlet of some sort peeking out. "What are those?"

"My playbills," he replied with a sheepish grin. "Guess I've got myself a decent collection."

The idea that he compiled a stack of playbills collected from various Broadway shows was completely endearing. Noah wished he could organize and display them for him somewhere, but he was going to guess that Will would frown upon that. It seemed the boxes had become a holding pen of sorts until...what? Suddenly, he wanted to know about all of Will's hopes and dreams.

"Will you show me?" Noah asked, sinking down on his firm mattress. His comforter was a warm blue that matched the pattern of the curtains strewn across his window.

Will slid a box toward them and bent down to open it. As he shuffled through the stacked playbills, he recounted his favorite plays, musicals, and performances he'd worked on. His voice had grown animated, his entire face lit up; it was a side of Will he'd never seen, and Noah loved hearing him speak with such passion.

"You miss it, don't you?" Noah asked as Will replaced the lid on the box and slid it back in place.

"Maybe sometimes," he replied with a shrug as he looked at the time on his phone. "Want to stay for dinner? We're only ordering in pizza."

Noah's heart squeezed. "I'd love to."

About an hour later, the three of them sat in the living room, eating pizza off paper plates and talking about random things. He found out Will's mom also had theater aspirations when she was younger, had been in a couple of minor productions, and had the same way of repeatedly brushing aside her bangs when she was telling a story.

Noah could almost picture her onstage, her beauty and charm, and he felt sad about the time she'd lost from such a debilitating illness. He understood now Will's protectiveness of her, as well as Will's fears about descending into the same darkness.

When she got stumped on a story about a celebrity she once met, she shook her head, her cheeks flushing. "My head's a bit cloudy." She lightly knocked her temple. "I sometimes wonder if there's some scar tissue in there that makes me so fuzzy."

"No worries," Noah replied with a small smile. "Besides, I have actual scar tissue on the outside of my body, so we're even."

When her gaze shot to Will, he nodded. So Noah ended up telling her about his accident and his fear of storms as she listened intently and patted his arm in sympathy. But Noah didn't take offense to it. It felt like they were both warriors recounting battle wounds.

She stretched and yawned. "I'm tired and heading to bed."

As she got up, she glanced out the window at the rain that persisted into the night. "You're welcome to stay with us, Noah. I think Will would like that."

"Um, thanks, Ms. Crossen," he replied as she shuffled down the hall.

"Call me Rose," she said over her shoulder. "Good night."

Will gathered the paper plates from the coffee table. "You don't have to stay; she was just—"

"Would you like me to?" Noah asked in an uncertain voice.

"I definitely would," he replied. "But my bed isn't as big as—"

"Will you cut it out?" Noah said as he helped him put the pizza box in the recycling bin. "Besides, I can tell how exhausted you are. Someone needs to make sure you get your butt to bed."

"Probably right," he said around a yawn. He was completely dead on his feet.

So after Will checked on his mom twice more and made sure the deadbolt was secure, they went to sleep in Will's bed, and this time Noah held him all night long.

Because Will needed it. Deserved it. Noah cherished the closeness and honesty between them because in many ways, tonight felt like a stolen moment. But stolen or not, he wouldn't trade it for anything. Even at the expense of his heart.

Noah knew then that he had fallen hard for him, and he wasn't even sure if Will felt the same way. But for the moment, it wasn't important. All that mattered was the warm skin and soft breaths of the man in his arms.

34

WILL

"I like him, William," his mother said the next day after Noah had gone home to change and attend to a few other things, including his online class. Home and Hearth was closed on Mondays, and Noah had promised to return early to spend the afternoon with Will and his mom.

"Me too, Ma."

It felt foreign sharing his mom with anyone. Plus, he knew that he and Noah still had some tough things to talk through. But for now, they had placed it on the back burner and were just getting to know each other better, as friends, he supposed. With the possibility of more?

Noah had slept in his bed last night. And even though all they did was cuddle, it felt more intimate than any other time they'd shared. Because Will was letting him in, no matter the consequences. It didn't change all the external factors that would invariably act as barriers between them, but it did make Will feel not so alone in his worry and grief about his mother.

The procedure she had undergone had terrified him, but now that she was coming out on the other side, he hoped they'd made the right decision. Only time would tell.

Later that morning, Noah returned with bagels from one of Will's mom's favorite shops in the East Village. She had completely lit up from that surprise and was more animated than usual. Or maybe Noah brought that out in her. After last night, the two of them seemed to have forged some sort of connection. When Will came back after checking the mail downstairs, he overheard Noah talking to his mom about his parents and the guilt he felt in recent years about the tension between them. His mom had given Noah some good advice, and it seemed he planned to reach out to them this week.

They played Scrabble, watched a couple of documentaries, and even got outside to enjoy the weather by walking to the new custard place in the neighborhood.

They had hit it off, and what Will realized was that Noah was the first guy who didn't treat his mom differently, like she might break or go off the deep end. He didn't know if it was because of Noah's own experiences with others' reactions to his injuries, but watching them made Will's heart sing.

By the time dinner rolled around, Will had to admit it had turned out to be a great day. His phone buzzed on the tabletop where he left it, and when he listened to the message, it was from his escort service for a job that night with a repeat customer. He tensed up, but Noah threw him a knowing glance.

The call left him reeling and completely torn. He needed the money. That was his whole reason for taking the job. And he had missed two shifts at Home and Hearth already.

As his mom got lost in a reality show, Noah followed him to his bedroom. "You should go."

"What do you mean?" he asked, trying to play dumb.

"You're supporting your family," Noah replied in a casual voice, but Will noticed the strain around his eyes. "I've got stuff to do at home. Go get ready."

"Noah, I—" Will fumbled as he retreated out of the room.

"It's okay. I get it now, more than ever," he replied in a firm tone. "I had a great day, so thank you. I'll say goodbye to your mom on the way out."

Before Will could form anything logical to say, Noah was already gone.

WILL MUSTERED ALL THE STRENGTH HE COULD TO MEET HIS CLIENT at a pub attached to the upscale hotel. He remembered this guy. He had requested him once before when he'd come in from out of town. He was a businessman from LA. Last time Will had spotted a wedding ring on his finger, but he'd ignored it, not wanting to know if the man was cheating.

They shared a couple of drinks at the bar and then went up to his room. The man turned on some porn and wanted them to jack off together, same as last time. Will eyed the tip on the nightstand. It was a generous one, but he never felt more conflicted than in that moment. It was different when he was single with no romantic prospects in sight, but now that Noah had turned his world upside down, it felt all wrong.

The fact that Noah had encouraged him to go was even worse. Because if the shoe were on the other foot, Will would feel twisted up inside and all kinds of jealous—not that Will had feelings for any of his clients or that he and Noah were even together. But in that moment, he wanted to be with him more than *anything*.

And that was what made this encounter excruciating for him. He didn't know how they were going to make it with new bills coming from the latest treatment. That was what kept him rooted to the mattress, watching two burly men screw each other on this guy's laptop.

Will couldn't get anything up regardless. Watching porn only gave him a half chub this time, purely a physical reaction. The man already had his cock out, and as Will focused on his gold wedding band for the first time tonight, warm bile crawled up his throat.

Somehow looking at that symbol of devotion on that man's finger decided it for him. He jumped up and backed away from the bed, knowing he couldn't do this shit for one more minute.

"I..." Will stuttered as the man's eyes widened. "I'm sorry. I have somewhere I have to be. Don't fault the company; it's totally on me."

"What the fuck?" the man growled, his eyes bulging. "Get back here. I'm paid up for the evening."

He wanted to argue that in the Gotham City rules, the escort had the right to refuse any portion of the evening, but he kept his mouth shut. It wasn't worth it, not when this man still had his stiff cock between his hairy knuckles.

Will wished he had a wad of cash in his pocket he could throw on the bed as payback, but he was as broke as ever. "I'll make sure they prorate your time."

When he shut the door behind him, the relief was so consuming that he sagged against the wall. There had to be a different way. It would take longer, but it wouldn't feel like this. Him entertaining a man for money while the guy he desperately wanted to be with felt a world away.

Once he got home and saw his mom was fast asleep, he slipped back out because he needed to see Noah. He had this crazy urge to hold him, smell him, taste his lips. He was nearly blinded by his longing for him.

By the time he got off the train on 2nd Avenue on the Upper East Side, his heart was thrumming. He wasn't sure why he hadn't texted Noah first, except maybe he was afraid of being turned away.

But he needed to bare his soul even if Noah refused him.

He knocked softly, considering that Noah might be asleep.

A few seconds later, Noah blinked up at him as he pulled open the door. He looked adorable in a pair of worn sweats and T-shirt, and Will grinned despite his nerves. Glancing over Noah's shoulder, Will noticed a wineglass on the table, along with a home-renovation show on the television.

"What are you—"

Before Noah even had time to process, Will's hand cupped his nape, and he sealed their lips in a heated kiss. There were things he needed to say to this man who had somehow wormed his way inside his heart. But he couldn't help himself—he needed to touch him and taste him and hold him close.

"Will," Noah moaned against his mouth as his hands clutched his waist. "Is everything—"

"Need you." Will walked him backward inside the apartment, shut the door with his foot, and then caged him against the wall. "God, do I fucking need you."

Noah trembled all over as Will's fingers grazed the hem of his shirt, then yanked it over his head. Will licked and sucked his throat, then dragged his lips down the center of his chest. He paused to flick his tongue against each of his nipples and watched them harden in response. "Every single part of you is gorgeous."

Noah's whimper turned into a growl as he dragged Will's mouth toward his own. There was merely a moment's pause before they were all teeth, tongues, hands, and lips. They sucked on throats and ears and jaws before fitting their mouths back together again, their tongues grappling for dominance.

Noah yanked Will's shirt over his shoulders as he urged him backward toward the couch. Will sank down with one foot flat on the floor, the other leg stretched out on the cushion. Noah fit himself between Will's thighs so they were aligned shoulder to hip. As soon as their cocks rubbed together through the material of their pants, Will groaned. His fingers latched on to Noah's ass as he dragged him even closer.

"Jesus," Noah groaned, burrowing his fingers into Will's hair. "It's not really fucking registering that you're here. What happened to your—"

"I couldn't go through with it. Not when *you*...when *I*—" Will crashed their lips together again, wanting to devour his mouth and lips and tongue. Their kisses turned greedy and desperate, and as he sucked Noah's tongue into his mouth, Will needed more. He needed to feel Noah's warm, pulsing skin against his own. He needed it more than his own breath right then.

"Unzip my pants," Will rumbled against his neck, and as Noah complied, Will took hold of the soft material at his waist and tugged Noah's sweatpants over his thighs to his knees. And then finally—*finally*—their cocks were angled exactly right to rub together. He felt the heat of Noah's bare skin over that hard steel as his stiff cock leaked against his groin.

Will had long ago lost track of when his want for Noah had crossed over into raw, unfettered need, but right then everything felt overwhelmingly right. *Noah* was everything he needed.

Will's hands clamped down on Noah's bare ass, his fingers digging into his flesh while he sucked the skin on this throat. Noah squirmed and moaned as he inhaled Will's collarbone, biting down and then soothing it with his tongue. Will's entire body trembled in response.

"Need your hands on me," Will pleaded in a strained voice.

Noah's fingers stretched between them to Will's erection, and he traced over a vein as his thumb circled the crown. He sighed as if in relief. "Mmmm, *perfect*."

"No, *you're* perfect," Will whispered against his ear before sucking the tender lobe in his mouth and thrusting upward, seeking input.

"Fuck, Will. You make me crazy." Noah curled his palm around both of their cocks and jerked his fist in long strokes, making Will hiss and leak like crazy.

"Yeah, that's it," Will groaned. "Make us come."

They thrust into Noah's fist in unison as Will panted and groaned against Noah's lips with every flick of his wrist. Their cocks sliding together created the perfect friction, and his balls drew up, a line of electric frisson traveling up his spine.

Noah moaned, his strokes turning choppy as his thighs went rigid above him. Will's legs quivered as his groin turned to liquid heat.

"Jesus." Noah's hips stilled as he rushed out a string of curses and spilled his seed over Will's stomach.

Will's eyesight nearly whited out as his orgasm careened off the rails, knocking his head back in a blinding fog.

"Fuck," he bit out in a hoarse groan as he shot all over Noah's hands. As Will slowly came back to himself, Noah had the wherewithal to stand up on shaky legs and reach for a wad of tissues to wipe them down. "Damn, I needed that."

Noah hummed in agreement as he sat on the edge of the couch and began tucking himself back in. Will tugged on his arm, forcing Noah to lie on top of him again. "C'mere."

Noah rested their foreheads together. The tips of their tongues flicked out and met in a slow and sensual kiss as their eyes remained open. Noah's gaze was soft and adoring, and it made Will's chest ache with longing.

"Noah, I—" His throat clogged with emotion as his fingers burrowed in Noah's hair.

"Why did you come here tonight? What happened to your appointment?" Noah's eyes took on a faraway look as he swallowed roughly. As if bracing himself for whatever he thought Will was going to say.

"I couldn't do it. Not anymore," Will murmured as he tapped their lips together. "Not when I'm in love with someone else."

"Wait...what are you saying?" Noah drew back and bit his lip, looking so damn adorable.

"Somewhere in all this pretending, it got real, and I fell in love with you." He shook his head, trying to get the words out as his pulse pounded in his ears. "And it's okay if you don't feel... But maybe we can still..."

"Oh, I *feel*," Noah said, clutching Will's jaw. "I feel every bit as in love with you."

Will's heart rose to his throat as he gathered Noah's face in his hands. They grinned stupidly at each other right before Will captured Noah's lips in a slow, deep kiss.

They stayed that way—lips and foreheads joined, hands winding in hair—for several long minutes.

"I'll have to figure something else out," Will eventually murmured.

"We can figure it out together," Noah replied, nuzzling his neck.

"Damn, I love the sound of that."

Will could feel Noah's heart beating right up against his own, and it brought him peace. Like he could share the burden on his shoulders, at least momentarily.

He grew motionless so he could soak in all of Noah's heat and breath in his scent as he wound his arms around him and pressed closer. He couldn't seem to find the right words for how overwhelmingly content and settled he felt in that moment, but the breathless silence between them crackling with raw emotion seemed enough for now.

"Do you need to get home?" Noah whispered against his ear. "Is your mom okay?"

Will loved him for asking. For knowing that he needed to take care of her no matter what. And he hoped like hell it didn't come between them, because he wanted so badly to have this man in his life.

"She was sleeping when I left," he replied, kissing Noah's hair.

"Can I hold you a while longer?"

"For as long as you want."

"What if I want to hold you for always?"

Noah whimpered against his neck, burrowed in even closer, and that was all the answer Will needed.

35

NOAH

SIX MONTHS LATER

"Is that it?" Will asked excitedly as he eyed the thick envelope in Noah's hand.

Noah had woken up to amazing morning sex, where he'd practically been fucked into the mattress. That was in contrast to the other night, when he and Will had made slow and sensual love, with caressing touches, lingering kisses, and whispers of devotion. He didn't know sex could be like that—hot and hard, or tender and profound. And he certainly didn't realize he would cherish both.

Afterward, Noah had gone down to the lobby to retrieve the mail while Will jumped in the shower.

"I think so," Noah replied as he sat down on the couch and gently picked at the seal on the back of what looked to be fancy correspondence.

Will sank down beside him and watched as he gently slid the vanilla-colored card stock out of the envelope. The writing was loopy and elegant, and Noah smiled as he read the invitation aloud.

Boy meets boy
And falls in love.
For the rest of the story,
join us
as
Anthony Malone
and
Matthew Collins
are pronounced husband and husband
Saturday, the tenth of May
The Pines, Fire Island
Flip-flops required

"It'll be quite a celebration," Noah mused as he studied the invite. Tony and Matt had stewed over dates the past few months until they finally settled on a spring wedding by the ocean. By then the weather should hold, and it would probably be pleasantly warm, unless Mother Nature had other ideas. Regardless, it would be beautiful. Noah would expect no less.

So far the winter in Manhattan had been a mild one, except for the surprisingly white Christmas and completely frigid New Year's. But Noah and Will barely noticed in the whirlwind of their newfound relationship, as they tried to fit themselves into each other's lives.

Not like it was a hardship. Anytime Will walked through the door, Noah's pulse would flutter and everything in his world would right itself again. He could scarcely believe that this gorgeous man wanted him. That he quit his escort job because he chose to be with him. He needed to knock on wood, or he was afraid he might wake up from some kind of mocking dream.

But Will had not only quit Gotham City, he also walked away from Home and Hearth a month later because of a chance audition Noah encouraged him to seek out. It was for the new Bronstein production his friend Oren had told him about, and Will scored a small role. The budget was larger, which meant the pay was better too. But that also meant his schedule was more hectic than ever. Regardless, it was where he was meant to be; Noah could feel it in his bones.

The production was currently in rehearsal mode, and Will usually worked an eight-hour day, six days a week. Opening night was still months away, but he'd signed a one-year contract, so he felt momentarily settled. And that took some of the pressure off.

Though Noah missed seeing him at work, they no longer had to sneak around, and that freed Noah up to throw himself completely into his job. He had even designed the winter-themed window display to rave reviews from customers and coworkers alike.

"*Look at you go. I love it,*" Samantha had said the night they revealed the exhibit, which featured a snowball fight on one end and a cozy fireplace scene on the other. Showcasing Home and Hearth furnishings, of course. *"And I'm still waiting for the real story between you and Will Crossen."*

By that time everyone knew they were dating but not the actual details behind their romance because it was sort of mortifying to recount. They had even concocted a white lie for Noah's parents, who had grown to adore Will, especially since he was working on a Broadway production. At dinner one night, Will told them that Max had been a stage name, but that he much preferred William, his birth name. They bought it hook, line, and sinker.

Will still worried obsessively about their bills, but his mom was doing much better since the outpatient treatment and had developed new friendships through her weekly knitting group. She had even made them matching scarves for Christmas.

Noah enjoyed getting to know Ms. Crossen during the dozens of evenings and weekends spent at their apartment. Sometimes he'd even visit her when Will was at rehearsal. He knew how much Will appreciated that—knowing she was safe with Noah while he threw himself into his performance.

More often than not, Will stayed over at Noah's place. So Noah offered him a key and plenty of closet space, hoping he'd feel like he belonged. Because he definitely belonged in Noah's heart, and Noah hoped that someday they'd make a more formal commitment to each other. But for now, he was okay taking it slow.

They tried to spend as much time together as possible, and some nights that included sexy surprises. Like the silky black underwear Will had worn with the new pair of fishnets Noah had purchased so that the older, tattered ones could enter into retirement.

And Noah loved just as much their tender, everyday moments —seeing the appreciation in Will's eyes when he walked through the door to a home-cooked meal or an open bottle of wine or any other number of ways Noah tried to pamper him and show his affection.

Over the holidays, Noah had Will's playbills framed for him, and now they hung near the balcony door. To Noah's surprise, Will had a similar gift idea with a hand-painted ocean sunset he'd purchased for Noah's bedroom, and which they'd placed right above the jar of seashells.

Noah smiled at the sweet memory as he slid out the small RSVP square that came with the invitation, and stared down at the blank space for the number of guests. This time last year that line would've taunted him, but now he saw it as an opportunity to make new memories with the man he adored.

"It'll be good for you to be at the ocean again," Will said, kissing his temple.

"Yeah." Noah sighed. He found the thorny edges of his memories had dulled even more, thanks to the man beside him, who made everything more bearable.

Fishing out a pen from the side table, he wrote the number 2, then slid the card into the complimentary envelope to mail back.

"Love you, babe," Will whispered into his hair.

"Love you too." Noah smiled brightly and pecked his lips. Will settled against the cushions with Noah draped over his chest.

"Need to get in the shower," Noah murmured into his neck.

"Five more minutes?" Will encircled him tighter in his arms.

Noah reveled in his boyfriend's warmth as his fierce emotions for this man took hold. The last few months had been surreal. And there had been times when he fought his own demons as the self-doubt invariably crept back in. Would Will's interest eventually wane?

But Will's adoration always held strong, knocking him back with the force of his resolve. His love reverberated louder than all of Noah's fears, tolling like a bell in all the uncertain spaces of his soul.

THE END

THANK YOU FOR READING LOVE ME LOUDER

Thank you for reading LOVE ME LOUDER. I hope you enjoyed it.

Reviews help readers find books, so if you feel compelled to leave a line or two about this book, it would be greatly appreciated!

Are you curious about **Tate Sullivan/Frieda Love** from Ruby Redd's? Tate and Sebastian's book is called **THE HARDEST FALL**. It's from the Roadmap series but can definitely be read as a standalone. Read further to find the blurb and first chapter.

OTHER BOOKS WRITTEN BY CHRISTINA LEE

There You Stand

Roadmap to Your Heart series
The Darkest Flame
The Faintest Spark
The Deepest Blue
The Hardest Fall
The Sweetest Goodbye

Under My Skin Series
Regret
Reawaken
Reclaim

Co-written with Riley Hart (AKA Nyrae Dawn):
Touch the Sky
Chase the Sun
Paint the Stars

Living Out Loud
Ever After: A Gay Fairytale

MMM
Last Call (co-written with Felice Stevens)

MF Books
All of You
Before You Break
Whisper to Me
Promise Me This
When We Met (anthology)
Two of Hearts
Three Sacred Words
Twelve Truths and a Lie

ABOUT THE AUTHOR

Once upon a time, **Christina Lee** lived in New York City and was a wardrobe stylist. She spent her days getting in cabs, shopping for photo shoots, eating amazing food, and drinking coffee at her favorite hangouts.

Now she lives in the Midwest with her husband and son—her two favorite guys. She's been a clinical social worker and a special education teacher. But it wasn't until she wrote a weekly column for the local newspaper that she realized she could turn the fairy tales inside her head into the reality of writing fiction.

She's addicted to lip balm, coffee, and kissing. Because everything is better with kissing.

She writes MM Contemporary as well as Adult and New Adult Romance. She believes in happily-ever-afters for all, so reading and writing romance for everybody under the rainbow helps quench her soul.

THE HARDEST FALL BLURB

After licking his wounds from a painful relationship, Tate Sullivan is ready to move back home. He picks up where he left off as drag queen extraordinaire Frieda Love in a West Village bar in New York City. He doesn't expect to be drawn to the mysterious man with the dark eyes who shows up to every single performance—flirtatiously eyeing Tate one second and disappearing on him the next. Why mess around with a guy who is clearly giving him mixed signals?

Sebastian Clark is on a mission the first night he shows up at Ruby Redd's. He doesn't anticipate his plan being flipped on its head by the charismatic drag queen and even more so by the mesmerizing man beneath the makeup. But the more he learns about the vibrant and brash Tate Sullivan the more intrigued he becomes. So he pushes aside his guilt about why he sought out the bar in the first place in order to get to know the guy behind the stilettos.

They're opposites on many levels, but as Tate spends time volunteering with Sebastian at the shelter, he begins to feel good about himself in ways he hadn't before. For Sebastian, Tate represents a sense of fun and freedom that is completely fresh and invigorating. Before they know it, their easy companionship catches fire, and Sebastian is kissing a man for the first time, while Tate is opening his heart to new possibilities. But Sebastian is still keeping a secret, and Tate will have to decide if he can trust again, or if the betrayal he feels from Sebastian's confession is too much to overcome.

EXCERPT FROM THE HARDEST FALL
TATE

My arm shot up and I pointed at the ceiling as I belted out the last note of a Gaga song. If I had her voice, I'd be rolling in the millions instead of lip-synching her pop tunes, wearing heavy purple eye shadow, and silver stilettos that pinched my freaking toes.

But I had a blast performing as Frieda Love, I was damn good at it, and the stage adored me. As did the crowd, if a couple dozen gay men wolf whistling had anything to say about it. Or that sexy man in the corner whose dark eyes tracked me two nights a week.

Dark Eyes looked straight as they come with his perfectly tailored button-front shirt that opened at the throat, exposing a patch of smooth tan skin and a fine silver chain. But plenty of het men and women came into Ruby Redd's Bar and Grille. Some stayed for the food, others for the entertainment.

As I exited the stage down the three steps to the dance floor, I spotted Dean and Callum near the bar. Making my way through a sea of bodies, fingers groped and voices carried as the audience congratulated me on a great performance. Frieda Love might screw around with one of her regulars tonight, but first I wanted to hang out with my friends.

"*Girl*," Jessica, one of the other queens who had already performed tonight, drawled in my ear. "You looked ridiculously fab up there."

Hazel Nuts, as she was known on stage, was in transition, drop dead gorgeous, and had a huge following in this crowd as well. Fuck the prejudice she encountered in her everyday life from the asshats that couldn't see how radiant she was in her own skin.

Here at Ruby Redd's we were strictly against the use of such language as *tranny* and *shemale*, which were not only derogatory but also encouraged the idea that transsexuals were men dressed as women. Any hecklers were immediately thrown out on their asses because the owner, Maurice, ran a tight ship.

I kissed her cheek as I walked by. "Thanks, sexy. My friends are waiting at the bar."

I hadn't seen Dean since he graduated from NC State last fall. He looked good, especially with Callum standing behind him with his burly arms wrapped around his waist and his face nuzzled in his neck. Dean and Callum were really good together and I couldn't be happier for them.

They were only in town so Callum could finally meet Dean's parents in Jersey. While here they had also planned to visit me and to see a Yankee game, since Callum was a huge fan.

I was back in the city because I didn't have many other options. This was my hometown, my mother lived on the Upper East Side with her new husband, and I was having trouble finding full-time employment.

It took me two additional years to graduate from NC State with a communications degree because some of the credits wouldn't transfer from NYU. Broadcasting jobs were hard to come by and though I had interned at an online publication there were no openings available at the time. I stayed as long as I could before finally coming home.

Now I did what I knew best—performed as drag queen extraordinaire at a bar on Christopher Street two nights a week. That, along with my graphic T-shirt business helped me contribute to the rent in the small West Village apartment I shared with my best friend, Tori.

"I always knew you could rock the stage," Callum said in his southern drawl as soon as I reached them. He looked so much more comfortable in his own skin then he had six months ago, which was really cool to witness.

"Of course I can." I spun around and shook my booty in my white beaded dress while they cracked up. I made sure not to bend too low and rip the seam because the cost of dressing in drag was not for the faint of heart. I went for demure Gaga tonight because her elaborate costumes broke the bank, probably even for her. Besides, I wasn't a fan of wearing meat, only packing it.

A man from a nearby table whistled at me and I recognized the dude after he slipped me a twenty at the end of my performance. The way he eyed me now told me he was hoping for some Frieda loving tonight, but I wasn't someone who could be bought. Still, I could flirt shamelessly with the best of them.

I hugged Dean and then turned toward the tall and hulking Callum to wind my arms around his shoulders. I couldn't help sniffing his cologne extra deep since he was plain gorgeous and just the kind of guy I got a boner for.

"That's long enough," Dean hissed in my direction. "Stop mauling my man."

"You mean I can't sneak in an ass grab?" I quipped before backing away. Seeing that possessive look in my friend's eye was humorous, but also gave me an ache in my chest that I couldn't quite explain. I didn't want to explore what that meant, so I brushed it aside.

When I glanced over Callum's shoulder the same man with the dark eyes and inky black hair was watching me and once he was caught staring, his gaze flitted away.

Maybe he appreciated the make-up, the blonde wig. I'd been told I had a nice jawline and could pull off my female counterpart pretty convincingly. Dark Eyes was probably a straight guy who enjoyed the female anatomy, even though my boobs were falsies, same as my eyelashes. Maybe he'd even been with a couple of queens who were asked to stay in full costume while he pounded them from behind so he could maintain his het status in his own deluded mind.

My gut tightened painfully remembering being in just such a precarious position.

I wondered how he'd react if I approached him without the getup, with a fresh face, clean of makeup. My bet was that he'd run in the other direction. Fucker.

He wasn't exactly my type so what the hell did I care? He might've been a bit taller and thicker than me but he matched me in build, with his solid shoulders and lean waist. He had a beautifully masculine face, not boyish in the least, with a strong brow and full lips. Compared to my blond hair and fair skin, we'd be quite the contrast.

But his eyes were the draw for me, especially when I was on stage. How they tracked me, made me wonder what he was thinking. They were soulful, a cross between forlorn and world-weary, and though I really had no patience for emo guys, for some reason the more I saw him the more curious I became.

"So what's new?" I asked the gorgeous couple standing in front of me, breaking my gaze from the mysterious man who did not deserve so much of my attention.

"Mom and Dad are warming up to Callum," Dean said, grasping for his guy's hand. "They're glad I brought home a *friend.*"

"Friend?" I scoffed. "Seriously?"

"They're slowly coming around," Dean said. "Especially after our argument on Thanksgiving when I told them they'd be losing another son if they didn't accept me for who I am."

"His mom kind of lost it," Callum supplied, after sipping from his glass. "Got herself together right quick. Called him and told him she wanted to be part of his life."

"Damn straight." I clapped Dean on the shoulder.

"And how's business?" I asked Callum because his family owned a hunting preserve in small town hick-country Florida.

"Doing great," he said, taking another pull of his beer. I realized how parched I was from performing as I watched him swallow. It had nothing to do with that enticing Adam's apple bobbing up and down.

"He's been making all kinds of furniture and his family is selling sugar cane syrup," Dean said, looking at his boy with pride.

"Cassie and Billie?" I knew his sister Cassie from NC State and heard his brother had a therapy dog that assisted him with his seizure disorder. But that he was also wicked smart, loved to bake, and hadn't yet officially come out to his family.

"Cassie is engaged to Dermot," he said. "And Billie begged to come to the city with us. I told him next time for sure because he's still in school."

"That kid has wanderlust." I grinned. "Maybe he'll decide to leave that town."

Something gloomy passed through Callum's gaze. I knew how protective he was of his brother.

"He could study abroad or attend culinary school," I suggested. "Have him come to the city. I'll look out for him."

Dean's eyes bugged out and Callum burst out laughing.

"Thanks for the vote of confidence," I huffed out, crossing my arms over my boobs, which felt like they'd shifted a bit during my performance. "I wouldn't let him get into any trouble. I'd slowly introduce him to the scene."

Just because I would never settle down didn't mean I couldn't be a good friend to somebody who needed support. I certainly would never want anybody to get burned the way I did. Gay dudes who pretended to be super straight to the detriment of everybody around them could go suck it.

That includes you, Dark Eyes. I could feel his heated gaze on me again. Bet his thumb was fingering the condensation on the glass. Gin and tonic with lime every single visit. I could ask the bartender who was scheduled most nights I was on stage. Phil always had a tall glass of water with lemon waiting at the bar for me after my performances. He would tell me if Dark Eyes was batting for the same team or if he seemed to swing both ways. But then I'd appear desperate, and queens were never desperate. We always had plenty of men to hold court.

"Let me get changed," I said, reaching for the cold liquid on the bar but refusing to look in Dark Eyes' direction again. "My feet are killing me, but I want to watch Candy Cane perform."

Dean pulled Callum toward the dance floor and then locked him in a kiss that made my toes curl. Well, fuck. I threw Dark Eyes one final glance as I sipped at the water and bit down on an ice cube. I would definitely find somebody to hook up with tonight. Somebody who was eager for a piece of this fine ass.

Just as I had the thought, one of my regulars crowded my personal space and made the motion to kiss my cheek before I had the sense to back away. How dare he think he could touch this queen without her consent?

"You were spectacular tonight," he mumbled with glazed eyes. He was already half-crocked, so I let him off the hook this time. Nothing worse than a sloppy fuck.

"Frieda Love always brings her A game," I cooed to him over my shoulder. "Better get yourself a cab ride home."

Printed in Great Britain
by Amazon